8.95

The Throne of Tara

The Throne of Tara

John Desjarlais

CROSSWAY BOOKS • WHEATON, ILLINOIS
A DIVISION OF GOOD NEWS PUBLISHERS

The Throne of Tara.

Copyright © 1990 by John Desjarlais

Published by Crossway Books, a division of
Good News Publishers, Wheaton, Illinois 60187.

Cover illustration: Chuck Gillies

First printing, 1990

Printed in the United States of America

Scripture references are taken from THE NEW ENGLISH BIBLE
© The Delegates of the Oxford University Press and The Syndics of the
Cambridge University Press, 1961, 1970. Reprinted by permission.

Excerpts on pages 42, 44-45, 46, 163 are taken from *The Ancient Irish Epic Tale:
Tain Bo Culange* by Joseph Dunn. Published by David Nutt, London, 1914.

Latin prayers and Irish poem on pages 79 and 209-210 taken from *The Celtic
Saints* by Daphne D. C. Pochin Mould. © 1956, 1982 by Devin-Adair Publishers,
Inc., 6 N. Water Street, Greenwich, CT 06830. Reprinted by permission.

Excerpt from poem, "The Altus Prosator," on page 130 taken from *Monks and
Civilization* by Jean Decarreaux. © 1964 by Librarie Arthaud, c/o Georges
Borchardt, Inc., 136 East 57th Street, New York, NY 10022. Reprinted by
permission.

Poems on pages 124 and 216-217 reprinted by permission from *Ireland:
Harbinger of the Middle Ages* by Ludwig Bieler, © 1963 by Oxford University
Press.

Library of Congress Cataloging-in-Publication Data

Desjarlais, John, 1953-
    The throne of Tara / John Desjarlais.
        p.   cm.
    ISBN 0-89107-574-7
    1. Columba, Saint, 521-597--Fiction.   2. Ireland--History--To
1172--Fiction.   I. Title.
    PS3554.E11577T4   1990
813' .54--dc20

90-80614
                                                                          CIP

For Virginia,
my wife and soul-friend

and

In memory of Dad,
a soldier for Christ

CONTENTS

ACKNOWLEDGMENTS

I have taken certain liberties with the written records of Columcille's life. The struggle with Broichan and the druids, for example, accompanied other contests of power. For the fuller story, see Adomnan's *Life of Columba,* the Ninth Abbot of Iona's tribute to his patron. I have introduced fictional characters true to the culture for the story's dramatic sake, such as Drummon, though the battlefield where he fell in fiction is today in fact called Coola-Drummon.

Otherwise, historical characters, beliefs, and details of Celtic culture and the Irish church are as accurately recreated as possible. I pray Columban scholars to forgive where I may have oversimplified or chosen a controversial interpretation of history. I also ask modern readers to allow for beliefs they may consider non-Biblical that are included because they reflect the actual thinking of people at that time.

I would like to acknowledge the assistance of library staff at Edgewood College, Gordon-Conwell Theological Seminary, Trinity Evangelical Divinity School, and the Madison Public Libraries for providing research resources.

I also thank Ellen Hunnicutt and Betty Durbin for their critique and early encouragement, Donald Brandenburgh for his persistence, Jan Dennis and Lila Bishop at Crossway Books for their courage, and Scott Wilson at InterVarsity for allowing me creative space. Above all, I thank my Irish wife, Virginia, who believed in me and my son Matthew, who at age seven acted out the sword fights with me.

John Desjarlais
Madison, Wisconsin

1

FEDLIMIDH

A.D. 521

 HAVE A SON," FUMED
FEDLIMIDH, WIPING RAIN
from his grizzled mustache, "and by the gods, he shall be High
King of Erin one day."

The chieftain punched aside the heavy hides at the entry
of his lodge and marched to the central hearth. Waterdrops
drained off his stout body, leaving a dark trail on the clay floor.
He held his battle-worn hands to the fire for a moment, and then
began peeling off his clinging tunic.

"High King," he said with a huskiness not from the winter's dampness but from the pride of his lineage, "Ard-Ri, king of
all the kings." He squeezed water from the sleeves. "Did you hear
me, Drummon?"

The broad-shouldered bodyguard, Drummon, finally
caught up and assisted his patron with his gear. Not minding the
pool he himself created on the floor, Drummon grasped the
chieftain's dented bronze helmet and gently lifted it off.

"Enough wars. Enough cattle raids." Fedlimidh's voice
rose with his temper. The hearthlight flashed in his narrow gray
eyes as sunlight glints on silver daggers. He gazed into the fire
with an equally burning intensity, the lines on his squint-eyed
face deepening to match the curvilinear tendrils etched on his
helmet. "It is no way to prove you are a worthy king."

"They didn't get any of the herd," said Drummon, wrapping him with a cloak. "The storm drove them off, and we found the missing cows in the woods."

"Stealing them is not the object." The gratuitous insult of the raid settled in Fedlimidh's muscular chest like phlegm. Reprisal—short, swift, and equally insulting—was called for by custom. But as he peered into the flickering blaze, he glimpsed a future, not of more petty raids on his own relatives to provide the banquet hall bards with more stories, but of his baby boy as a grown man taking the furry cloak and massive gold brooch of kingship at Tara where the chief of the Celtic chieftains ruled and judged. When a log popped, Fedlimidh's dream merged into the angry red coals and was lost. The growling in his stomach returned. "Did you get any idea who it was?"

"No," said Drummon, "the rain covered them well. I couldn't see the bridles. But it must have been your cousin, Cadoc of Cinell nEogain."

"He has always been jealous of me." *He may be elected overking of the Northern Hy Neill for now,* Fedlimidh thought, *but I am descended directly from Niall of the Nine Hostages. Fedlimidh macFergus's son is in line to be the Ard-Ri of Eire, and Cadoc will in due time be counting out his cattle and sacks of grain very carefully as tribute to my son, according to the Brehon Law. Raids will not be necessary any longer.*

The chieftain savored the thought of his long-range revenge, and as the winter rain, driven sideways in solid drenching sheets, rattled the lodge walls, Fedlimidh grinned. *Fate is on my side. Cadoc and his men are out there in this.*

The singing from the other end of the lodge broke his line of thought. Fedlimidh's mischievous grin widened to a pleased, gentle smile at the soft woman's voice, lifted in a lullaby. Fedlimidh's wife, Eithne, wrapped and rocked their infant son in the sleeping room beyond the dark deerskin hides. Her music swirled in the main hall like a welcome breeze, echoing playfully off the timber walls in time with the drumming of the rain, which now dripped in rhythmic thumps on the long oaken bunks where the household warriors slept.

"Do you hear that, Drummon? One of the psalms, no doubt. The boy will have them all memorized before he's five."

The singing continued, dropping to a hum now and then.

"She's preparing him for baptism," Fedlimidh continued, "but all we'd have to do today is hold him outside the door."

Even as he said it, the rain lightened. The Atlantic squall pressed eastward, leaving behind a pearly mist which caressed the deep green countryside. The abbot would probably make the trip from the abbey after all.

"She wants him to be a man of the Church," the chieftain grumped. "Perhaps his hair will grow down the back and not on top, and then we'll know he was meant to be one." He glanced anxiously at the curtain, lowering his voice. "She says it's God's will. How does she know what God's will is? Can she see the future like a druid?"

Drummon warmed himself by the fire, palms outstretched to the glowing cinders. "It is what *you* see that matters."

Fedlimidh clapped his square hands. "She can't even see the past. She too is descended from kings. Why can't she see he is destined to be the Ard-Ri?"

"She perhaps sees only the present."

"Then let her see that our marriage not only secures peace between Ulster and Leinster, but points to the uniting of all kingdoms under our son."

Drummon shifted his weight to face his foster brother and chief. "You know what she'll say," he whispered. "Your father, Fergus, was baptized by the blessed Patrick himself. A sure sign that his destiny is in the Church."

But Fedlimidh knew the real cause of Eithne's dreams for their son. It is the son they waited so long to have, and only when Eithne left the annual rites of fertility at the druids' wells and turned to the monks in earnest, embracing the new faith as a grapevine wraps a trellis, did she conceive. Fedlimidh remembered the many nights of her shaking sobs over her barren curse and the angry helplessness he felt lying silently next to her in the dark. He had refused concubines, to the consternation of his men. "They may be permitted by the law," he had said, "but I will not disrupt the royal line."

And now the boy seemed a gift of God, and Eithne had promised to return him to God in the service of the Church. How could she when it was also apparent the gods had favored his fidelity? Could their son not worship Eithne's God along with the others at Tara?

13

Fedlimidh recalled his own baptism at an early age with the whole household of Fergus and his warriors. It seemed to please his irascible father, but the belief was never deep. No god should be offended or go unappeased.

Eithne's pure, clear singing continued. "What's keeping her?" Fedlimidh grumbled. "Will she pray all day?"

"Probably putting him into extra wraps," comforted Drummon. "The church will be cold. And wet."

"Prayer won't help that," Fedlimidh grunted. He pulled at his bronze torque, the sacred collar of heroes he refused to remove. It lay cold against his leathery skin. The chill awakened the pains in his back and neck, reminders of all the petty raids to keep his hereditary holdings secure and his fluctuating allies satisfied. "Check on the guard in the pasture," he said with a wave of his hand. "We'll want no interruptions during the service. It's not beyond Cadoc's men to try again. I would consider the baptismal ceremony to be an excellent opportunity."

Drummon nodded, rose quickly, and slipped through the thick hides to the outside. A cool gust entered through the flaps carrying a few loose leaves, which briefly eddied and then settled. Yes, the wind was picking up again. The winter squalls hit and run as quickly as cattle raiders. Fedlimidh rubbed his chin, coarse with the night's stubble. He would have to shave before the abbot's arrival. Would that it were soon. Then perhaps he could make a speedy foray into the hills to clear them of thieves. Thank the gods, the abbot's trip from the abbey was barely a half-day's ride. *But, of course, the gods of Erin and the God of the abbey are not on good terms,* smiled the chieftain. *But I would sooner trust in Neit and Nemon, gods of war, than the God of Eithne, who gives His royal son a crown of thorns. My son,* he burned, *will have a different crown. My son will not be humiliated, as I have been. Eithne must understand that.*

The singing suddenly stopped. The sleeping-room curtains snapped open. The rush of the deerskins bestirred the bats in the smoke-blackened rafters, and the flutter of their leathery wings filled the hall. Fedlimidh stood with a start, his sword scraping the earthen floor. His reflexive movement, like that of a surprised badger, sent a twinge of pain through his back, but he grimaced inwardly.

Eithne strode into the main room of the lodge, servant

girls giggling behind her. With royal bearing, tall and graceful, she seemed to float. Her copper hair shimmered in the hearthlight. Her white cape, fringed with bright fox pelts, flowed behind her so that she seemed an angel. The wide-set eyes, green as springtime, glanced happily from Fedlimidh to the bundle she held against her embroidered bodice.

The chieftain came forward to greet her, pressing his helmet over his head as if preparing for battle. His quick strides on short legs, tough as oak, carried his stocky frame to his loved ones in the space of a few blinks. His swinging fists opened to gently hug them. His eyes, cold as slate and piercing as one of his prize javelins, softened as the baby squirmed and bubbled. As the proud father playfully poked at the child's tummy, a tiny hand reached out from the woolen folds to grasp his scarred finger.

"He has a good grip, as a warrior holds a sword," beamed Fedlimidh.

"Or as a scholar holds a quill," countered Eithne.

"As a horseman pulls the reins."

"As a priest raises the cup."

"He shall be Crimthann, the wolf, filled with strength and speed."

"He shall be Colum, the dove, filled with the Holy Spirit."

Fedlimidh's voice took an annoyed tone. "He is of the royal family of the Hy Neill."

"He is to be of the family of the High King of Heaven."

The fire snapped. The room seemed noticeably warmer. Fedlimidh's forehead began to bead with sweat, and his jaw tightened. *We may have married to settle an old rivalry between our tribes,* he mused, *but the battles go on.*

"Your back is bothering you again," Eithne said quietly. She bent down to kiss her husband's forehead. She stroked his dark hair, still matted against the back of his neck from the rain. "What happened? You left in such a hurry. There were shouts in the dark, and then you were gone."

"Cadoc and his men raided the herd."

"I would have gone with you, the baby . . ."

"I know," Fedlimidh smiled, grasping her shoulders in an understanding squeeze. "They got nothing."

Eithne pinched her eyes closed in a fleeting prayer of thanks. She had brought many of her own cattle from Leinster when she joined Fedlimidh in marriage. She herself had beaten off wolves and thieves in the cattle-drive north to Donegal. She looked over Fedlimidh's shoulder, as if looking through the walls into the hills. "Then they're still out there somewhere."

"Yes."

"Shall we go after them?"

"No," he snorted, like a horse in the gate at the tournament races, seeing the track and chomping the bit. He shook the baby's fists. *But my son will. In due time.*

◼

The church of the dun presided on higher ground over the timber-and-sod huts surrounding it, like a teacher over a group of attentive schoolchildren. It now commanded the altar space of a sacred grove once claimed by the druids. Sunken, soggy holes remained where the oaks had been ripped up from the ground and milled into the lumber to build the church. The wood now absorbed the chants of psalms rather than the screams of criminals burnt as sacrifices inside animal-shaped wicker cages.

Inside, the old priest with a face as craggy as oak stood in undyed wool, with his Tiaga satchel containing Scripture portions and the Order of Baptism slung over his frail shoulder. He was shaven from ear to ear in the distinctive tonsure of the Irish church. A few wisps of sheep-white hair hung freely down behind his drooping ears. His bony finger traced a sign of the cross as Eithne and Fedlimidh stepped forward in the church to present the boy.

"Oh, a fine one, a fine one," the abbot beamed, opening his gnarled hands in welcome. Eithne knelt before him to receive the blessing of his extended hand, but Fedlimidh stood firm, arms folded.

"Dear Cruithnechain," said Eithne, head bowed, "are you well? I've missed you. How long now?"

"Since your last time of instruction, Child, since the first news of the boy."

Fedlimidh's cheeks warmed, and his lips pressed together. He disliked the easy rapport and intimate respect Eithne gave to her soul-friend, or confessor.

The abbot noticed the chieftain's discomfort. "Fedlimidh,

sons are a gift from the Lord, and children a reward from Him. Like arrows in the hands of a warrior are the sons of a man's youth. Happy is the man whose quiver is full of them; such men shall not be put to shame when they confront their enemies in court."

The quote from the Psalms raised a brighter flush in Fedlimidh's face. All morning he had dwelt on the day when he would bring his son to the court of the High King, not to the oratory of some churchman.

Eithne rose, the swaddled boy squirming against her bosom. She gently pushed back the hood from the baby's head. Tufts of fine, reddish hair peeked out.

"Have you decided on a name?" asked the abbot.

Mother and father glanced at each other, her eyebrows raised and his lowered.

Cruithnechain understood. "Two names, I imagine," he sighed. "Well, why not? One a name. One a title. Everyone can guess which is which. Let's begin."

The boy was transferred into the baptismal gown. Eithne and Cruithnechain carefully wrapped the white linen around the protesting kicks of the child. Fedlimidh tugged at the huge silver brooch pinning his cape. The abbot began to intone the rite of inclusion into the kingdom of God, his tired eyes suddenly brighter and his wizened face cracking into a toothy smile. "*In nomini Patris, et Filii, et Spiritu Sanctus . . .*"

Fedlimidh's hand tightened on his enameled sword hilt. He could not imagine his son, destined for glory, in the company of quiet monks with their strange language, strange shaven heads, and stranger disposition towards books. How could he explain to the other chieftains of the north that his son might not be the fulfillment of their hopes to wrest the power of Tara from their southern rivals? What then would prevent Cadoc from positioning his own sons for the honor, since he already sat as the elected overking of the Northern Hy Neill? But worse, what would he say to his own father in the Otherworld, who faced his enemies even in death, buried upright in full battle array? Fedlimidh still heard his dying words: "Return glory to the Dun Con Conaill. Do not fail me."

"What shall be the child's names?"

The familiar Gaelic pulled Fedlimidh back into the

church. Once again, he exchanged a questioning glance with Eithne. His palms dampened like the stones tucked between the church's timbers. The baby fussed, tiny fists punching the air. Eithne was leaving it up to him, and there could be no argument in the presence of the villagers gathered at the door. The abbot's right thumb remained poised over the mouth of a small glass cruet filled with the chrism oil.

Fedlimidh's mouth, dry as winter hay stubble, twitched. Glowering, he said, "He shall be Crimthann, the wolf." He caught Eithne's darkening eyes. "And Colum, the dove."

The rain clattered once again on the steep slate roof as Cruithnechain anointed the crying child and led the parents in the litany to renounce Satan and his works and pomps and declare belief in the triune God. The abbot took the child in his robed arms, gripping him tightly as he would a full chalice. The boy pumped his legs and drew a deep breath for a piercing scream of protest. "Howling and flapping his arms like wings," called out the abbot above the din. "He lives up to his names already."

As the boy splashed into the font three times, water spattered to the broad, flat stone under the abbot's feet. The deep brown bloodstains of former druid sacrifices glistened with the spray and seemed to steam.

■

When the seasons turned, Fedlimidh left for his annual obligatory attendance at the overking's court. He arrived late, as always. Cadoc's round hall, filled with a pungent hazy smoke from the cooking fires, stank of roast boar and spilled beer. Loud conversations, plump with boasting, crisscrossed the crowded room. Chieftains and champions from the many scattered kingdoms huddled cross-legged with their women on gaudy pillows and wolfskins, trading tales of prowess.

No one noticed Fedlimidh's arrival. With Drummon at his side, he took his customary place beneath the prize stag heads, away from the door where the lesser nobles squatted, but also far from his cousin, the king of the northwestern clans of the Hy Neill.

Cadoc sprawled in a wicker throne-seat woven of yew wood and covered with otter furs. The chair creaked each time he lifted his meaty fist to his mouth with food. He wiped his long, drooping mustache and licked juice from his gem-studded finger and thumb rings, one for each king killed in battle.

Fedlimidh took note of the number and position of Cadoc's household warriors. Most were feasting, but a few stood stiffly behind the king. Brawny and bare-chested, the warriors' blond hair flowed down past their thick necks, collared by gold heroes' torques.

A throaty snarl pulled Fedlimidh's attention to the far corner where the hearthlight barely reached. An enormous wolfdog, big as a mule, lay in an iron cage. The shaggy beast, no doubt, had helped Cadoc track and kill the boar everyone enjoyed, as well as the magnificent stags whose heads adorned the rafters. But the animal was asleep. Beside the cage crouched the king's champion, ripping the boar thigh meat noisily. It seemed by the absence of blood on the clay floor that no one had challenged him for the prize this year.

The other choice parts lay half-eaten before the king's poet. Standing near the king, bright with the six colors allowed for his Ollave, or doctoral, rank, the poet plucked at a lyre.

Clustered around the king's knee-high table sat the judge, the bishop, the historian, and a guest musician, trading exaggerated accounts of the year's exploits, outdoing one another in boasting. The judge's black robe and the bishop's chestnut cowl contrasted with the king's seven colors which no one else was permitted to wear. The colors bounced as Cadoc guffawed at the historian's stories. About cattle raids, it seemed.

While everyone reclined, sucking bones and swigging beer and mead, the physician patrolled the floor. His yellowed eyes, shifting like a bird of prey, looked for signs which required his gruesome attention. His nervous, knotty fingers caressed the bag of herbs and poisons pinned to his belt. His darting eyes seemed to be asking, "Was that a cough over there, not a laugh? Does his skin seem yellow? Are his eyes more watery than usual?" Many turned askance as the doctor made his covert rounds. Too much of his art had been learned from the druids. One could either end up cured or changed into a sea gull.

The musician joined the poet, experimenting with a new song. The harp's brass strings, old and stretched, hummed and screeched alternatively.

Cadoc spat out fat into his bowl and hailed the musician.

"What is that?" he bellowed. "It's enough to make our enemies beg to surrender."

"We shall go to battle armed with harps and led by bards," said the historian.

The guests roared, toasting the idea with their goblets, spilling more beer. A few threw bones at the bard.

"That is not far from the truth," said the musician. "I have been employed many times in war to hurl satire rather than spears."

"A powerful weapon, indeed," acknowledged Cadoc. He swirled the amber mead in his cup. "But I would rather have a hundred warriors than a hundred harpers."

"Perhaps they could be trained to be both," said the bard.

"Such a man should lead them into the battle," said Cadoc.

"Such a man will."

"And who will that be? And mind your words, you don't want to give up your warm bed for the night."

The bard stood so fluidly that it appeared he had hardly tensed a muscle, as if he'd been lifted. The company quieted. As the bard rose he cast a long shadow on the wall, a new presence in the room. It hovered over the stretched hides like a specter, outlined in the golden light of the fires. Cadoc stopped chewing and swallowed with a loud gulp. His champion stirred in the corner as though suddenly aware of danger, his greasy hand sliding to the ornate dagger handle by his hip.

The bard locked his eyes on the king's and held him hypnotically. His rich voice, high and melancholy, swirled in the hall, punctuated by crackling from the fires. The voice seemed to come from the shadow, from another world and time, singing:

> A man shall be born of your rage,
> > A poet, a prophet, a sage.
> Pure, a lovable lamp, and clear,
> > Never in falsehood, ever held dear
> As a pious king of the graces,
> > Known in the heavenly places.

The bishop crossed himself, and several warriors followed him in the gesture. "It's the prophecy of Patrick," said the bishop in awe, "given to the clans of the Hy Neill."

The bard sat down slowly, wheezing. The court poet steadied him under the shoulders, easing him onto a cushion. He passed him his own goblet and helped him to sip it, for the bard's hands shook too much.

Cadoc looked over the company of guests who were buzzing in hushed tones. He spied Fedlimidh and stabbed his finger towards him. "Perhaps he is speaking of you, Cousin," he called. "You have had a son this year."

Fedlimidh straightened, ignoring the ache in his back from the long ride. "Yes, we have had a son born into the royal line of Niall of the Nine Hostages."

"Is it well?" croaked the physician, slinking closer.

"Yes, he is well," said the chieftain between clenched teeth. His icy stare froze the physician, who smiled thinly.

The bishop leaned forward. "Perhaps it is your son of whom the blessed Patrick spoke," he said.

"There have been many sons born this year in Erin," retorted Fedlimidh.

"Is his training prepared?" asked the bishop.

"Crimthann shall learn the ways of the horseman and warrior, as is our custom."

"Crimthann?" The bishop rubbed his chin. "Is he not also Colum, pledged to the Church?"

"He has been pledged to Cruithnechain of Abbey Douglas in fosterage at the proper age according to the Brehon Law."

"And then?" pressed the bishop.

"Ask the bard. He seems to know the future," said Fedlimidh.

Cadoc drummed his fingers, round and ruddy as blood sausages, taking pleasure in his rival's discomfort. "It is your right, Cousin," he said, "to raise the boy a warrior-chief. He must have your lodge and lands one day as the eldest. You would not so easily allow him to forfeit his inheritance to serve the Church, now, would you?"

"He can be a chief and serve the Church at the same time," said Fedlimidh. "Why not? There are still many druids who are also chieftains. Is that not so, historian?"

The historian nodded. "But they also go into battle. Could he uphold the honor of the Hy Neill and also uphold the word of this God who has made you weak and afraid to fight?"

Fedlimidh bristled, but restrained himself. He controlled his right hand, itching to draw the bronze dagger from its sheath and send it spinning into the historian's throat. He quickly gauged the distance but dismissed the thought. This was no way to win power over the clan and unite the dozens of scattered duns.

"My son will learn everything necessary to be a king."

Cadoc drained his cup. "And who will he learn from, to be a proper warrior? Surely not you, Fedlimidh. We can hardly trust you to join our raids anymore."

"I have all the cattle I need," said Fedlimidh, muscles tensed. Drummon laid a hand on his patron to calm him, but it was like trying to cap a hot spring with a stone. "Why fight among ourselves?" Fedlimidh managed. "It keeps the southern clans in power at Tara."

Cadoc laughed. "Southern clans? Cousin, you have married into the house of Leinster. You are practically southern yourself."

Fedlimidh rose with a start, and Drummon could not grab his arm quickly enough to restrain him. The flaxen-haired warriors behind Cadoc stiffened, and the champion in the corner growled. "I am a man of Ulster," thundered Fedlimidh, "and I am sworn to see a man of Ulster take the cloak of Tara. It may or may not be my own son, but nonetheless I will train him in all the skills of a warrior-king as the gods will."

Cadoc sounded a wet belch. "Which gods, Fedlimidh? Lug who carries a club, or the bishop's Christ who carries a cross?" He wiped his bowl with a handful of flatbread. "And king? He will do well in your house, Cousin, if he can protect the royal chessman in your care. But he will not protect the Hy Neill."

"And you?" boomed Fedlimidh, taking a step. The warriors' jewelry jingled as they felt for their sword handles. Fedlimidh held out his arms, scanning the guests. "Are you protecting our people? You incite the chiefs to raid each other for land and women. Is it not enough to receive the tribute due you by the Brehon? Must you sneak in the dark like a weasel to steal from your own family? The men of Meath and Connaught laugh at the men of Ulster pecking each other like roosters." He paused to catch his breath. "We will teach the boy how to fight," he said sternly, "and we will teach him who to fight."

Cadoc bent his head down slightly to assess his soldiers from the corners of his eyes. Then he shook his head as if merely annoyed. "Sit down, Fedlimidh, dear cousin," he said. "Let's not fight here. I killed a boaster every day last week, and to keep the Sabbath holy, killed two on Saturday."

The guests clapped and hooted. The court poet struck up a tune. Drummon helped Fedlimidh find his seat again and nearly wrestled him down. Fedlimidh's searing gaze fixed on the chuckling Cadoc, never turning to the doorway where the rowdy band of cockfighters invaded the feast.

Two glossy birds in separate cages scratched and fluttered while pillows were kicked away to make room. The cages were joined and the latches thrown to remove the barrier between them. And as the squawking roosters clawed at each other, one bright with colored feathers and one dark with a menacing forward-leaning comb, Fedlimidh continued to eye the king who laid his bet with vigor on the bright cock, "for it has the colors of a king!" But when the colored rooster, badly bloodied and retreating, fell to the furious talons of the dark opponent, Fedlimidh knew that he, not his cousin, would have the power to weave the northern Hy Neills into a shield of strength to advance to Tara. And Crimthann would lead the way.

2

EITHNE

A.D. 529

EDLIMIDH'S DUN STOOD
BRIGHT AND SHINING ON THE
hill, its limed drystone palisade overlooking long, narrow Gartan
Lough, whose waters reflected the darkness of the deer-filled,
wooded mountains. With morning, the wolves had stopped
their trilling and yips, and the cows returned to the boulder-
strewn pasture.

Inside the round fort, thin threads of blue smoke from
peat fires began to curl upward through the thatch. The outer
gate opened, and the stableboy let out the horses to mark the
beginning of the day, according to the Brehon Law. Urging them
forward with playful shouts, a group of kilted boys dashed out
for a swim in the lake, a blur of bodies pushing through the fragrant fuchsia and vaulting the fiery rhododendron, kicking up
puffs of pollen, splashing each other in the cold brook that wandered to the rugged, rocky shore.

Colum led the noisy pack, his long, thin legs pumping like
a mischievous colt's. His red cheeks puffed with determination as
the other boys wheezed at his heels, laughing. For Colum had
now spread his arms like a sea gull about to dive for breakfast.

Eithne watched the race from the gateway, a wicker
sewing basket balanced on her hip. "Look how tall he is already,
Collain," she called over her shoulder to the house servant.

"I see," said Collain, resting her basket of clothes bound for the brook's washing rocks. She pressed her deeply-lined palm to her forehead.

Eithne admired the glint of her son's copper hair as he disappeared over the slope leading to the lake. "He may look like me, but he has his father's temper."

Collain didn't answer. She hefted the basket with a sigh though it only had a few soiled garments.

The women followed a well-worn path to a wider place in the brook shaded by hickory and apple trees. Soon the nearby slopes would be white with their blossoms, rivaling the distant white quartzite cone of Mount Erigal, sovereign of the Derryveagh Range.

The women settled by the brook's edge where the waters glittered with the springtime sunlight, bringing life to the thirsty gorse bushes clinging to the rocks. Collain smacked the clothes on the wet stones and began kneading the dirt out, pounding them mercilessly. Eithne sat nearby, bone needle in one hand, the other digging in the basket for the proper thread. She noticed Collain's furious wringing and put the sewing aside. "Please let me help, Collain, you know I always do . . ."

"No, no, it's all right, just these couple of things to do," Collain objected, her voice thin and strained.

"I can leave the trousers for Colum for another time," said Eithne gently. "His birthday is months away."

"No, I'll manage." Collain bit her lip and twisted the cool water from the cloth as though wringing a foul's neck. She snapped it out to dry on a nearby boulder and lifted her puckered hand to her temple.

Eithne, with her needle threaded, began to stroke calmly through the linen fragments. "Something is on your mind, Collain," she said. "It's Colum, isn't it?"

"It's just an ache in my head."

"Is Colum the ache?"

"Well, he . . . ," she hesitated.

Eithne nodded to encourage her onward. She kept the steady pace of the needle to control her own fear that perhaps Colum had gone too far with his temper this time. In the years past, she had seen Collain try to beat the temper out of him, but now he was getting too big for that. He was a good seven-year-old, really. Bright, eager to learn, robust, and full of mischief, and full of mystery. Eithne remembered how his angered face set ablaze to match his hair and how he growled when the younger children kicked the pile of stones he'd carefully stacked, an immense fort complete with ramparts and water-filled ditches. The deep concentration he used to build the model turned instantly to a deep drive to revenge, and after being restrained, he had brooded in the church for hours.

A haze of other memory-pictures passed through her mind: the broken play arrows, the spill on his servingplace. How many bruises and cuts had she and Collain nursed because Colum had lashed out with tooth and slashing fingernail, like a cornered wolf, only to be smiling and humorous the next moment, hardly remembering his outrage? The calm that settled on his face was as eerie as the choler.

◼

She must know, thought Collain as she rubbed at a stain, her lips rehearsing what she could share with Eithne. She had only asked him to chop the wood, which he'd done many times before. "I had a dream," he had said. "I cut thousands of oaks with just a word, and they were all crying. What does it mean?"

"Dream your way straight to the woodpile, young man," she pointed. She would be firmer this time and ignore any tantrum. Fedlimidh would not snatch him from his chores today to learn swordplay. *How like him,* she thought, *compulsive and quick to anger that comes and goes like a summer storm, spent in a moment, giving way to a sunny affection. Spirited and free as a dove one moment, fierce as a wolf the next. He was named well.* "Pick up that ax and go." Her pointing finger shook a bit, but she determined not to give in or call out to Eithne again.

"But father promised to teach me with real swords today."

"Ax now, swords later."

His silver eyes, at first inquisitive, darkened like thunderclouds. "Father is waiting for me," he said slowly. "A prince of the household has more important things to do than chop wood. That is work for a commoner."

That was it. She picked him up by the ear and pulled him outside. "Now," she stammered, "chop this wood and carry it inside."

The boy grabbed the ax with vigor and turned towards her. She stepped back with a gasp when she heard the low growl. A headache struck with a stab, and she nearly fainted. Somehow she managed to point to the woodpile, and the boy attacked it with a ferocity likely meant for her. Chips spun in all directions, and by the time Fedlimidh rushed out to see about the crying and hacking, he found the boy flushed red, covered with sweat and flecks of bark. Collain knelt by the lodge, choking back sobs. Fedlimidh helped the woman to her feet, soothed her with a few words, and turned to the boy. His son was smiling now, wiping his brow with his sleeve and streaking it with dirt. "I think that's the fastest I ever did it," he had said proudly, planting the ax in a stump with a thud.

"Let's get to the field now, Wolf," Collain overheard. "But first you must learn that a true chieftain cares for his household. Say you're sorry to Collain."

The boy ran to her, hugged her skirts and burst into tears. "I'm sorry," he moaned sincerely, face buried in the linen folds.

But Collain's temples still pounded. "Go practice now," she whispered, smoothing his red hair with one hand and holding her own forehead with the other.

Fedlimidh put a hand on her shaking shoulder. "Collain, are you all right?"

■

"Collain, are you all right?" Now it was Eithne asking, her hands suddenly still, her green eyes puzzled. "Collain, are you ill?"

"No, no. Just, my head hurts. I'm worried for Crim . . . I mean, for Colum."

"He was a wolf with you yesterday?"

"He lives up to both his names." She rubbed the cloth faster, afraid to reveal more. An idle curse, a mean-spirited prayer, could be disastrous.

"He's like our own countryside," said Eithne, looking up at the clouds galloping across the blue sky, throwing shadows across the rolling pastures. Deep, gloomy grays and tans gave way to vibrant shades of purple and green. The patches of color chased each other over the flower-matted meadows. "Head in the clouds one moment, like a dove," she mused, "and furious as a beast the next. Just like his father."

27

"Don't you worry for him?" Collain said.

Eithne's eyes misted. "The time for his fosterage with Cruithnechain is near. Soon after his birthday, we must take him to the abbot according to the Brehon Law. According to my promise." The thought of leaving him in the woods with Cruithnechain sent a pang of emptiness into her stomach. "We have taught him all we can here. Train up a child in the way he should go, and when he is old, he will not depart from it," she quoted.

"But which way have we taught him? The way of Laegaive the Victorious, Keltar of the Battles, Cethern of the Brilliant Deeds, Conor of the Red Brows, CuChulainn . . ."

"Joseph of Egypt, Moses the Lawgiver, David the Shepherd-King. . ."

"And warrior."

Eithne nodded, remembering how many times she had told him the story of David and Goliath. "Our people love heroes," she admitted, "and they are madly fond of war." She began to gather her sewing into the basket.

"From the beginning I knew he was to be different though," she continued. "I did not give him his first solid food on the tip of Fedlimidh's sword and vow he would find no death but in battle. Fedlimidh was, shall we say, displeased?"

"I remember."

"But yesterday Colum behaved like every good warrior," said Eithne, recalling the hunting party's return from the forests. When the men entered the dun with their game roped to their spears, Colum joined the victory procession, whirling his wooden sword, beating it on his little shield just like the burly hunters. He strutted and hollered in his high but pleasing voice, composing a song on the spot about their brave deeds. The men laughed and hoisted him up on their bare shoulders. And when he had come scampering to Eithne, hopping with excitement and grinning gap-toothed, she wiped his face that was streaked with white lime from the dazzling, drummed shield, and sent him off to play. But he followed the men and watched with deep interest as the game was skinned, cleaned, cut, and hung in the curing house. Then she had to wipe off the blood, pierced with a cold premonition that there would be men's blood on his hands one day.

Yet she shook off the vision with better memories of her recurring dreams where God's Spirit, like a dove — soft, radiant, pure, and free — descended on her Colum. And the voice always came next, a reassuring whisper: "He will lead many into the heavenly country." Then she would always awaken, strangely warmed but newly worried.

"Is it blasphemy?" she had cried to Cruithnechain. "It is too much like the baptism of the Lord."

"Do you not wish the boy to be like Him?"

"How so, Father?"

"Is he not a king? Called to be a servant?"

"No questions, please, Father," she interrupted. "Just tell me what it means."

"Only you know. It is not my dream."

God will honor my vow, she thought. *Colum, born to be a king, will lead many into the kingdom of God, not into the battles of Erin's warring kingdoms.*

The distant splashing of the boys' swimming stopped, and above the trickle of the brook, Eithne heard the clicking of wooden swords.

"I'm going to watch him over there," she said, bundling up her things. "Just leave the clothes to dry awhile and go rest, Collain."

Collain dropped the cloth to a rock sure to get the sun as the day advanced, stood slowly, and turned for the dun. Head low, she still rubbed her temple.

"Collain," Eithne called, "whatever happened, I know you did what you were supposed to do. You always have."

"Thank you," Collain whispered.

"He's a bit unpredictable now," Eithne continued soothingly. "He's just discovering how he must live with the consequences of his choices. It must be frightening for a seven-year-old."

"It frightens me," said Collain.

Eithne watched her scuff over the path up the hill to where the spiked stockade of the settlement began.

She is faithful, thought Eithne. *She cares for Colum as if for her own, which her brave old husband Boite had never given her. Killed in a raid.* She shook her head sadly.

Eithne bent her ear into the breeze. Faintly, she could hear

Drummon lecturing the boys about something or spinning a tale of his former glories. Teaching them to brag and embellish. She sighed. She followed the brook down the knoll toward the lough. Still no snap of flint-tipped practice javelins. No twang of bowstrings. Drummon must be up to something else today.

She picked her way around a circle of rocks where Colum often strayed alone. Many a time she had come to fetch him from this quiet retreat, worried that alone and outside the ramparts, he could fall prey to roving wild dogs or a jealous rival interested in a royal hostage. Scolding had long lost its effect, and the brooding boy still sought refuge in this tiny, natural roofless cell.

In this way he differed from the other boys, always with their tongues wagging. He could chatter with his endless "whys" and be as annoyingly verbal as any other bright child, but he was also quiet and curious, capable of long concentration — examining flower petals, counting stars, drawing animals with charcoal in the margins of his wooden letter-board.

Eithne stopped and looked around in a broad sweep. Crowning the knoll was the great somber circle of the hillfort, rising from the green, the thick stone walls challenging the stony hills and rugged coast. What did he think about when he sat here to survey the rolling pasture dotted with cows? The upland forests filled with deer and danger? The deep blue bays patrolled by monsters? Did he sing his memorized psalms, as the shepherd boy David sang when out with his sheep?

As she moved on and reached the edge of the grass where the earth dipped steeply to the pebbly shore of the lough, she caught sight of the boys with Drummon.

A half-dozen young boys, their knee-length tunics dancing, crowded the annoyed champion. Colum stood above the rest, tall for his age, the hair golden in the morning sun. With the other boys, he jumped and squawked, scrambling like a sparrow competing for crumbs, trying to get a better view of whatever Drummon pulled out of a large burlap sack.

"Let me see."

"Are they real?"

"Are they yours, Drummon?"

"Did they ever kill anyone?"

Fedlimidh's captain of the household guard stood up, towering over the skinny youngsters. His curling flaxen mustache flowed back to join his long hair, pushed behind the earrings and hanging over the hero's bronze collar. Laughing, he brushed away the boys with a slow sweep of his bronze-banded arms.

"Back now, step back, you bunch of peeping chicks. No one gets a chance with these until I have more room."

The boys backed off, chattering, clustering around Colum. He stood quite still now, eyes fastened on Drummon, listening intently as though waiting for a command to attack. The others bumped him in their excitement, but he did not seem to notice the jostling and shoving. His attention was fixed on the shiny swords Drummon drew reverently from the sack.

Eithne pressed her ruby lips together when she saw the gleaming weapons. Her long fingers wrapped absently around an imaginary hilt of the blade she had wielded in defense of her cattle. *It's in our blood,* she thought as she found a weather-worn boulder for a seat.

A squat, overweight boy with greasy hair elbowed Colum. Padarn, the blacksmith's eldest, pointed proudly to the weapons which Drummon now stacked in a circle. He raised his hammer-like fists in a show of strength, pummeling them on an anvil of his imagination, for the swords were the products of his father's forging.

Colum just rolled his eyes, unimpressed by the act, much to Padarn's annoyance. Instead, he concentrated quietly on the long, narrow blades, dulled in drilling and unsharpened. Wider at the handles, which were capped by small carved heads, the blades showed signs of wear — chips, discoloring, scratched enameling.

"How many heads have they cut off?" wondered Padarn out loud. "Who wants to bet how many?"

Colum stuck out his tongue at the thought while the other boys chuckled and called out numbers.

"Three times fifty!"

"A score each!"

Eithne shifted her position uncomfortably. Few warriors took such cedar-oiled trophies now. But rumor was that the smith, who made the swords, preserved a few in a chest to show proudly to relatives, customers, and foreign visitors. "It's why the Romans never came to Erin," he would boast.

Padarn continued to swagger, gaining the attention of the other boys who left Colum's side and gathered around the big boy at a respectable distance. Many villagers still considered his father a wizard, working magic with metals amid a spray of sparks. The boys imitated Padarn's struts, much to his pleasure.

The commotion broke Colum's thought, and he turned to catch a view of Eithne among the rocks. They waved happily to each other. She motioned him to pay heed to Drummon, and then rolled down her sleeves as the cooler lakeside breeze blew in.

"Eyes front now," commanded Drummon, lifting a sword.

Colum blushed. Eithne blanched. Would she just distract him? Embarrass him? Would the others tease him because mother was watching? Or was he proud that his warrior-mother took interest? Drawn by Drummon's storytelling, she stayed.

"Men of Ulster," Drummon bellowed, his voice deep and gallant, "which of you will be like CuChulainn, the great hero, whose dearest love, the beautiful Emer, cried for him behind the walls of her fort while the men of her tribe laughed?"

Drummon crouched as if to spring upon the boys, who leaned back and giggled. They had heard the story in all its variations and exaggerations many times.

"So CuChulainn leaped over the walls! In a single thrust, he cleared the tops, sharp as wolves' teeth. His sword glowed with the love he had for Emer."

He passed the sword in a slow arc at the boys' eye level.

"Then he struck down groups of men in single strokes, grabbed his love and her foster sister, and leaped over the walls again. Emer laughed for joy! Her sister squealed in fright!"

Drummon made a falsetto screech that sent the boys into a fit of giggles.

"The soldiers flung their javelins! The slingers sent their stones! But they bounced off the pot of gold CuChulainn had stolen along with the women. And now," he continued in a more somber tone, "which of you will be the hero next?"

"Me, me," they all chirped, eager as sparrows awaiting their meals. Drummon held up his calloused palms to quiet them.

"Today we drill with iron. I want you to get the heft and feel of these pieces. They are smaller than what your fathers use, but will prepare you well for the tests of the Order of Knights."

He motioned for the boys to separate, and then began to distribute the swords among them. Each received it as a prize, a trophy, a sacred charge. They eyed them with both disbelief and delight that at last they had graduated from wooden sticks in tin scabbards.

"Feel them," Drummon urged. "Lift and lower them. Know their weight and balance." After correcting two boys who swung them about carelessly, he went on to extoll the Order of Knights which they would aspire to enter if they kept discipline. No one was assured a place in the honored roll of Erin's finest warriors, not even the well-born. The knights voted on new members at the trials the boys would soon undergo. Competing with sons from the other duns and tribes, they would display their skills in mock combats to win favor. Only the best were chosen.

As the drills began, Eithne watched Colum with mixed feelings. He glanced up now and then, seeking her approval, and she waved weakly. His agile aggressiveness disturbed her. His intense eyes, his serious scowl, his coolly deliberate footwork set him apart from the others who shuffled and snickered. Whatever pride she may have felt for his aptitude blended into a fear that he would too easily enjoy his power.

As the boys panted for breath, Colum pressed on, his mental conditioning extending his endurance. He refused to falter with Drummon watching.

Padarn, sweating heavily, whined for a rest. The other boys, tired to the point of stabbing at each other carelessly, followed suit. Drummon frowned.

"All right, we'll rest," he said, displeased. "There's water in the wagon."

The boys cheered, and still gripping the swords, they pushed and pummeled their way to the four-wheeled chariot, a short scamper away. Colum dashed after them, sword firmly in his hand.

The dappled gray horse tethered to the hickories pricked up her ears at the boys' noisy approach. She flicked her tail, whiplike, as they greedily scooped up ladlefuls of cool water from the barrel behind her in the chariot. The boys splashed

33

each other between drinks. Then the horse stamped and whinnied.

Drummon left the boys and their horseplay to calm the beast and to fetch two wicker shields hanging over the front of the chariot. Then he heard the hoofbeats. He lifted his head to catch the rhythm. Eithne heard them too, and tensed.

Fedlimidh and two stable-keepers rode shiny stallions over the knoll toward them. Eithne recognized the familiar jingle of the harnesses with their bronze finery, the thump of the iron horseshoes on the earth. Eithne stood. The boys raised their swords and voices in salute. Drummon grinned broadly. "Welcome, welcome! We are honored."

Fedlimidh pulled up the huffing horses, crunching the pebbles underfoot. He praised the boys with upraised hands. They returned the salute again.

Drummon came alongside to help settle Fedlimidh's horse.

"I came to see the match," said Fedlimidh, leaning down closely to Drummon. "Who have you chosen?"

"No one yet," said Drummon, patting the horse.

"See to it," said the chieftain, straightening in the saddle.

Drummon turned to the boys who still jumped with excitement. "Enough," Drummon barked. "Everyone sit, over here, now." The firm voice sent them all scurrying for a place in the sand. "Except you, Padarn," he called, picking the big boy, "and you, Wolf."

Eithne winced. She knew the men and boys called him by that name. But each time she heard it she felt dismayed. And now the dismay settled in more deeply as she realized that Drummon was about to arrange a match on the first day of drills with iron. She stood quickly and hurried to Fedlimidh's side.

The chief greeted her with a wide grin, the kind he displayed when about to present her with a gift. "Are you out so early, my love?" he said, extending a hand.

She took it and squeezed it, shaking slightly. "It's their first day with the irons," she protested. "How can you agree to a match? How can he be ready?"

She glanced to the open space on the beach where Padarn strutted front and center, pounding his fleshy chest.

"He is ready," said Fedlimidh calmly.

Colum, trying to puff out his own narrow chest, pranced to the big boy's side, chin up, but with self-conscious eyes. Drummon stood between them, nudging them apart for his arm's length, and placed his hands on their heads as though appointing them to a task.

"In the tests for the Order of Knights," he bellowed, "you will be matched with another of your skill level. In the drill, no skin contact is allowed. Just blades and shields may touch. Touching or breaking the skin disqualifies you." Then more directly to the chosen opponents, he said, "You must control the blades so they almost touch but never do."

He held Padarn's sword tip to Colum's chest to demonstrate. "Like this," he said.

Padarn smiled cruelly. Colum measured the distance of the blade and then measured the demeanor of his opponent.

"Now show me that you understand." Drummon had the boys practice their thrusts and parries slowly and kept his own hands close to theirs, guiding them. "That's it. Almost touching, but not."

Each time the big boy's blade came closer than permitted, he apologized falsely.

Eithne wiped her smooth palms on her skirt as the boys squatted into position. Her heart beat faster, and her breath quickened.

Drummon saw Fedlimidh nod, and then said, "Begin."

The two boys circled stealthily. The other boys stood, shouting.

"Come on, get him!"

"Fight!"

Drummon hissed at them sharply, and they whimpered into silence. Drummon kept his eyes on the combatants. "Feet further apart," he called. "Keep the point up."

Now there was only the dusty shuffle of the boys' leather footwraps on the dirt. With wood, they had slashed and swung more freely, but now they hesitated, unsure of the swords' weight, feinting, keeping apart.

Fedlimidh leaned forward on his mount as though trying to whisper instructions to his son. "Watch the eyes. Always watch the eyes. You can tell where and when he'll strike." He mouthed the words he had given to the boy in many private practice sessions, and the words fell to Eithne's hearing below him.

Padarn snickered with a forced pompousness, "You bean-pole! Dried up cornstalk! I'll cut you down! I should have a scythe, not a sword!"

Colum stared coldly into the big boy's eyes, steady as a cat sizing up a rodent.

Padarn shook his head to clear it. He dared not catch his opponent's eyes again.

Padarn advanced and cried, "Come on, you skinny hen! I am CuChulainn, and I'll cut you in half!"

He swung with surprising speed, and Colum danced back. Padarn ran forward, his wide feet kicking dust and his chunky fist slashing. Colum raised his blade.

The shock stung his hand, but he held on. He swung the shield forward, catching the big boy's shoulder. Absorbing the hit, Padarn whipped his blade to the side without restraint. Colum ducked as the dull edge chipped his shield.

Eithne clenched her fists. She saw that Colum wanted more time to size up his opponent, to outwit him rather than overpower him. But Padarn, accustomed to swinging a hammer beside his father, pressed the attack. The short swords clunked and pinged, the iron singing. Padarn lashed and lunged left and right; Colum poked and parried. Coolly deliberate, Colum let the big boy exert himself. Uncharacteristically silent, he let Padarn continue to hurl insults, the Celtic custom.

Padarn looked confused, annoyed that the match was taking this long. His face sweated as if he were boiling in a pot, and his chest heaved like a bellows. Impatient, he screamed shrilly as though in pain and rushed forward.

With a vigorous overhand blow, Padarn split Colum's shield. The blade penetrated the splintered reeds and grazed Colum's forehead. Yelping with pain and anger, Colum stumbled back. A crimson trickle spilled over his eyebrow to his down-turned lip. When he tasted it, he stiffened.

Drummon stepped forward, but Fedlimidh froze him with a curt command. "No. Let him finish."

Eithne glared up at him incredulously. Then she heard the snarl.

It came from Colum. Teeth bared, veins bulging in his reddened forehead, knuckles white with fury, Colum growled at the big boy. Padarn stopped up short. His eyes bulged like a hunted rabbit's when he saw Colum's silver-lined pupils.

"Wolf, wolf," chanted the other boys in unison, shaking their fists.

Colum dropped his split shield and pounced with such a feverish flurry of strokes that Padarn could only hold up his blade to protect himself.

"By Belanos, you're crazy!" cried Padarn.

Colum crossed their blades near the hilts, holding them aside, and kicked with a fully extended leg. The heel crunched into the boy's kneecap. Padarn collapsed with a scream. The shock sent his sword spinning in the dirt.

Now Colum leaped on him, blade pressed to the throat. Suddenly Drummon clawed him off. Padarn panted in the dust, eyes squinting as blood stained his collar. The dull sword had only scraped him badly in a sensitive spot, and the boy's fat had probably saved him.

The other boys crowded Colum to cheer him, but he burst from the noisy group and bounded across the sand to Eithne. She knelt to catch him as he flung himself into her embrace, shaking with sobs. Fedlimidh's smile of pleasure turned to a scowl of puzzlement.

Over the shouts, Padarn croaked, "He has a devil! He has a devil in him!"

Eithne basked in the springtime sun which hung above the timber church of the dun. Had the ancient poles been in place, the sundial would have traced the shafts of light through the day to predict the Spring Equinox and the Season of Plantings.

The high sun burned off most of the morning mist, leaving only a halo hugging the hills, and a brooding cloud of thought filled the church where Colum solemnly recited his psalms.

Eithne stood quietly outside the church near the well. She listened to the pleasant pitch of her son's Latin cadences. At her feet, Iogen the toddler played with stones, throwing them with awkward thrusts towards the church door.

The steady phrases of Colum's song rolled out the open door, the music of his voice joining the rhythm of the stone milling quern, the stamping of the stable horses, and the unruly choir of children drumming on the earth with their hurly sticks.

A bustling trio of boys tumbled and kicked their way to Eithne. They looked up at her with eager, dirty faces, their third visit in a short while.

"Has Colum come from the church yet?" they chimed, almost pleaded, needing another player to round off their teams.

"Soon," she said. She had said it the last two times.

The boys shrugged, disappointed, and let out an impatient moan. They sped away, hooting to their friends, "Columcille will come soon!"

"Soon!"

"Soon!" they called, mimicking Eithne's empty promise.

She smiled as she held on more tightly to the bundle of her son's clean tunic, the three-colored garment of his rank — red, green, and brown — fit for sons of chieftains. *It may be warm for wool today,* she thought, *but it must remain clear whose son he is. This morning he was Wolf, and at noon he is Dove of the church: Columcille.*

She listened again to his flawless notes, a flowing soprano with a promise of future richness, intoning the lyrics with a fervor and affection for Scripture she had only heard before in Cruithnechain. Other boys stumbled dutifully through the exercises when required. But Columcille found special refuge, even recreation, in the daily drills. And today he extended his sojourn in the church longer than usual, practicing as diligently with the sword of the Spirit as with the sword of the soldier.

When he emerged, skipping, the little wood play sword in its tin scabbard slapped against his thin thigh, and he raised above his head the hurling stick with its shiny brass rings.

"Mother!" he sang, hugging her vigorously with his free arm. He bent to loudly kiss his little brother's blond head. Iogen fussed.

"They're waiting for you," said Eithne, unfolding the tunic. "Put this on."

He squirmed out of his dirty tunic, smudged from the morning's match with Padarn. When he had bolted into the church and begun the high-pitched chants, Eithne let him be.

Now with the conflict within him finally resolved, he pulled on the prince's colors and stood back to be admired.

"Very good," said Eithne. She offered him a chunk of stone-hard cheese. "Now go play."

Colum snatched it gratefully and ran off to join the hurly game. Iogen whined as he watched the cheese disappear with his brother. But Eithne had a piece ready for him. He gnawed on it sloppily.

"There's much more cheese to be cut for the feast," she told Iogen. "Gemman, my old teacher, should arrive today. And we will have a proper way to show him hospitality, won't we?"

Iogen babbled.

Eithne lifted her chin to see the boys beyond the horse fences, churning up the sod and grimacing in tangled-leg collisions. Their flat-clubbed sticks chattered and clicked. The blur of the ball flew from side to side in their makeshift field. The old fishing nets, serving as goals, shook with hard-earned scores.

Colum handled his stick with skill and speed, crunching and being crunched in the fray. With a spirited leap, he smacked the ball home from the midst of a twisted group of elbows, knees, fists, and kicking feet.

One boy flipped into the air and smacked into the dirt face first. The shouts abruptly stopped, and the players gathered cautiously around the injured boy. Some of them snickered, whispering into each other's ears.

A frail, freckled youngster with stringy hair lay still. Stunned into a brief silence, the boy now released a pitiful, muffled moan. Blood bubbled from his nose as he cried, and his little mouth opened wide in a wail. His pale hands reached to his skinned knees, but he drew them back with a wince. Colum pushed through the huddle, bent to the boy, and tenderly turned him over.

Eithne ran to the scene, followed by Collain and two other servant girls, their hands yellowed from grinding corn. But before they all arrived, Colum had wiped the boy's face clean with his tricolor tunic. He spoke quietly in his ear, and the sobbing relented.

The other boys covered their mouths to mask their giggles from Eithne. *I should scold them,* she thought, displeased with their insensitivity towards the weaker playmate. His sobs were as much from pain and failure as from a sense of insult, When she helped him up and brushed off his clothes, she saw the nose-bleed had stopped. The rough, pink scrapes she had first noticed on his knees were smooth and freckled.

"He'll be all right," said Colum matter-of-factly. He traded crescent grins with the boy, as though they shared a secret.

"Let's all get cleaned up now," said Eithne. She took Colum's hand and gave it an affectionate, approving squeeze. Colum blushed while the other boys continued to cup their mouths in whispers.

Colum's hand was unusually warm.

■

Late in the day at the time of long shadows, the poet's procession approached the hillfort, heralded by the music of the bell-branches. The happy jingling announced that soon there would be a night of songs and stories told by a distinguished master of the Aes Dana, a learned man of high rank and six colors, free to travel and teach.

Gemman the Bard in a long mantle of bird feathers rode tall on horseback, a stately figure in his early fifties. With his ecais, the stiff, short whip, raised before him like a scepter and a retinue of pupils behind, Gemman appeared to be an envoy from a distant, distinguished kingdom.

The music and commotion gathered an eager crowd at the gate. The poet's party pranced across the settlement to Fedlimidh's lodge. Gemman greeted by name many who ran alongside. He hailed them with bright hazel eyes and a hearty laugh. His ash-gray hair fell to his shoulders, thick and joyful, bouncing with the horse's high steps. The smooth-shaven face, patchy and etched with thin lines of experience, nodded continually, acknowledging the well-wishers on all sides.

Eithne's household hurried out to meet the noble traveler.

"Hot water for their feet!" commanded Fedlimidh. "Stable-masters!"

The poet dismounted with a jump. Eithne was first to greet her old teacher with a hug.

Colum stood shyly in the shadow of his stocky father. But Gemman spotted him right away. Gemman pointed a slender finger to him and winked. "You don't remember me, do you, my boy?" He laughed. "I sang you many a lullaby."

"I still use some of them," said Eithne.

"I make up songs, too," said Colum, suddenly bolder. "Would you like to hear them?"

"I'll play the harp if you'll sing the song," said Gemman, pleased.

■

A roaring fire and plenteous supper awaited the bard and his traveling school, a shower of hospitality due to one of such station. Pungent pressed cheese, thick sour milk, bowlfuls of berries and hazelnuts, and kettles of salmon spread over the serving tables and laps of the guests.

Fedlimidh's household warriors, weighted with nobly wrought armbands, collars, brooches, and the rings of valor that bound them to their chief, stretched on the hall's benches where they slept each night. Their ashwood spears stood in a line, one per berth, bronze-tipped and straight, each with a name.

Eithne passed from warrior to warrior, pouring to each a portion of honey-sweet mead from a jeweled flagon. Ending with their ring-giving lord, she raised her own cup to Fedlimidh. The gold bracelets slid up her smooth arm to click at her elbow. "I wish you joy in the feast."

"Blessing on the fare which the Almighty brings from the earth," saluted Fedlimidh, raising his own cup. With his other arm, he hugged Colum closer.

Gemman showed Colum his four-cornered harp, letting him pluck the strings and put his ear close to hear them vibrate. Wiping his fingers carefully, he adjusted the harp in his lap and stroked the silvery strings, the trimmed, chipless fingernails gliding over the instrument as a child caresses a household pet. He wove stories with the colorful threads of his words, the syllables and stresses flowing as a well-placed warp and woof.

Colum sat attentively, fully engaged, his ears tuned to the magical meter in Gemman's baritone. Colum's inner sight roved into the distant past of the brave kings Gemman described, and his smile broadened as the bard sang of Ulster's hero, CuChulainn, at age seven.

It was a familiar tale of the gallant, gaudy hero. At age seven, CuChulainn is introduced into the palace of King Conchobar. He defies all rules of the palace, irking the other 150

41

boys in training. Refusing the protection of his elders, he wields his wooden toy weapons against the boys of the court who come to chastise the brash newcomer.

The harp struck sharply while Gemman drew a quick breath. The cheerful clinking of cups stopped for everyone to hear the climax of Gemman's story.

> They cast their thrice fifty hurl bats at the poll of the boy's
> head. He raises his single toy-staff and wards off the thrice
> fifty hurlies, so that they neither hurt him nor harm
> him. . . . Then they throw their thrice fifty balls at the
> lad. . . . and he catches them. . . . They throw at him the
> thrice fifty play-spears charred at the end. The boy raises
> his little lath-shield against them and fends off the thrice
> fifty play-staffs, and they all remain stuck in his lath-shield.

The harp rejoiced and Colum stood, grasping at the air in mimic of the hero. The guests applauded his pantomime and resumed their feasting.

Drummon drew his whistle and blew a heel-kicking tune. Colum watched his quick fingers dance over the holes, his cheeks puffed and his eyes winking. But when Colum turned back to Gemman and peppered him with questions, Drummon's face fell, the whistle stuttered a brief moment, and then renewed its rhythm reluctantly.

Why is he so jealous, Eithne wondered. *Does he think Colum shows more interest in the harp than in the sword?* She denied the impulse to reassure Drummon and turned to Gemman instead.

"That was beautiful," she said. "Just as I remembered."

"You have an excellent memory," said the bard. "Always did. And your son has it too, Eithne. Did you hear him singing along?" He looked into Colum's excited eyes. "Do you like that story?"

"I'm seven," said Colum, thumping his chest with his thumb.

"Just like the hero," laughed Gemman. "Then you'll be receiving your first horse soon. What will you name it?"

"I don't know yet."

"It will be whatever you name it, so name it well. And of course, it will have its own secret name."

Colum cocked his head, intrigued.

"And will you be a warrior on it, or a poet?"

Colum looked at his father. "I'm going to be both," he announced.

"Then you'll have to study hard," said the bard, "both battle and books. Can you manage that? Sometimes I must."

"How?" asked Colum, eyes wide, shuffling closer to him.

Eithne felt a story coming. She folded her hands and relaxed, pleased that Colum was taken with her childhood teacher. *How old he now looked,* she thought, *wise with many winters but visibly worn, ready for a warm bed, yet eagerly earning it with his warm stories.*

"Once on pilgrimage to Armagh," the bard was saying, "I was surrounded by robbers shouting on every side, swords out and teeth showing. And I turned in my saddle to the bags stitched to the sides, and I pulled out my books, the kind on wood plates, plaited with leather thongs, and I swung them in quick circles like a sling." He spun his spotted hand. "The books sang in the wind, bashed the robbers so they yelped like injured wolves, and off they ran, holding their dented heads."

"Why didn't you just ride off?" asked Colum.

"I could see they needed to learn something from books," said Gemman. "But that's not how I usually teach with them."

The young men of his entourage laughed with him.

"Gemman, come now," Eithne shook her finger, "you're beginning to sound like one of the warriors, boasting about a victory."

"But it really happened," shrugged Gemman, gesturing for support from his pupils. "And you, young prince, will be in books soon, so you may as well know all their uses."

"A prince," said Fedlimidh, "uses a sword for a weapon, not books."

"Of course," deferred the bard. "Whatever cuts deepest. And perhaps he'll carry both as he rides." He patted the boy's bright head. "Where will you be in training?"

Colum looked to Eithne, who answered for him.

"He is promised to Abbot Cruithnechain for fosterage. After that . . ."

"After he has learned to read and write," interrupted

Fedlimidh, "he returns to his training to be a chieftain. He is in training now under my champion."

"Drummon, is it?" said the bard, scratching his chin. "Good with a whistle, too."

Drummon, hearing his name, tucked away the long whistle and sat closer to his patron.

"My son is a very good warrior already," said Fedlimidh. "You should have seen him in a match today."

"And he has memorized a fair number of psalms," said Eithne. "You should have heard him sing today."

"A very talented boy," said Gemman, watching Colum's self-conscious shifting. "What is a 'fair number'?"

"I did Psalm 140 today," Colum said. "Mother sings it first, and then I practice it."

"You must like King David," said Gemman. "As good with a sling as with a song."

"May I sing for you now?" asked Colum, bouncing.

Surprised, Gemman sat up. "I did promise to strum along, didn't I? If, of course, your father permits."

"Oh, please, Father! Please, please?"

Eithne suppressed a laugh. *Is a psalm appropriate here?* she wondered, but she nodded to Fedlimidh, deferring to his decision. *How can he refuse to show off his son? Even if it is with a psalm rather than a sword.*

Fedlimidh waved his hand towards Colum, a gesture of approval.

Colum stood with a jump, expanded his chest, and contorted his face in a grotesque grimace. Eithne drew a startled breath and felt her neck tighten, for now it was too late to change his choice of poems. He crooned with an impish gleam:

> Then took place the first twisting-fit and rage
> > Of the royal hero Cu Chulainn,
> So that he made a terrible, many-shaped, wonderful,
> > Unheard of thing of himself.
> His heels and his calves and his hams
> > Shifted so that they passed to the front.
> He stretched the sinews of his head
> > So that they stood out on the nape of his neck

And as large as the head of a one-month-old child
Was each of the hill-like lumps.
He gulped down one eye into his head
So that it would be hard work if a wild crane
Succeeded in drawing it out on to the middle of his cheek
From the rear of his skull.
He drew the cheek from the jawbone
So that the interior of his throat was to be seen.
His lungs and his lights stood out so that they fluttered
In his mouth and his gullet!

Gemman's fingernails slashed the strings, a shocking punctuation, a spasm of angry pentatonic notes. Eithne saw the warriors tensing their own tendons in imitation of the fire-filled boy.

His hair bristled all over his head
Like branches of a redthorn
Thrust into a gap in a great hedge.
Had a king's apple-tree laden with royal fruit
Been shaken around, scarce an apple of them all
Would have passed over him to the ground,
But rather would an apple have stayed stuck
On each single hair there,
For the twisting of the anger which met it
As it rose from his hair above him.

Gemman strummed brightly again to give the boy a breath. But Colum only drew a deep draught of smoky air and coughed until Eithne embraced him and held her own cup to his lips for a soothing sip.

He wiped his mouth and looked to the clay floor. "I forget the rest," he apologized. "Except that after the fight, they kiss three times."

Gemman laid down the harp. "Who taught you this?"

Colum coughed again. "Drummon."

The bard looked at Drummon. "Then you are as good with words as you are with swords," he complimented.

"Both are necessary in battle," said Drummon.

"And equally powerful," said Gemman. "You taught him the whole story?"

Drummon munched an unleavened honeycake. "Yes. The whole duel. To the death of Ferdia. When CuChulainn mourns for him."

Gemman repositioned the harp on his lap and played a melancholy introduction. He looked at Drummon, inviting him, perhaps challenging him, to recite.

Drummon swallowed his cake, cleared his throat, and said:

> *What avails me courage now?*
> > *I'm oppressed with rage and grief,*
> *For the deed that I have done*
> > *On his body sworded sore!*

> *O Ferdiad, in gloom we meet.*
> > *Thee I see both red and pale.*
> *I myself with unwashed arms;*
> > *Thou liest in a bed of gore!*

> *Woe, what is befel therefrom,*
> > *Us, dear Scatach's fosterlings,*
> *Thee in death, me, strong, alive.*
> > *Valour is an angry strife!*

The sad notes melted into the hiss of the hearthfire. Gemman let the vibrations fade away. "Very well done. Like it might have been spoken by the hero himself. Fedlimidh, your house is already well supplied with poets, and one who even knows the *Tain Bo*. There is no need for an old bard here."

"Not so, dear teacher," said Fedlimidh. "That's all my champion knows, while you have the 350 tales of an Ollam."

"Of course, you'll stay a few days," said Eithne, "to help prepare our son for his fosterage." She still felt uneasy with the grisly pagan poems and hoped for Gemman to give Colum the perspective of the holy faith to his ancient heroes.

Gemman seemed to understand. "Am I to be the bridge between two worlds?" he asked, sounding honored. He smiled at the boy.

Colum returned the smile but looked confused. "What do you mean?"

"I mean, dear prince, that there is a place between the dun

and the oratory where the gods meet. Take, for instance, the sea-god Lir, known to the people of Erin from many invasions ago."

Eithne furrowed her brow, confused. *How can he teach of the Almighty with a song about Lir?*

Gemman lifted the harp again. "Perhaps this will help. Let this be my parting gift of the evening before we retire."

The old bard bowed his wrinkled face to his hands, folded over the harp as in prayer. Then, opening his palms in a gesture of welcome, he sang:

> *The four children of Lir*
> > *Shone with a skin that was fair*
> *As the swans on the lough where their father would go*
> > *To grieve for their lost mother there.*

> *Put in the care of Aoife,*
> > *His second wife, filled with jealousy,*
> *She cursed how they shone far more fair than her own*
> > *Children, so the sorceress said,*
> > *"Swans you shall be!*

> *Fly to wander, fly to roam,*
> > *For nine hundred years, without any home!"*

> *The four children of Lir*
> > *Covered their faces in fear*
> *As they sprouted their beaks with hideous shrieks*
> > *And the feathers began to appear.*

> *Into the clouds they arose*
> > *To wander the earth's lochs and loughs,*
> *Awaiting the day when the spell fade away*
> > *And the song of the swan-children go,*

> *"Fly to father, fly to home,*
> > *For nine hundred years we wandered alone."*

> *The four children of Lir*
> > *After the nine hundredth year,*

Made flight for the glen where their father had been
Where all had been joyful and dear.

But below, shrouded in fog
  Their meadow had turned into bog
Their castle was gone, not a stone upon stone,
  And the dead had fled to Tir na'n Og.

"Fly to the islands! Fly from home!
  Exile forever!" was their song.

The harp mourned; Eithne closed her eyes with a rush of
grief at the inner sight of the sorrowing swans. Gemman tweaked
at the strings, evoking the images of other birds flying to their aid.

The four children of Lir
  Alight on the Isle Inishglaire,
Their mourning song sweet; all other birds meet
  Them and join in their tears by the shore.

But lo, in the distance, a bell!
  Matins of St. Caemhoch! It tells
Of the end of the charm, and their wings turn to arms
  Just as Caemhoch strides over the hill.

But what Caemhoch sees stops his breath:
  Four shriveled, bent figures near death.
He runs to the sea and baptizes three,
  Then the fourth, as their souls rise from earth.

Young and radiant, pure as the swans,
  Follow the moonrays; then they are gone.

"Fly to heaven! Fly to home!
  To Almighty Father! Never to roam."

Eithne pressed down the burning mist gathering in her
eyes, seeing Colum's own tears wet on his pure cheeks. Reassured
that the old gods would not prevail, she took Gemman's hand
and squeezed it thankfully.

Colum stretched, eyes blinking away sleep.

"I didn't mean it to be a lullaby," said Gemman with a grin.

"Master Gemman, what's exile?" Colum yawned.

"It is the worst thing that can happen to a man of Erin. Besides excommunication," he added, aside. "It is to be sent away forever. It is a punishment for the lowest of men, for the highest of crimes, for the longest of times."

Colum yawned again.

"Time for bed now," Eithne said, helping Colum to stand. "Let's go together. Say good night."

Taking his protesting arm, she excused herself and passed through the deerskins with the reluctant boy to the family sleeping berths. Eithne wrapped Colum snugly in the furs, gently humming to quiet his excitement. She turned to the taper on the wall to blow it out.

"Please don't," Colum pleaded.

"Go to sleep. It's been a long day for you. You can be with Gemman again tomorrow."

"I'm afraid."

"Of the dark?"

No answer.

"It's all right. If we weren't afraid of the dark, there would be little love for the Light of the World, our Lord Christ." She kissed his forehead, quoting, "'His light shines on in the dark, and the darkness has never mastered it.' He will post his angels of light round your bed, Colum, strong and swift as fit champions of the royal Son of God. They shall guard you well." She kissed him again softly. "I'll leave the light on as a reminder of their presence."

"Good night, Mother."

Eithne went to the doorway. Behind her, she heard a gentle brush of wings.

Just some pigeons in the thatch, she thought.

3
CRUITHNECHAIN
A.D. 529

OLUM RODE HIS BIRTH-
DAY HORSE THROUGH THE
woods into the abbot's simple settlement. The ironclad hoofs of
the dappled gray stallion crunched on the grass, still stiff with
frost. Chin high, Colum searched for an open space for racing.
He pressed his trousered knees against the horse's side to lift
himself higher.

"I can run Angel Wing over there." He pointed so his
father riding beside him could see.

A silvery meadow glistened just beyond the dark earth of
a dormant cornfield. Colum tucked in his elbows and crouched
in the saddle playfully, as if to race. He waited for Fedlimidh's
smile, the same proud look he received at the summer tribal
assembly when Colum flew Angel Wing around the boys' track
with the skill of a seasoned warrior. Other boys, though stronger,
older, and emboldened with offerings to Epona of the Horses,
could not catch him.

He would gallop off now, eager for the wind-whistle in his
ear and the hoof-drumming underneath, were it not for the
oxen they towed, the down payment for his fosterage. The oxen
thumped forward sluggishly. The packs on their backs swayed
with the weight of food and clothing brought for the abbot in
accordance with the Brehon code.

Fedlimidh surveyed the meadow. Colum watched his experienced eyes searching for ditches, fences, rabbit warrens, any obstacles which might injure his son and disqualify him from a future kingship.

"It looks fine," the chieftain said. "But we'll inspect it more carefully later. And I doubt the kind abbot will appreciate a horse in the cornfield except to work."

Cruithnechain hobbled out of his small oratory, bending through the coverless doorway. He raised his knobby cane in a spirited greeting and quickened his pace towards the visitors. His undyed brown wool smock swished in the grass, and Colum noticed the bare toes peeking underneath. The abbot's craggy face, lined deeply as oak bark, cracked into a toothy smile.

"Peace," he hailed hoarsely, "peace to Fedlimidh MacFergus and his son."

"And peace be with you, Father," said Fedlimidh, suddenly alert.

A contingent of teenaged men in chestnut habits emerged from the low huts clustered around the oratory.

"Come, come." Cruithnechain beckoned to the boys as though to his own children. "Tend the horses. Unhitch the oxen. Fine beasts. God be praised."

The boys obeyed without speaking, gently holding the huffing animals while Fedlimidh and Colum dismounted. The oxen were disengaged and led with their packs to a small woodplank barn beyond the oak grove, nearer the cornfield.

Like his father, Colum surrendered his horse reluctantly to a shrugging teen who looked intimidated by the prince's suspicious stare. Watching every move, hand on his bronze dagger hilt, Colum surveyed the plot of land his father had bequeathed to the monks. The sacred grove, once the scene of sacrifice by the family druids, now featured a square timber church, its door facing sunriseward. It was smaller than the church in the dun. Colum wondered how the altar-table and other implements could fit inside with the abbot and his students. *Perhaps it is only for the abbot,* he thought.

Along a path to the barn stood a kitchen, evident by the high stone chimney and piles of peat and wood nearby. The guesthouse, a single-room stone structure, stood near the kitchen. Across from the church's door sat Cruithnechain's rude oratory, squat and simple, arched at the top with mortarless, fitted stones. Through a hole in the roof rose a thin line of blue smoke from a peat fire that was his only light and heat in the damp winter. Colum already missed the snapping hearth of his father's hall.

But the boys' beehive huts intrigued him most, woven with flexible hickory branches and packed with straw-stiffened mud. Patches of waterproofing turf had broken away from several of them. They looked as though they were trying to huddle together for warmth. Colum counted two to three boys coming from each hut. He already ached for the secure skins and familiar furs of his own sleeping berth.

It was quieter than the dun. No shouts of children arguing. No chatter of hurly sticks. Just the twitter of sparrows and the rustle of the cold wind through the brittle brown oak leaves.

"Come, see the guesthouse," said Colum's new teacher. "I'm glad you're early." He reached out for Colum's hand, but the boy held it back.

"A bit anxious. Of course. I know. But you'll like it here. Much to learn. New friends. Like brothers."

Colum watched the teenaged boys with the oxen. "Are there other boys my age?" Colum asked. His head jerked side to side searching for them.

"In their houses. All around there," Cruithnechain swung his cane. "Inside. Learning letters. As you will. You'll meet them at the midday meal. In the refectory."

"What's that?"

"Where we eat. In that kitchen. Fits twelve or so. Just right for us."

"When is the meal?"

"Hungry already?"

Colum thought it odd that they should be kept waiting.

"Mother gave us biscuits early this morning."

"And it is a long ride over the mountain," sighed Cruithnechain, looking sympathetic. "We'll eat soon enough. We'll get the oxen settled."

"Are there horses in there too?"

"We have no horses except for yours."

Colum felt his stomach squeeze in disappointment. *Everyone will want to ride mine.*

"But we do have some cattle for milk and some sheep for wool."

"Where are they?"

"Outside the settlement. Like at the dun."

"No pigs?"

"No pigs."

No bacon, Colum thought, stomach growling.

"Is this where I'm staying?" Colum asked, astonished and dismayed as they reached the tiny stone guesthouse.

"Oh, dear boy, no," said the abbot gently, aiming his cane towards the larger oratory. "You'll be over there."

Colum took heart, seeing that the building had preeminence over the huts and looked heated. His bright gray eyes followed the line of the cane to fix on the wood-and-wattle huts.

"One of those," said the abbot, "I haven't decided which."

Colum's knees weakened. He heard his father grumble.

"We'll need our provisions," said Fedlimidh, stepping into the guestroom and inspecting it with a scowl.

"My children will bring . . ."

"No, we'll get them ourselves," said Fedlimidh gruffly.

"As you wish. Then you can see the grounds."

Passing through the settlement, Colum spied evidence of what his chores would be. The woodpiles meant chopping. The bundled stalks in the cornfield meant sowing, reaping, stripping husks, kiln-drying, and grinding corn — the work of low-born women.

Would he hunt with his foster father as he did with his father? *Only for obscure Bible passages,* he thought. Didn't he say Angel Wing was the only horse? And there were no barking dogs at their arrival. And no stag antlers or boar tusks hanging in the guesthouse where one would want to make a good impression.

And where was the hurling court? Perhaps those oaks over there would do as goals. But the circle of huts left no room for a field; besides, it was too rocky and the grass, though now bent with cold, obviously too long in season, with well-worn paths from each hut converging at the church door. *Maybe the meadow would do.*

No archery or javelin targets or smashed wicker shields dangled from any limbs. *Do I have the only sword in the settlement, too?*

Perhaps the abbot disapproved of weapons. But how could they protect themselves against bandits or wild animals bent on taking a lamb or calf?

When they returned to the guesthouse with their satchels, a fire crackled in the center of the floor. The abbot tested its warmth with his hand. "It will catch on. And so will you, my boy. Midday meal is at the second bell." He shuffled out.

Fedlimidh dumped his bags on the hard-packed floor. "This will be a good place for you."

Colum sniffled.

"You don't think so now, Crimthann, but perhaps you can see it as a long hunt."

"I don't think the abbot hunts, Father."

Fedlimidh gripped the boy's upper arm with a gentle, reassuring shake. "Remember how we stayed in the woods for the deer hunts?"

"And we made shelters from branches."

"This is like that." He untied one of the bags. "But I brought a few extra comforts for the son of a chieftain."

He displayed two honey-wheat biscuits. "These won't last seven years," he grinned, "but they'll help us to last till the midday meal."

Colum bit into the crumbly treat just as a dull bell rattled outside. He poked his head out the door, mouth stuffed, to see a cadre of younger boys scurry for the church. Curiosity rolled through him, but he stopped in the doorway. Their leather-shoed shuffling quieted quickly. The strains of a familiar psalm lifted, drifted to Colum's ears. He cocked his head as a hound to the sound of its master.

Colum sang along under his breath, no longer conscious of the biscuit crumbs on his lips, tasting only the sweet words:

> *The heavens tell out the glory of God,*
>> *The vault of heaven reveals His handiwork.*
> *One day speaks to another,*
>> *Night with night shares its knowledge,*
> *And this without speech or language*
>> *Or sound of any voice.*
> *Their music goes out through all the earth,*
>> *Their words reach to the end of the world.*

The comforting cadences did not transport him out of the chilly guesthouse, but sharpened his senses within it — the sweet hay, damp moss, and charcoal cinders perfumed the room. The grass outside lay humbly prostrate to heaven, and the mighty oaks raised their bare-fingered branches in obeisance. The crisp air, God's own breath, filled his chest with the settled sensation of a fatherly Presence in the room, more loving, more powerful, more cautiously approached than his own royal father.

When the singing stopped, the air chilled, and Colum smiled at his father as though he'd just returned from a journey. "This will be a good place for me."

Now the boys tumbled out of the church, chasing each other and jumping over rocks. Colum brightened.

The bell clapped again, and Cruithnechain, standing beside the kitchen door, beckoned to Colum.

"Midday meal, Father," said Colum. He stuffed the biscuit into a pocket and ran outside to the refectory. The other boys, filing past the abbot, glanced Colum's way with no greeting. A few pushed as though more eager to evade him. Last to enter, with Fedlimidh beside him, Colum felt the abbot's hand on his head, mussing his red hair affectionately. "It's not boar," he smiled, "but it's still quite good."

Inside, Colum took a seat near the head of a long oaken table. He craned his neck as he sat on a plain, uncushioned stool, examining the gray-shadowed room.

There were no engraved pots bubbling with stew, hung by chains over a central hearth. No spits of meat turning on stakes. The plank walls were bare without the ornate carvings or hung shields which adorned his father's hall.

Even the table was plain, not inlaid with parquet designs or decorated with paints made from meadow flowers.

The boys dressed in the drab of serfs, not the crimson, cyan, and saffron tunics of the dun. They stood in straight rows at the table. Stood.

Colum felt his cheeks flush, and he snapped to a standing position. The stool screeched on the packed floor. He hunched his shoulders, suddenly conscious of his contrast in colors. His princely tunic seemed very bright.

The abbot spoke. "Today we welcome Fedlimidh MacFergus. Of the Clan Con Conaill. He has been generous to us. In land and cattle. This is his son, Colum." He put his hand on Colum's head again. It felt like a great weight though the palm barely touched him. "We've all been looking forward to your arrival."

Colum forced his chin up to regain the composure of his rank. The smiles around the table were coldly polite.

The abbot intoned the blessing. "*In nomini Patris, et Filii, et Spiritu Sanctus . . .*"

The boys' right-hand fingertips shot to their foreheads, hearts, and shoulders in a dutiful sign of the cross. Colum followed, more slowly, aware that eyes were still criticizing him.

The blessing continued in Latin. Mother often prayed the blessing in a musical Gaelic. Colum choked slightly but dared not sniffle.

With the "amen," everyone sat. Conversation became lively, to Colum's surprise; he had heard of silent meals in such places. The abbot engaged Fedlimidh in talk about Colum's coming studies: phonics, penmanship, the Psalter, support of the settlement. The boys seemed to be sharing about their chores, but a few whispered out the corners of their mouths and looked his way from the corners of their eyes.

A server made the rounds, ladling steaming stirabout with bits of salted fish into grateful wooden bowls. Colum studied the brown porridge, spattered in his bowl like acorn mix tossed to swine. The table lacked honey, or salt-butter, or flat wheat cakes to mop up the meal.

He picked out a fish bit with his finger. Common trout.

"It's in there today because it's Friday," said a round-faced boy sitting next to him, "and because you're here." His low ears wiggled when he talked, making his smile more comic than friendly. His feet scuffed the floor, barely reaching, just like Colum's. His freckled hands dug into the meal hungrily. "Watch for bones," he said, trying to bait a conversation. "Eochaid over there catches them well, but can't clean them like I can."

"Where do you fish?" asked Colum.

"There's a stream over there." The boy waved his hand westward.

"It runs into a pond where the cows drink and where we wash our writing boards." He wiped out more stirabout with his fingers. "I'm Grilaan," he said. "Can you fish?"

"I can hunt better than I can fish," said Colum proudly.

"Do you hunt with that?" Grilaan asked, pointing to the sheathed dagger hitched to Colum's leather belt. The boy grinned enviously, his new teeth oversized for his face.

At this, Colum straightened on his uncomfortable stool, buttocks still smarting from this morning's ride. He told Grilaan eagerly of hunting in these very hills, dogs baying, horses bolting, arrows singing, stags succumbing. He recounted archery and swordplay with Drummon, hurly, and chess with his father — then he saw the boy's blue eyes wander.

"And where are you from?" he asked, ashamed he had spoken of himself so long.

"Near Dun Kineely," said Grilaan, "on a farm by Inver Bay."

Colum leaned closer. "Where are these other boys from?" he asked, already afraid they were all free-farmers' sons, well-prepared for the agrarian chores of the settlement.

They were.

"But I'll show you what to do," promised Grilaan, "if you can teach me what you know."

Colum promised him turns with the dagger and rides on Angel Wing if Grilaan would show him the hoe and the sheepshearer.

"But what we mostly do is practice our letters and memorize God's words," Grilaan said with a bored look. "In the language Father speaks at the blessing."

"I already . . ."

"It's so hard," said Grilaan, pushing more fish pieces into his pouting mouth. "But I guess easier than our own language."

Colum nodded, remembering the runes scratched into rural gravestones, the mysterious, cumbersome scribbles invented by Ogma, the honey-mouthed god of literature. "It shows you what was in his mind," Gemman had told him, "crammed-tight confusion."

"We practice our letters so much," whispered Grilaan, "I sometimes feel my hand will fall off."

"It couldn't be harder than Drummon's sword drills. That makes the thighs ache."

"Your fingers will ache here. You'll write so much Latin, you'll be dreaming in it."

"I already have strange dreams."

"What kind?"

Colum leaned even closer to Grilaan's ear. "Last night before coming here, I dreamed I was fighting with candles."

Grilaan covered his mouth. "Candles? Did they cut?" Food squirted between his fingers as he laughed.

"No," giggled Colum, amused at Grilaan's attempts to keep his food in his mouth.

The abbot hushed Grilaan, and Fedlimidh gave his son a rebuking look.

Colum hung his head over his bowl, reddening while the others at the table pressed their lips together and pointed at him with their eyes. Colum dipped quietly into the meal and decided not to tell Grilaan he had had the same dream for the last three nights.

■

Colum hopped up and down when Cruithnechain assigned him to Grilaan's hut. He stayed near Grilaan's side all day, within his father's sight but growing in his distance as the day progressed. At first proud but now embarrassed by the tricolor tunic and swinging scabbard, he wondered when he could change to plainer, inconspicuous homespun.

At the evening office, Colum nearly fell asleep from the day's stress. But Grilaan poked him awake. After prayers, Colum headed for the refectory until Grilaan caught his collar. "One meal in winter," he said. "And you might as well know that there's usually none on the sixth day. Unless there's company — like you."

Now the hard bunk sheathed in sheepskins was welcome. Colum and Grilaan lay in the dark, trading hushed secrets, yawning, whispering, unwilling to end the day. Colum shared honey biscuits he had smuggled into the hut. They rejoiced that Colum's father had approved of the field for horse-running that afternoon.

The other boys, groaning in protest from the neighboring huts, threatened to call in the abbot on them. So they quieted.

Colum pulled up the wool to his chin, trembling not with the chill of the late winter night, but with an uneasy anticipation. The hot tears came back, unchecked in the dark, and he rubbed his burning eyes till his knuckles were wet and his visions of home were crushed to a dull, white glare.

But in the haze of his itching eyesight, he saw the swan-feather quill with the pure, inkless nib, camouflaged in the reeds by the cattle pond.

"Grilaan," he whispered, "I see your quill. It's under the tall grass where you washed your letter-boards yesterday."

"Oh, good!" Grilaan cried. "I thought it was lost forever! My father gave it . . ."

"Shh!" scolded a boy at their hut's door. "Do you want us all to be punished?"

Startled into silence, the two boys slunk under their sheepskins. The reprimander left.

Colum whimpered off to sleep, his ears tuned to the distant snore of his father in the guesthouse, his chest hollow with homesickness for his mother, and his mind frightened as much by the newness of his surroundings as by the fact that Grilaan had never told him he had lost anything.

■

The timbered banquet hall gleamed with burnished shields, silken banners, and mounted javelins. The royal Synod Room of Tara filled with knights and nobles by the dozen, champions by the score. Harpers. Singers. Serfs. Roaring torches sparkled on the gold collars of tight-waisted warriors, dressed in loud tunics and trousers, weighted with Erin's famous embroidery, rivaling each other for the finery of their bracelets, brooches, and battle gear, all carefully measured to the limits of the Brehon code.

In procession up the five avenues that led to the Hill from every point on the broad plain of Meath, the chosen kings of each clan's ruling family marched, diadems dazzling, sword scabbards shining. From among their ranks, the lesser lords of Erin and the rulers of the Five Ancient Provinces elected the Ard-Ri, the High King. His authority, guarded by loyal knights, lauded by skilled poets, and established in the collective memory by historians, would unite the scattered duns and tuaths.

The Coronation Stone, LiaFail, planted by divine invaders of a misty past, screamed as the new king stepped on it. Knees bent and swords saluted as the massive gold brooch was pinned on the new king of kings: "Hail Crimthann MacFedlimidh, Colum of ConConaill!"

The skin-drums pealed, rolling, rolling . . .

The thunder awakened Fedlimidh. It faded in the distance, an angry growl like a wounded boar in retreat. He swiveled his feet, still leatherbound, to the floor. There were no planks of Tara, only the clay of Cruithnechain's guesthouse. He patted his side for the reassuring bump of his dagger. He crouched at a crisp sound outside the door — feet snapping a stick? — but it was only waterdrops plopping into puddles.

Fedlimidh stepped out and drew a lungful of the moist night air. The rain clouds fled eastward to seek new trouble. Water pattered into barrels beside the church walls. On the roof, bleached with moonbeams, he saw the cross looking like a sword pointing down. "Upside down, they do everything upside down," he mumbled. "Of course," he noted, "even the moon has a halo here."

He spotted Colum's colorless wicker-and-wattle hut, repressing an urge to carry in his own cloak to cover him.

But someone had a fire going — smoke itched in his nostrils. In the stone oratory, lights flickered through the chimney hole, and a few sparks skipped into the starry sky. The subdued chant of the boys' voices also rose from the chimney, like an offering mixed with yew-wood smoke rising to the moon goddess. It was totally unlike the cry of boys in the dun, boasting, cursing, threatening during their games, just like their fathers. The song was peaceful, confident, an insistent force. The dark clouds retired in fear from the undulating assault of their song.

Fedlimidh crept closer to the building, pausing by twin oaks to catch his breath. He palmed the small of his back. *It's the damp air,* he thought. *I stood up too fast. The one meal in the day.* He cleared his head with a shake and stepped ahead. The singing swelled as he approached the low, doorless entry.

He stooped to enter, humbled by the low archway. He saw the boys at prayer. They gathered in a circle which included Cruithnechain. The abbot's thin arms embraced the youngest boys to his left and right — Fedlimidh's son and his new friend. Every head was lowered, each boy's fingertips steepled and raised to the forehead. Their drab shirts anticipated vows of poverty. Their bare knees dented the earthen floor, damp in spots where the roof leaked. A few high voices cracked here and there, signs of coming puberty, while Cruithnechain's smooth baritone paced the nocturnes.

Fedlimidh could not make out the Latin of the abbot, but the boys were responding in a homely Gaelic. The sight of his own son, wrapped in sheepskin and not the prince's colors, barefoot and bowed in the company of farmers, stung Fedlimidh. The warmth of the room was not enough to cause the sweat on his lip; the glow of the fire was not enough to prevent the chill in his spirit, and the closeness of this little family brought not comfort but a constriction to his chest, the dread of a Presence he did not understand and the portent of a future he could not accept. He slipped out and stumbled back to the stone guesthouse. The haunting call and response of the abbot and his children reached out to him, raising goosebumps which he tried in vain to rub away.

"*Pater noster, qui es in coelis.*"
"Our Father, who is in heaven."
"*Sanctificetur nomen tuum.*"
"Holy is Thy name."
"*Adveniat regnum tuum.*"
"May Thy kingdom come."

■

Cruithnechain took the chieftain's son into his poor family as an equal with the others, to Colum's annoyance. Within several weeks, by the corn planting, Colum settled into his humbler role. Following Prime, the morning service of creation, the boys tended the animals and rotated chores of the kitchen and cornfield. Colum swung his hoe with the same vigor as he had swung his hurly stick. Cruithnechain plunged him into the hard work, not sparing his well-born charge from any menial task. The repetitive physical labor quieted him; it channeled his enormous energy, and his complaints gave way to an infectious cheerfulness, especially when allowed to run Angel Wing.

Under Cruithnechain's watchful eye, Colum squatted for hours in the cool oratory, scratching out his letters with charcoal sticks on a smooth board, which was washed and dried between lessons. He'd only broken two writing boards out of frustration, but the penalty of collecting ten species of insect each time seemed to correct the outbursts.

On the simple diet of the refectory, he sprouted as fast as the corn. The monthly visits by his mother, loaded with provisions, eased the transition. He'd stopped moaning about only bread and milk on the fourth and sixth days, coming to appreciate the anticipation of fuller fare on the Lord's Day.

On those Sabbath mornings, Colum kneaded out the cornmeal dough, rolling it into long strings and shaping them into Latin letters before baking them under the hot hearthstones. Cruithnechain helped him arrange the edible letters into words on the table, one letter per place setting — PACEM IN TERRA or IN EXCELSIS DEO. The boys looked forward to each tasty combination. "How sweet are your promises to my taste," quoted Colum, and the boys laughed.

The rhythm of the meals and the ritual of the six daily offices paced each day. In Vespers, Colum recited his Pater Noster, TerSanctus, and Gloria as well as any novitiate. Most of the Psalter was familiar to him already in Gaelic, and now the meaning of what Latin he had memorized pressed into his prodigious memory. When he prayed those musical lines, the hearthfire seemed to leap, and when he left the oratory, it darkened. Cruithnechain no longer dismissed it as a draft.

The daily rote transcription of the psalms made the new language dearer to Colum; he was privy to the thoughts of God's own bards. But he still sang the old stories of the dun. They poured out of his mouth sometimes during mindless exercises, leading to vulgar doodles along the edges of his board.

"When CuChulainn went to train with Scatach the Shadow Woman," he recited one day, the boys staring dropjawed, "he paddled his coracle to the Island of Shadows beyond Alba, away from time. From her he learned the feats of sword-edge and the swing of the sloped shield, the feat of cat and the heroic salmon-leap, the noble chariot-fighter's crouch, the feat of the chariot-wheel thrown on high, the feat of the shield-rim, and the feat of snapping mouth and the hero's scream . . ."

"Colum."

"The feat of . . ."

"Colum," the abbot repeated gently, as though waking him. He stood in the doorway, arms folded.

The boy looked to his feet, then to his mentor, as though

he was suddenly aware that he was in Donegal and not on a distant island.

"I'm sorry, Father."

"Another time," smiled Cruithnechain. "Do your letters."

"You aren't angry?"

The abbot shook his balding head. "Those who tell the stories lead the people."

So Cruithnechain made certain to weave the stories of Scripture into the boy's precocious memory in outdoor sessions on stone seats or during walks in the woods. Cruithnechain often overheard Colum rehearsing them aloud during his chores, reviewing his pronunciation with Angel Wing listening patiently, sometimes nodding as though encouraging the boy to continue.

Each year Colum's voice and conviction sank deeper, as determined as his stubborn attempts to perfect his technique with the sheepshears and the corn-kiln. He was best at fishing, thanks to Grilaan.

"But I want to be a fisher of men," he said.

"You will catch them with a quill," said Cruithnechain. "Practice your letters."

By his sixth year in the settlement, Colum's calloused fingers yearned for smooth vellum and a real quill. The dagger lay long forgotten under his bunk.

■

Cruithnechain wiped the bronze chalice, buffing the sides with his brown sheepsmock. The rubbing could not smooth out the pitting of age, and parts of the cup refused to shine any more. His own reflection in it was now dull, diffused at the edges as though he were fading from the earth.

His finger joints ached almost constantly now. The cup wobbled when he put it down. The night-long vigil in prayer, capped by the morning Mass, had refreshed his spirit, but revealed no course for Colum. With the end of his seven-year fosterage at hand, a twofold path lay before the young man. He could return to the dun for further training in the ways of a king — archery, horsemanship, forays against his own family. Or he could move on to Moville as an oblate for the priest-scholar's life.

The bishops he had visited to present the boy and to pray

with for guidance all pressed for Colum's priesthood. A fine mind, they said. Curious. Determined. Hardy, with a poet's instincts, they observed. Impetuous, perhaps, a kicking colt. And that voice. That heavenly voice.

Only Bishop Brugacious doubted a vocation for the prince. "Hear how he keeps interrupting your psalms, Father," he cautioned, "finishing them for you, correcting you?"

"It is his way of serving me," said the abbot. The memory lapses, the frequent fog that lulled his concentration into a waking dream, embarrassed him. "He knows them all so—"

"He is a show-off. Teach him to control his tongue."

"He only—"

"A boaster is not fit for the tonsure."

"How has he—"

"He says he learned his letters by eating them."

"That's because—"

"Send him to the dun where he belongs. He is not one of us."

You judge him by what you dislike in yourself, he thought. Did that also explain Fedlimidh's ambitions for his son? Which of his own shortcomings would he press to realize in his son? His lack of education? Or his lower station? Would Fedlimidh stop his support if Colum moved to Moville to study? Perhaps Eithne could give him a hint.

Cruithnechain listened for the footfalls of a horse, expecting Eithne soon. "It's today," Colum had announced at the morning worship. Somehow, he always knew. So the abbot waited.

When she arrived, Cruithnechain was not surprised to see her alone. In six years of visits, Fedlimidh rarely came along. His warrior-wife was capable of dealing with any difficulty en route. The embossed battle-ax hung from her saddle, as beautiful as its owner and as potentially deadly. In his mind, Cruithnechain heard the gentle clip-clops quicken to a war-gallop. Eithne's sunset-colored hair brightened to a blaze, and her eyes became a bilious green. The sweet voice strained to a shriek, the full lips taut, calling out the name of her prey . . .

"Cruithnechain? Are you well?"

The abbot rubbed the bald dome of his pate. "Daughter, it is good to see you again." Arms open in welcome, he moved forward, more stooped, less steady.

Two boys, told in advance to keep watch, approached to water and tether the horse. They stood nearby to help the frail man avoid any appearance of impropriety with a woman. It was best to be careful.

Eithne beamed. "Father, I always feel that I've come home." She took his gnarled hand and genuflected slightly. "Why, your hand . . . It shakes so."

"I can still fold them in prayer," said Cruithnechain. "Come to the refectory. Refresh yourself."

"How is Colum?"

"Taller. If you can believe it. With a few whiskers. Very proud of them." He grunted in his effort to walk, the knees grinding.

"Father, I worry for you." She offered a steadying hand.

Cruithnechain raised his deeply grooved palm. "'Fret not thyself,' says the psalmist. I don't worry about myself. Neither should you. I do worry about Colum sometimes."

"Isn't he learning well?"

"Very well! Bright boy. Tries hard. Gets angry."

"Angry?"

"Only with himself. Doesn't hurt anyone, if that is what concerns you."

Eithne looked relieved. "Where is he now? Can I see him?"

"Where else would he be? In the church."

They shared a chuckle. "I won't disturb him now," Eithne said. "Columcille. My prayers are answered."

"So are his," said the abbot. "We have found more lost things because he has prayed to find them. He dreams about them."

"Is that bad?"

"No, dear daughter, no. Didn't God tell Joseph in a dream to take the Holy Child to Egypt? Didn't He tell the druids from the east to avoid King Herod?"

They reached the refectory door, and he motioned her inside. "And He still speaks to you, Eithne?"

She blushed. "Everyone dreams, Father," she said.

"Nobody listens," he said.

■

In the church, Colum polished a tall brass candlestand by torchlight. Tiptoed, he rubbed the long neck that spread out to three spikes, pitchfork-like, which impaled three fat altar candles. *Mother is here*. He could sense it. But perhaps she wasn't feeling well or was troubled. Alongside the pleasant warmth of her presence, Colum felt a dull ache, a tightness that numbed his neck until he kneaded it. No matter, she was here, and he had much to show her this time. He picked at the lone whisker curling from his chin. *Not just this*. He smiled. He had practiced letters on sheepskin-vellum he had made, cured with resins still staining his fingernails, rubbed smooth with pumice stone till his broad shoulders hurt. With Grilaan's quill and some inks the abbot had borrowed from Finbar of Moville, Colum had first felt the words flow out of his arm onto the page, a creation of permanence and power.

He shook out the polishing cloth, folded it, and hurried to the narrow alley behind the altar where he stored the cleaning cloths in a small chest. When the church's door squeaked, Colum leaped up, expecting Eithne.

A shadowed figure prowled in the doorway, the features blurred by the harsh backlighting. Colum shaded his brow while another figure stole inside, twitching and turning often for a look behind his back.

"Who are you?" challenged Colum.

"If you were a real wolf, you could smell me," said the silhouetted intruder. The door closed, and the torchlight revealed the face of Padarn, the blacksmith's boy.

At sixteen, Padarn had filled out in his chest and shoulders to match his waist. The pudginess had turned to thickness, and he stood sturdy as a stump. The bare arms, short and muscular, banded in bronze, spoke of his standing in the Order of Knights. In each meaty hand, he gripped a dagger. He passed them before his boarlike face near the spare brown bristles of a mustache beneath his round nostrils.

"What do you want?" Colum's hand searched for the scabbard by his belt. He felt only the hemp hugging his homespun smock. "Looking for gold?"

"Looking for you, Wolf," said Padarn. "I want a rematch." He laughed with his mouth pinched shut, head bent back. Under his chin, a pink scar remained from the bout on the beach. "I've been practicing. A lot. Have you?" He waved the blades.

Padarn's companion, a stranger to Colum, also produced a dagger and waved it in the same manner. He breathed in short, nervous gasps, glancing at the door.

Colum's mouth, suddenly dry as an August cornhusk, opened but said nothing. He swallowed hard and muttered hoarsely, "Get out. This is God's house."

"Which god?" teased Padarn. "Lug, god of war?"

"I don't want to fight you."

"Is that what they taught you here? How to be a coward? Like your father?"

A fire kindled in Colum, a slow burn deep inside. "Don't say that."

"It's true, isn't it?" Padarn stepped forward, stalking, turning his blades to catch the torchlight. "Afraid to use your sword? Or you just use it to cut corn now? Where is it? And your quiver? Are you the son of a chieftain or not?"

"Fighting is all you know about."

"What else is there for a real man to know?" sneered the boy. "Look at you, cleaning candlesticks like a woman. No one will ever say that about me. And no one will ever say that I can't get even."

He shook his dark head to the side, and the companion nodded. He split off to his right in a move to outflank Colum and trap him behind the altar. Padarn threw the bolt into the door frame. "This is just between us," he said. "I'll cut you into pieces so small you can fit through a cornsifter."

Padarn ran forward, knives raised.

Colum reached for the candlestand, pulling it across his midriff in time to parry the first thrusts. The iron blades screamed on the bright brass. Padarn stabbed again. Colum's sleeve tore away roughly, pulling him to the floor. He dodged another slash, and then pushed out the candlestand, forcing his opponent back.

The other boy rushed upon him from behind, now that Colum seemed vulnerable. Arms straining, Colum swung the base up behind him. The heavy disc cracked into the boy's chin. He howled and staggered back, hands to his jaw. His knife clattered to the floor. The candles broke off their prongs and rolled on the altar.

Padarn puffed, showing his teeth. "I'll put a scar on you,

holy boy," he hissed, rearing back to throw. The flying dagger clanged off the candlestand.

The door thumped. Colum heard his mother call out his name. His new brothers put their shoulders to the door.

"They can't help you," smiled Padarn.

"You'll be caught and punished," huffed Colum. "The Brehon Law—"

"The law stands by me!" shouted Padarn over the pounding on the door. "There is a new king at Tara who will no longer ignore what you did to me."

Colum's biceps burned; the candlestand seemed heavier. He lifted it like a lance and poked it at his opponent. Padarn leaned to grab it. Colum jerked it away, but not in time. Padarn latched on like a lobster. The candle prongs, flaked with beeswax, slipped. Padarn stumbled forward just within range of Colum's swinging leg. The shoe smacked into Padarn's ear.

The boy snorted in pain and cursed, tripping to the timber wall. The thud shook loose some mortar and nearly rattled the torch free from its holder. Padarn plunged his finger into his ear, wiping out blood. His companion, still stunned behind the altar, spat out bloody teeth.

Colum stared at his attacker. "Many rise up against me," he recited in Latin, the thoughts like thunderbolts, "many there are who say, 'God will not bring him victory.' Rise up, Lord, save me, O my God. Thou dost strike all my foes across the face and break the teeth of the wicked."

"Stop it," growled Padarn, "no magic! Fight like a man fights!" His eyes, pinched in pain, watered heavily. He swished his dagger left to right. "Where are you?" he yelled.

"Thine is the victory, Lord, and may Thy blessing rest on Thy people," continued Colum.

"Stop it!"

The door thumped again, bits of mortar-pebbles peppering the floor.

Colum pounced, the trident turned just enough to catch Padarn's sweaty neck in the curved arm between the spikes. He pushed with a tremendous effort. The points planted in the planks with a splintering crunch. Padarn sat helplessly pinned against the wall, trapped but unharmed. He grasped at the imbedded prongs to loosen them. The candlestand held fast.

Colum checked the other boy. Assured he was harmless, Colum sank to his knees.

"Answer me when I call, O God, maintainer of my right," he recited, "I was hard pressed; Thou didst set me at large . . ."

The old door frame groaned and split. Three fellow students, the abbot, and Eithne burst into the dust-clouded sanctuary. The light beams fell on the intruder, kicking like an animal in a trap and on Colum at prayer.

"Know that the Lord has shown me His marvelous love—"

"Colum, Colum!" cried Eithne, running to him, hugging him. Her cape wrapped him, the warmth of her empathy filled him, and with her touch he felt the burning in his arms subside.

"The Lord hears when I call to Him," he continued, his breath slowing.

The other boys disarmed Padarn and wrenched him free, locking him in their arms.

Cruithnechain calmly picked up the knives from the floor. He turned them over in his hand. "Formidable weapons," he smiled. "No match for candlesticks in the right hands."

"I'm sorry," said Colum, his hands tightly clasped in Eithne's fists. "I'll make new candlest—"

"No doubt you will light up Erin with or without them, my son," said the abbot.

Padarn, squirming in the armlock of the boys, squealed, "Let me go! He started it! I only came to tell him about the trials for the Order of Knights, I swear, but he went crazy. He's jealous and angry he couldn't go, he's—"

"Enough," hushed the abbot, raising his cane.

Padarn paled at the sight of the yew-stick.

"It is anger that brought you here," said Cruithnechain. In Latin, he chanted, "However angry your heart, do not do wrong."

Colum recognized the line, the next line of the very psalm he had been praying. He pushed down his resentment, whipping it back to its unseen cage deep in his conscience.

"What kind of curse are you putting on me?" wept Padarn.

"Get a dressing for his ear," ordered Cruithnechain, ignoring the question. "Find and freshen their horses. Send them home." He bent his wizened face to Padarn, widening his eyes like an owl preparing to strike. "Worse things await you if you return or harm this family," he warned Padarn. "Leave now."

The boys in drab, gripping the two intruders' colorful shirts between the shoulder blades, escorted them out.

Eithne stuttered, "Father, I . . . the boys must have followed me, I . . ."

"Say nothing of it when you return, Eithne," said her old soul-friend. "It will only fan his fire." Then he stooped to look Colum in the eye.

Colum turned away, fearing a flame lingered there.

"My son, are you hurt?"

"No, Father."

"Look at me."

Colum faced his foster father slowly. Controlled. Trying to let the fury drain from his cheeks, but knowing he could not hide the glow he still sensed in his silver eyes.

"You look fine," the abbot said. Colum knew he lied. "No cuts. This time."

■

As Cruithnechain led the group across to the kitchen, he hid his frown from Eithne. *He will go to Moville,* the abbot thought. *He is in danger. And he is dangerous.*

4

FINBAR

A.D. 538

OLUM KNELT OPPOSITE FINBAR, ABBOT OF MOVILLE. They measured each other in silence, hands folded in prayer. Despite a summer sun beating on Finbar's stone oratory and a sweltering humidity that slowed the chip-chipping of the monks' hoes outdoors, Colum felt a bracing coolness on his skin. Reciting a psalm with the abbot had refreshed him, putting the interview into perspective. Breathing deeply, he drank in the cool oratory air, hoping the abbot's first question would not be too difficult. His plain wool tunic, worn at the knees, began to itch at his bare ankles. But he dared not move and betray a lack of discipline.

Finbar raised his puffy eyes which had seen more of the world than Colum knew or could name. The thin mouth, arched between hints of sagelike jowls to come, had tasted exotic foods in Egypt and prayed with bishops in faraway Rome. The tight ears had been filled with strange music from curious instruments. The wide sandaled feet had tramped on ship decks and cobbled roads in places unpronounceable.

Finbar unfolded his round, ruddy hands and brushed back his hair, still black as a new-moon night and thick behind the shaven forehead. He smiled with the deference of an ambassador.

"Why have you come?" he asked.

Colum stiffened. "To seek after God."

"For what purpose?"

"To know Him and to serve Him who made all things and to whom all things rightfully belong." Colum quickly indexed his memory for a proof text. "The earth is the Lord's and all that is in it, the world and all who dwell therein," he said in Latin in his lowest register.

Finbar appeared pleased but not overly impressed. "You speak of rights," he said. "Why do you renounce your birthrights?"

"Christ did."

Finbar furrowed his bald brow quizzically.

"Was He not," Colum explained, "a descendant of kings, the Son of David? Was He not before all worlds the royal Son of God? He lay aside His rightful position to serve us and to save us." He took a breath for emphasis. "So I, more than others, can truly follow Him."

Finbar blinked and widened his eyes at the bold statement. Colum knew why. This kind of talk would send the Roman bishops ripping their clothes. They'd even be taken aback by his name.

"Do you think that by giving up much you can follow the Lord better than he who gives up little?" asked the abbot.

"Whatever a person gives up is considered by him to be much. If the Lord has given him much, much more is required of him."

"Is this why you do not wish to live in the free-farmer's house which your father arranged for you?"

"My father has arranged many things for me before. It is time I made some arrangements for myself."

"Are you not grateful?"

Colum watched Finbar rub his double chin in curiosity. "If he ordered me to do so, I would. I will submit to whatever you advise."

Colum guarded his deeper motives. *Why should a noble prince associate with free-farmers when he could be with scholars? If one bed of straw is as good as another, it is better to be closer to those of your station.*

Finbar smiled warmly. "You need not be so humble in

this, my son. Many students stay with local villagers in exchange for a little labor. The settlement is large, but it cannot support the hundreds who come. So it is an acceptable practice."

"I know."

"You know you must build your own hut then?" said Finbar.

"Yes," said Colum, a bit annoyed at the obvious question. He thought of his mother's engraved battle-ax tucked away in his pack, and he was eager to stroke off the hickory branches he would weave for his bothy.

"Cruithnechain tells me you know your letters well and that you are skilled in the Psalter."

"Yes, Father. I can recite all 150."

"Bishop Brugacious of Kelkennan tells me you can be boastful."

Colum held his breath. "I pray the Lord will hold His servant back from presumptuous sins," he quoted from Psalm 19, suddenly shamed that it was his quick memory which had provoked the bishop. But Finbar did not seem offended.

"I also hear you commit hours in prayer and like to be alone."

"Yes, Father."

"Here you will pray in the appointed hours, study in the appointed hours, and labor in the appointed hours. And there is not much time to be alone here. This is a busy place. Hundreds of students of every age. We do things together here."

"I understand," Colum said, eyes drooping.

"But I expect we will put you to work immediately as an apprentice in the Scriptorium."

Colum straightened. His fingers twitched, joined at the tips, anticipating the curve of the quill dipping into inkwells and scratching out the words of God. When he felt his hard calluses from years of tilling, he reminded himself that cows must be milked and grain cut. "Where in the fields shall I work?" he volunteered.

"You won't," said Finbar, looking amused. "This is a much larger settlement than where you're from. Everyone has his own tasks. There is some rotation, but you shall be in the Scriptorium when not in lessons or in worship."

"Thank you, Father," said Colum, nearly cheering.

"Now, two last things. Cruithnechain passes rumors to me that you can . . . well," he searched for the right expression, "see the future." The abbot shifted, his skeptical frown showing his discomfort with his word choice, with even the need to broach the subject. "Leave that to the druids. This is an academic community. Divinity. Astronomy. Arithmetic. History. Writing, grammar, spelling. We produce scholars, not magicians."

"But if God gives me visions, how can I . . ."

"Enough," waved Finbar. "Do not presume what comes from God and what comes from your own active imagination. God speaks in His written Word. It is the only voice from Him we have, or need."

Colum sucked in a breath to control himself. As his folded hands tightened, the fingertips turned an angry red.

"Do not be deceived, Colum," continued the abbot. "The devil speaks in whispers and appears as an angel of light. Therefore, you must tell me when you see such things. I will not have one of my children misled."

"The law of the Lord is perfect," recited Colum. "His Word is complete to make us wise."

"This Word tells us to cleave to Christ and love His cross. Are you ready for these things?"

"Yes, Father," said Colum, his fingertips lightening.

"Then you will learn to desire nothing but to know Him. Consider all things of this world to be weights which hinder your flight to God. Learn from nature how to praise Him. Remain a virgin in your thoughts, pure and fit as one betrothed to Christ, unstained and unsullied by the lusts which war within us men." He spoke with a knowing tone. "You are in a time of your life when your body will be at war with your will. Come to me in your battles, and I will help you. You cannot win alone."

"Yes, Father," said Colum, aware of the penances he might prescribe to dull his drives. Already Colum had chopped stacks of wood to corral his wandering thoughts. Only by intense memorization had such mental meanderings been squeezed into submission, time after time. With a burning concentration, he cauterized the leaks of his bent nature. But on those mornings when he'd awakened with a start and a stain on his sleeping-smock, a panic of impurity hastened him to the brook for a discreet dousing. "Like steam from a covered kettle," reassured

Cruithnechain gently. "As long as the whole pot doesn't boil over."

But Finbar's fixed smile said he would not be so glib concerning spilt seed. "Build your hut near the church door," instructed Finbar. "You will find stacks of branches already cut there."

"But, Father, that spot is only for your best scholars."

"I know," said Finbar. "Do as I say. I will see to your father's cattle and horses which you brought. It is a generous endowment."

The abbot rose from his knees with a grunt, refusing Colum's hand. He stood over the young man and capped the novitiate's head with his palms and began a blessing in Gaelic. "Now may the High King of Heaven, Maker of all that is seen and unseen, grant you eyes and ears for the Seven Orders of Wisdom . . ."

Colum closed his eyes, but a bright shape hovered before him — a young woman, hardly fifteen, in noble dress, with button breasts, bold eyes, and a heart-shaped mouth parted in invitation. Her headband, studded with amethysts, was of a design he'd never seen in Erin. She walked forward, milk-skinned arms outstretched, but she receded farther away with each step. She called out a name. It was not his.

When the abbot finished his blessing and removed his hands, Colum felt the girl disappear in the distance, and with her an unsatisfied, long-ago longing.

It was a vision he knew he must never confess to Finbar.

■

After securing the sod roof, Colum inspected his round hut for potential leaks. Much of the clay was still wet and beaded due to the humidity. Colum shaped portions with his ax, shaving off excess, smoothing bumps with his palms, patting lumps into place. Only a few branch-humps of the expert wickerwork showed through the gray-brown sealant, like ribs in a thin cow. If plated in bronze, the hut might look like a helmet with a faint corrugated design.

Colum stepped back to admire his work, his hands dripping with cool mud. Passing brothers, tools to their shoulders, smiled in approval. Colum stood closer to it so there would be no question as to its fashioner.

His smock, soaked in sweat, stuck to his sore back. The orange sun kissed the tops of the pines on the western hills, yet the steamy air, still and stifling, offered no relief from the heat. Only a haze, not a breeze, drifted in from the lough.

Colum swished his hands in a bucket of water. It was luke-warm. Still, as he lifted his arms to let the water run over the rusty hairs to his elbows, he blessed God for even this small comfort. Cooler water from the lough, though, would be better.

He walked towards the shore, the grass soft under his bare, muddy feet. At the large refectory, just past the deep washing pool, the land sloped to a pebbly beach. Colum followed a smooth trail to the water's edge, scooped up water in his bucket, and then genuflected to splash his neck and arms in the lake.

Away to his left, gray-silhouetted in the oppressive haze, were great half-circles of students seated on rocks. They were young and old, a good threescore of them, whom Colum had seen leaving the smithy, kiln-house, and barns shortly after Nones, the mid-afternoon worship.

Standing on a flat-topped boulder shaped like a fishing curragh, Finbar taught his pupils. On occasion, a recitation or song wafted over the water, but mostly Finbar's fluent phrases, rolling with a rhythm to aid the memory, merged with the mist in a dim echo. Soon Colum would join those solemn, scholarly circles in his own shift for the novitiates and deacons-in-training, to receive insights of one who had traveled so far and journeyed so deeply into the mysteries.

"The cook cleans his pots," called the abbot, pointing to someone in the crowd, "because stains which remain pit the pot. An unclean pot poisons those who eat from it. And the warrior cleans his sword. Stains which remain scar the sword with rust, and it becomes dull and useless. So you must be clean. Holy vessels for holy work. Chaste, fit for His service. For from inside, out of a man's heart, come evil thoughts, fornication, greed, malice, indecency, envy, slander, arrogance, folly; these evil things come from inside, and they defile the man."

He spoke of these qualities as though they were lifelong enemies, as Colum's own father spoke of road bandits. It was the same message given to the group before this one. The outdoor lessons had touched on prudence, diligence, humility, and obedience, but chastity dominated Finbar's firm admonitions.

Touch no woman. It is good not to look on a woman. Eve fell first and led the man into sin.

At Cruithnechain's, many a noble's daughter came to learn letters. "Male and female created He them," Cruithnechain affirmed. "We are one in Christ. Together, we reflect the glory of God."

But there were no females in Finbar's fold. The only woman here was the nubile maiden in Finbar's mind, yearning for him hopelessly. Had his own youthful presence awakened the powerful memory that had passed through his palms? How had Finbar resisted her, so alluring and desiring? Or was it a fantasy which plagued him? No matter. If ever he was to become a priest, Colum knew he must protect the unintended confession in secrecy.

■

The oak chapel, squarish and stout, conforming in size to the Brehon Law, was choked with the smoke of altar candles. The bluish streams, unmoved by any hint of wind, rose in straight lines to the ceiling.

Finbar, draped in pure alba vestments, the virgin white of the celebrant, hovered over the altar. He carefully aimed three drops of well water into a jeweled, bowl-sized chalice. As each drop fell, he called, "*Peto te, Pater. Deprecorte, Fili. Obsecro Te, Spiritus Sancte.*"

On a wooden bench along the sunrise-facing wall, Colum sat with six senior brethren, elders of the Scriptorium who always took these places at the evening Eucharist. Outside the door in the dimming summer light, Colum heard the twitter of hungry birds and the rustle of the great company of the other students, standing dutifully prompt and quiet.

For the Gospel reading, Finbar would step outside. But few now heard his reverent blessing as the Host appeared and the wine mingled with the water, "*Remittat Pater. Indulgent Filius. Misereter Spiritus Sanctus.*"

With the Introit, Gloria, Collect, and Augmentum, Colum and the community lifted their hearts above the temporal plane. When they chorused, the little chapel vibrated with the energy of a transfer point between two worlds.

With the chalice and Host half uncovered, the mystery of

Christ's sacrifice not yet clearly revealed, Finbar's reading of the
Epistle pricked at Colum:

"Anyone who eats the bread or drinks the cup of the Lord
unworthily is guilty of desecrating the body and blood of the
Lord. A man must test himself before eating his share of the
bread and drinking from the cup. For he who eats and drinks,
eats and drinks judgment on himself if he does not discern the
Body . . ."

After hundreds of repetitions, Finbar's reading still
sounded crisp and convinced. The words slapped Colum like a
sharp wind in winter, sending an iciness through his conscience.

He had been thinking of his hut, admiring its perfect, circular base and the frame to rival any barrelmaker's. His content-
edness with his craftsmanship had been poisoned by pride and
had abscessed into adulation. He had lusted for recognition. As
always. He had forgotten that foxes have holes, and birds have
nests, but the Son of Man, who left His Father's heavenly lodge,
had nowhere to lay His head. Sickened, he even admitted to
himself that he had hoped to see a crowd of men circled around
his hut afterwards, resolving to improve their own, wondering
aloud who in their midst could sculpt such a fine work out of
clay.

I am only clay, he mourned, pushing aside the anger with
himself for having fallen again to arrogance. Did not Finbar's
warning come over the water just as he was washing himself?
Now I must be washed again.

He blessed God for revealing it to him, just as the abbot
fully revealed the Host and cup, the assurance of forgiveness.
Finbar pulled aside the pure napkin and led the brethren
through the next litany, Colum joining with a newfound fervor,
"How meet and just it is that we should always and everywhere
give thanks to Thee, Holy Lord, One and Immortal, God incor-
ruptible . . ."

Colum let the praises purify his own corruption.
Repentant tears wet his face. As a cool gust of air chilled his
cheeks, he heard heavy raindrops hammer the roof. A clean,
sweet feeling swept through his chest, renewing and relaxing
him. With an upraised hand, he joined his brothers in song,
"God living and true, God great and good, God blessed and just.
Sanctus, sanctus, sanctus, Dominus Deus Sabaoth . . ."

When concluded, Finbar took three steps back, beating his breast for sins in thought, word, and deed, and then took three steps forward to rejoin God at His fellowship table as a guest in His banquet hall, welcome to the feast mirrored so dimly in the leather-lined lodges of the chieftains.

After dipping the Host into the chalice, Finbar placed the wafer on the square paten, snapped it apart, and then joined the pieces together again. "His broken body was raised," Colum prayed, "so too can You mend us when we are broken. A broken and contrite heart You will not despise."

While the communicants came forward to Finbar in the doorway to receive a share of the elements, they sang the hymn so beautiful that men thought angels must have first sung it:

> *Sancti venite*
> *Christi Corpus sumite*
> *Sanctum bibentes*
> *Quo redempti sanguinem.*

Over and over the prayer was raised in defiance of the downpour. The music spiraled skywards, spinning the chapel in the vortex of their voices. Who could feel the pelting rain with such supernatural strains weaving a canticled cloak? In thankfulness, the monks turned their faces to the sky and its baptism. When their voices hushed and only the pattering in the puddles was heard, Finbar signaled his dismissal with a broad, open-palmed crossing. "*Ita Missa Est.*"

Colum bowed quietly to readjust himself to the material world. A low murmuring outside drew him to his feet.

A circle of brethren, several men deep, surrounded his hut. Colum swallowed hard, suspicious of his own reaction to their attention. He gently maneuvered through the crowd to stand near his creation.

The hickory ribs dripped with soggy clay which peeled off in thick chunks, dissolving into the drainage trough. Clumps of sod and mud slipped to the puddled floor.

Tears in his throat, Colum sloshed through the brown streams to lean on the bent frame. The brothers, silent and soaking, stood in their places, unmoving. Colum heard the low murmur of many prayers for him.

A hand squeezed his wet shoulder. Finbar gave his new student a fatherly hug and watched the hut's walls melt away for a moment.

Colum cleared his throat. "The things we do by our own strength wash away," he managed.

Finbar hugged him again as though he had answered a question correctly.

◼

The Scriptorium smelled of cured calfskins. In the low light cast by the lonely rushlamps, Colum saw the empty benches where the senior brothers sat for their copying. With summer, most had gathered up their inkhorns, goosequills, and boards to work on short pieces outside, their faces cooled and their words dried by the breezes off Lough Foyle. In winter they would blow on their own hands to stay nimble in the heartless room.

With books few and precious, most students copied their own in the quietness of their cells. But this hall housed an impressive collection of finished books, encased in finely tooled leather satchels which hung on pegs along the walls.

At the only desk, reserved for the illustrators, sat Erc the Master Illuminator. Thin and straight as a quill, he etched his lines much more slowly than the regular scribes. On the fine-textured, unblemished vellum stretched flat below him, Erc traced tendrils with the secret-recipe colors which filled the horns at his side. He changed pens frequently to vary the thickness of the lines.

Observing a strict rule of silence, Colum dared not disturb him. Just to be near Erc was inspiration enough to continue practicing the repetitious letter-lessons. Even with silence, the company of one brother was more welcome — and the work area more spacious — than working alone in the hut which Finbar had helped him rebuild.

Colum slipped the long, narrow tablets of wax-coated yew wood off his shoulder. He leaned them quietly on the bench and unwound the leather bindings. He tiptoed to the supply table and chose his usual sharp stylus. Seated, with a smoothed board on his knee, he crossed himself with the metal-pointed graib and asked for patience. Then the hard tip dug into the wax and carved the Latin lesson he had already memorized.

The hanging satchels of the library urged him onward. Within those worn covers, the classics of the continent called to him, coaxing him forward to qualify for their wisdom.

Colum had watched with wonder as the senior copyists unrolled the delicate, brown-edged sheets for transcription onto fresh skins. Most were Biblical books, passed through generations, each with its own stories and secrets. Some, partially burned and still smoky-smelling, had miraculously escaped barbarian looters. Some, hastily sketched, were smuggled to eager congregations in dangerous circumstances. Some, bearing Egyptian markings, held the voices of the Desert Fathers and patristics, models of learning and longing after God, defenders of the holy faith in the face of hatred and heresy. Some may even have been in Alexandria's great library, Colum mused.

All these had found refuge in Erin, carried by scholars escaping the tribal marauders who in turn fled a worse horde, the Huns, who were fathered by devils and determined to destroy the Word.

Certainly a good collection of classics came from Candida Casa, Ninian's great school where the gentle Finbar had studied under elders whose learning lineage looked to Martin of Tours. The brothers of the Scriptorium felt especially blessed with these — works of Aristotle and a few Greek histories, Roman law scrolls, and even a partial *Aeneid*. But even this was a modest acquisition. Finnian of Clonard in Meath, it was said, possessed Syriac Gospels, Arabic works of astronomy, an *Almagest* of Ptolemy, and the works of Julius Caesar, Livy, and Juvenal, as well as other Roman playwrights.

"You shall not covet," quoted Finbar with a smile, but he would not easily defer to the south and disappoint his family of the north. Though he had brought many satchels from Candida Casa, many others were prizes from his far-flung travels. The abbot insisted on the highest quality and integrity of text, braving steep slopes and strong storms to pursue the rumor of an errorless document.

A stone crypt of discarded, corrupted scrolls sat sealed behind the Scriptorium. Finbar hoarded the useless books, refusing to pass them along to lesser-endowed schools. "Why propagate the errors even if we know where they are?" he argued.

And so only the best manuscripts remained in the room, each correct word in its correct place with correct spelling.

Colum made his letters with consistency and caution, in imitation of his spiritual director. Finbar's stringent standards had even shown in the construction of Colum's cell. Waist-deep in water, the abbot selected well-shaped stones from the riverbed. He perfectly fit each stone into the foundation and discarded many that Colum found adequate. The task had taken several days, with much of Colum's work redone to meet the abbot's exacting specifications.

Though precise and precious, the books of the Scriptorium were not the most valued in the settlement. In the locked sacristy beside the church, Finbar stored his most sacred souvenirs, which no one had seen but his servant. Some believed even more beautiful books lay within, held in jewel-encrusted containers, and that the abbot copied these treasures privately. The practice explained Finbar's own stunning script.

There was so much to read — so much to know. Colum picked up another board and pressed more letters into the wax.

■

The hour for Sext approached, the sixth hour service, in homage of Him who at that hour ascended the throne of the cross, and the sun at its crowning height darkened.

A darkening would be welcome today to staunch the searing flow of heat from the sun. With the corn crisping in the fields, meals were more meager than usual, in order to store up for a lean winter.

As the timber Scriptorium warmed, sleep tempted Colum's baggy eyes. Though no one might see him close them for a moment, he resisted and took heart from Erc's steady work. By mixing, dipping, and tracing with unslowing strokes, Erc encouraged him to persist. His habits, formed over many years alongside his friend Finbar at Candida Casa, propelled him onward in the enervating air. *How quickly his ink will dry today,* thought Colum. *It will bake onto the sheets.*

He rubbed out a whole line of sloppy errors on his waxboard, disgusted with his carelessness. He rubbed his eyes with the heels of his hands. It made them burn more. Even the disciplines of the offices at Cruithnechain's had not prepared him for Finbar's rigorous schedule. Worship every three hours — never long, never missed — never allowed for more than three hours of uninterrupted sleep.

Colum stretched his dry cheeks, blinked, and shook his head. The penance for sleeping in services was severe — meals denied, strokes on the hands. Except for the Scriptorium brothers.

Erc propped his pen into a hole and turned to Colum. He rose and approached the novitiate with the stiff gait of one who has sat for so long. When he reviewed Colum's letters, he patted the young man's shoulder, smiling so his rotted yellow teeth showed. He beckoned to Colum to follow him to the desk.

Colum glanced over the work with an admiring gasp. The calligraphy was beautiful beyond words. Still gleaming wet in spots, the majuscule script marched across the sheet in orderly black rows, the letters round and rolling in unbroken columns. The consistent curves featured an occasional flourish at the end of lines to justify the neat margins. Colum studied the decorative capitals at the head of paragraphs, separated by their large size and elaborate embellishment — spirals and flowers, delicately drawn into the body of the text by a gradual diminishing of the following letters' sizes, blending, not dominating, pulling the eye across the page.

Erc reached to the penholder, selected a new goose feather, and handed it to Colum. Pointing to where he left off, he invited Colum to continue with a wink.

Colum's heart raced in his chest. He waited for a confirming nod. Erc pointed again. Disbelieving, Colum gripped the quill like a weapon and plunged it into the inkhorn. The pure carbon stained the sheet in even, dark lines, each letter merging gently with the next. A thrilling energy streamed through his sleeve, empowering the pen as it glided like a prow-boat on a waveless lake. His unhesitating, unerring quill followed a marvelous line, curving and twisting again and again. The steadiness of the script surprised him, and as he inked the nib he thought that surely an angel guided his hand.

Erc only interrupted to remind him to stir the ink and to count the letters. Beauty and accuracy, held in equal high regard, must not be compromised to mere speed. Erc spread a new piece of vellum on the board, pinned it in place, and with a look of surprised satisfaction, motioned Colum to press on.

Colum left a space for the capital letter, and in subtly declining sizes, began drawing his descenders and cross-strokes with a swift, sure movement. He began to hum the hymn which he copied, a familiar psalm from one of the day's offices. But Erc cleared his throat in a friendly warning as Finbar entered the Scriptorium.

After an affectionate stroke of Colum's red hair, the abbot leaned in for a closer examination of his star student's work. He immediately fingered several letters, incorrectly spaced by mere hairbreadths. The rumble in his throat voiced various criticisms of curves too thin or crosses too thick.

When Finbar reached for a stylus, Colum surrendered the seat to him. The abbot demonstrated a line of uniform copy. He then put his eye close to the blank space reserved for the capital letter. He noted the texture of the skin, calculated its absorbency, and then selected a new penpoint. He inked it and began to etch a serpentine figure with strange, twisted coils, forming a grotesque yet graceful letter. Finbar changed pens. He crowned the creature's head with feminine, flowing hair, held by a fragile noblewoman's headband. He bent the waves of her tresses to join the spirals of her serpent body. Beautiful and bizarre, it seemed a vision had captured him, and he was compelled to record it. When he scratched the last, soft stroke, he wiped the perspiration from his lip and blew on the ink. Removing the pins from the corners, he rolled up the sheet, tucked it under his arm, and left. He paused in the open doorway.

"The text is very good," he said. "But it is not for you to practice on the skins. We cannot waste them. Go back to your boards. First the blade, then the ear, then the full-grown grain in the ear."

He disappeared to the outdoors, his footfalls heavy on the turf.

Colum quickly slapped his tablets together with a pivot pin through the base-holes, whirled the leather thongs around them, and slung them over his shoulder as he hurried to exit.

Erc stopped him in the doorway. "Don't be upset," he said. "It is my fault."

"It seemed so unlike him," said Colum angrily.

"I have known him for many years," said Erc. "He has only been this way since our last year at Candida Casa when Rae of Galloway tempted him."

"A woman? At Candida Casa?"

"Aye. A nobleman's daughter came for instruction. Her lips dripping honey but full of hornets' stings."

"And he came here to escape her?"

Erc measured his words. With admiration for his lifelong friend, he said, "Great virtue is subjected to great tests. But can a man hold a torch so close without burning his clothes? Blessed be God, who always provides a way of escape. A highborn man took her from him."

"Why do you tell me this?"

"So you will more easily forgive him."

"It is God who forgives."

Erc blushed. "He did not touch her. But to purge himself of desire, he went to Alba in the north, taking a party beyond Hadrian's Wall."

"Into The Wilds?"

"To bring the light of God's Word to the darkened Picts. Where Ninian had worked long before. We barely escaped with our lives."

"How so?"

"It is Satan's stronghold," he said, his eyes filling with fear. "Filled with uncleanness of sun-worshipping savages. They raid the south for jewels and furs and for women to fill their brothels."

"But why? Are they not also Picts, like our cousins of the northeast?"

"Aye, but those of the north are filled with devils. They killed ten men in our party. Split their ribs and pulled out their hearts. The devils."

■

With Finbar's frugality and the frequent fasts, the winter brought a deep hunger which demanded the most concentrated diversions. In the chilly, cheerless Scriptorium, Colum dragged his quill across a horny strip of vellum. He flexed his fingers, stiff with cold, and pulled up his hood. He dried his stylus and tapped it mindlessly. He rebuked a yawn. His restless eyes wandered to the walls.

The classics and patristics still hung on their pegs, untouched by him in a year of copying. Only through Finbar's lectures did he know anything of their contents. While productive and promising as a scribe, he could not yet probe them personally. It was like hanging sweet apples just beyond the reach of a tethered colt.

When he saw Erc walking toward him, he wet the quill again and wrote. Erc placed his palm on the writing board, a signal to stop. Cocking his head, Erc motioned for the young novice to follow him.

Outside the door, a brisk wind flopped Erc's long hair over his forehead. He pushed it back and left dark streaks on the bare spots. "Colum," he grinned, "I want you to take a long walk."

"To where?"

"Just a long walk. To refresh yourself." His expression told Colum that he understood his boredom.

He decided to visit his old friend, Angel Wing, in the barn. At this time of day, the tenders would be in session with the abbot somewhere outside despite the raw wind.

The old horse whinnied and widened its white eyelashes when Colum came into the stable. The novice patted the smooth hair on the horse's neck, stroking tenderly. He examined the leg muscles, still well-defined and hard from plowing many cornrows. In a nearby bin lay a pile of dried kernels. Colum scooped some up and held them to Angel Wing's twitching nose.

"Old friend," he said as the horse lapped up the treat, "I think you eat better than I do. The teacher has been more frugal than a squirrel." He fetched more corn, a precious store denied to the men. "Are you happy here? Of course. As long as you get corn," he laughed. The horse pushed its hairy nose into his palm, searching for more.

"Perhaps you are content here," Colum continued, "but you were made for racing. And so was I."

Colum poked his head into a couple of straw-strewn stalls to check for lingering stable-servants. There were none.

"I feel my mind racing," he said, "but I'm plowing furrows like you. Line after line. Day after day. But there's so much more. Isn't there?"

The wind whistled outside and set up a flutter of bird wings in the hay piles.

"I wrote from the Proverbs today, 'Wisdom lifts her voice; She stands at the crossroads, by the wayside, by the top of the hill; At the entry by the open gate, she calls aloud, "It is to you I call.""'"

Angel Wing snorted and shuffled, his eyes ranging as though alert to the presence of a stranger. Colum glanced about, and seeing no one, soothed the horse with nose rubs.

"Do you suppose God is speaking to me?" he asked. "Is there an open gate that I should enter — or leave through — to find wisdom?"

The fear of the Lord is the beginning of wisdom, he knew. But what lay beyond the beginning? He searched his soul for direction. The dreams that might have helped him had stopped long ago. Only Finbar's lectures filled his energetic mind, stunting his other abilities. "The Word of God is all you need," he repeated, yet inside he felt like new wine in an old goatskin, bubbling in a ferment of wanderlust. *God's voice will only come if I am pure,* he thought. *As the abbot says, the Spirit of God fills only those vessels who are holy as He is holy.*

He stroked the horse's nose a last time and found a place to kneel in the hay. The silent prayer of his heart rose into his throat with song, building in vigor and volume, setting the thrushes aflutter. Without the cracks of earlier years, his voice settled to a baritone of hypnotic power, resonance, and range. He did not mind that the far-reaching notes might reach the Scriptorium. If only they might reach high heaven and transport him through the unseen plane which, when folded through prayer as fingers of the one praying, could become seen. His energy built; the sagging feeling from the Scriptorium transformed into strength. The joy of music and meter and the making of poetry as one made in the image of the Creator lifted him. Perhaps his love for the Psalter was that of a bard, not only a scholar. The poetry of the Proverbs moved him as surely as their wisdom.

Gemman would understand, he thought. The budding idea bloomed to a firm resolution. *I must see Gemman.* To travel with the scholar and singer would rescue him from roteness.

His chants had drifted to a thankful whisper when the perfume, sweet and subtle as new apple blossoms, filled his senses. His song choked in his throat when looking up, his eye followed the figure of a tall, graceful woman. She petted Angel Wing, pursing her full lips in a soothing, kissing sound. Her simple robe, secured by delicate gold chains crisscrossed over her chest, appeared to be a thin, bluish silk. Like a veil, the opaque folds followed the long, curving shadows of her legs. Her golden hair, glittering with tiny jewels, curled around her narrow, swan-white neck. When she turned to face him, the hair-stones spun off little rainbows. Her sky-blue eyes looked through him with a deep and endearing recognition.

Colum fell over from his knees to his seat, fascinated and frightened. Her disarming smile did not comfort him. He shivered and realized she had no cloak or shoes despite the cold.

Speechless, he gasped when two more young girls, in flowing silk and with bejeweled black hair, emerged from behind the haystacks. Their bright, friendly eyes fixed on him. Their bare feet, smooth and soundless, advanced towards him in careful, deliberate steps. One raised a slender hand to touch him.

"Stop," ordered Colum, struggling to stand. "Who are you?" Blood rushed to his face. His temples pounded with Erc's caution, "Great virtue is subjected to great tests." He crossed his forehead to ward off the temptation, but the comely intruders advanced. He knew none of them and guessed quickly that they must be highborn daughters of a local lord. The hair on the back of his neck bristled with the thought that under their filmy robes may be daggers. Were they on a mission for their father? But for what? For Finbar denying the noble's daughters an education? A defilement by an aberrant monk? Had they been lying in wait for him, as for a stray foal separated from the herd, in hopes of subverting his pledge of purity?

He pushed the girl's hand away roughly as though parrying a sword blow.

"What?" cried the golden-haired girl. "Do you not know us? We are three sisters whom our father gives you."

They moved forward again, their arms open to embrace him. Or devour him.

"Who is your father?" Colum cried, backing away.

"Our father is the High King of Heaven," replied the golden girl, her deep eyes sparkling. "We are Wisdom, Prophecy, and Purity. Did you not ask our father for us to come and never leave you?"

Their robes rustled open in the backs as their magnificent

wings unfurled. The horse reared. Colum felt the hay stubble on the floor prick his flushed face as he fell in a faint.

◼

Perhaps it was a delirium, as Finbar said. Colum's drivenness and hunger, coupled to a bardic imagination trying to compensate for his boredom, had probably exhausted him. After confining him to his hut for a rest, Finbar squelched the rumors of a supernatural apparition, though he could never fully explain the lingering fragrance. "Wet hay in an advanced state of decay. Releases all sorts of ill humors," he said. He ordered the barn inspected for evidence, and then cleaned by the stable-hands who found Colum.

Still, the tongues wagged, and a parade of inquisitive brothers gathered at the novice's hut, asking for prayer and instruction. Embarrassed, Colum sought the silence of the Scriptorium more eagerly. Yet even there the brother's quills quieted when he entered.

When he asked the abbot for an extended leave, Finbar most readily agreed. "It always does one good to travel," he encouraged.

But Colum detected a fear in the abbot's jovial voice. Did he feel threatened by the shower of attention given to his own favorite student?

In a parting ceremony, Colum took the tonsure of a deacon, submitting to the shears as Finbar intoned a blessing. As he watched his locks fall to the floor around his knees, Colum thought the abbot's prayer for him sounded less regretful about his departure, and more relieved.

5

MAIRE

A.D. 541

OLUM'S BOOKS AND BATTLE-AX HUNG SIDE BY SIDE ON
the saddle. He carried the memories of his parents' good-byes.
He smiled at the thought of his father reaching up to hug him.
The chieftain had looked troubled by his son's tonsure, yet
relieved to see Colum leave the monastery of Moville. "Have
Gemman introduce you to many chieftains," he said.

His parents had given him a farewell feast, a pack of provisions, and directions for the south road to the bard's winter
quarters in Leinster. "It is also the road to Tara," Fedlimidh
reminded him. "Get to know it well."

The triplets had surprised him. Cloistered as he was in
Finbar's regimented school, buried in books, Colum had lost
contact with his family. When his three new sisters hugged his
rough knees and lifted their little hands to their towering
brother, he gathered them up and occupied them with songs.
Mincloth, Sinech, and Cuimne cuddled closer. "It is a very good
omen," noted Fedlimidh, clapping his hands with glee. "Three
girls. See how they come to you. Like the kingdoms of Leinster,
Munster, and Connaught will come."

To add the honors of a poet to the rank of a prince would
make the young man an irresistible leader. But Colum wrestled
with a different set of thoughts, the disturbing vision of the three

girls in the barn. He pushed these pictures aside to enjoy the attention of the toddlers.

Drummon had polished the ax for him. Collain cut a bagful of herbs to take. She said they were for sour stomach and fever, but they were really to ward off the fairies. Eithne prayed with him a long time before she gave him final directions for her native Leinster.

It was just as she described — undulating green plains, patchwork pasture aplenty, wild groves of apple trees, and scores of small streams carrying away the winter wetness.

At each monastic stop along the route which his own mother had taken years before, Colum received hospitality and letters of passage through the quiltwork of quarreling kingdoms. "The Lord will guard you," he sang to the hills. "The Lord will guard your coming and your going, now and forevermore."

When he at last found Gemman's log house in the woods of WestMeath, he hugged the old man as though he had found a long-lost relative.

Gemman had aged considerably. His embrace, though warm, was weak. He walked with a painful, bow-legged stoop, and his hands, still skillful on the strings, were knotty as old pines.

The house seemed too large for one man, until Colum realized Gemman's twenty-four pupils had all gone to their own homes for winter, leaving the aging bard on his own. He was like a king without his warriors.

"I am glad for your company," Gemman said, stirring some hot soup. "I have prayed for your safe journey."

"I didn't meet any robbers," Colum said. "So I didn't get to use these." He pointed to his board-bound books with the long leather straps.

Gemman laughed till he wheezed.

■

After several weeks into early spring, Colum resupplied the household with game. Gemman's bow had not been used for a long time. But the strings on his harp were well-tuned.

The memory work in the twelve forms of poetry began immediately. Song upon song, story upon story, poem upon poem, Gemman added to his student's prodigious Biblical repertoire. Colum could see that his clear voice pleased Gemman. The old stories danced in his native tongue, setting the bard's foot tapping. The memorized melodies recalled the glories of heroes and the pangs of impossible loves. The powerful Gaelic chords chased winter away, and the very buds seemed to spring open with his commanding words. His bellowing notes vibrated the air violently, wobbling pottery and forcing Gemman to cover his ears. His psalms shook the hills. Clouds of crows took to flight with his exuberant shouts:

> *Prope est Dominus omnibus invocantibus eum,*
> *Omnibus invocantibus eum sincere.*
> *Very near is the Lord to those who call to Him,*
> *Who call to Him in singleness of heart.*
> *Custodit Dominus omnes diligentes se,*
> *Et omnes peccatores disperdit.*
> *The Lord watches over all who love Him,*
> *But sends the wicked to their doom.*

"King David may not have done it better," smiled Gemman to his lone student, uncovering his ears.

Colum bowed his head gratefully, his palms calming the strings of the four-cornered lyre. Their vibrations tickled his hand.

"You know the Psalter very well, young prince," said Gemman, "but there is much more to know."

"That is why I came to you."

"Latin may be the language of the church, but music is the language of the soul," said Gemman. He touched his bony fingers to his breast. "God is a poet. Why else would He give us such a large songbook?"

"Our people believe the god Lug gave us music."

Gemman rolled his eyes. "So you remember. Your nurse told you the story? Or your father's singing champion?"

Colum remembered how Drummon, despite Eithne's warnings, taught him the old legends. The warrior saw it his duty to keep the prince current with the other children of the dun. "Lug got it from the Dagda," said Colum. "When the Dagda's wife, the goddess Boann, was in labor, he played upon his harp, crying with her in her birth pains. When the three sons were born, he brought laughter to her through song, and then he made the sounds of sleep to bring her rest. She named the sons for her husband's music — Crysong, Smilesong, and Sleepsong."

"Boann is nearby," the bard teased, pointing a thumb toward where the River Boyne meandered through the meadows of Meath. "Perhaps she will help you spellbind your hearers into tears, laughter, and slumber at will. But if not, you can surely help them worship the true Creator of music with all their heart."

"Can the music of an Ollave really charm a person?"

Gemman paused to ponder his reply. "Usually it just warms a cold night, and the only magic is the swifter passing of time. But words have a force of their own. The long training of an Ollave Poet is not to teach him charms and spells, but how to responsibly use the weapons of his words. A warrior can hurl insults, words which may wound a man's pride. But a poet can hurl the glan dicend — the hilltop curse — words which can kill."

"Words that—"

"Words may also create," Gemman hurried on. "'The Lord's word made the heavens; let the whole world fear the Lord and all stand in awe of Him. For He spoke, and it was.' Surely you have copied the psalmist's words many times."

"Yes, but the words that—"

"And man, made in God's image, also creates through the word in a lesser sense. Adam named all the animals, and then named the creature that came from his side using a poem: 'This is now bone of my bone and flesh of my flesh; she shall be called Woman.'"

Flesh. Woman. Finbar's fiery fulminations suddenly streamed through Colum's thoughts. Gemman looked alarmed, as though he watched someone in a seizure. He puzzled for a moment, aware that his words had taken a potent effect on the young man.

"What is it, Colum? Are you well?"

"I am," said Colum. He handed over the harp to end the lesson. He stood and walked away from his teacher. He poured rainwater from a pitcher into a plain ceramic bowl, dipped in his hands, and patted his hot face. Bent over the bowl, dripping, he asked, "Have you ever known a woman, Master Gemman?"

For a moment, there was only the sound of the water drops. "Have you?" asked the bard.

"No. That is not why I asked." He raised his voice in imitation of the abbot, "A woman is a pit of vices, a snare—"

"That's enough," Gemman said sternly. "Is that what you learned at Moville?" He harumphed. "Our Lord did not regard women as such. He touched women. He taught them. He healed them. He honored them. For He made them our equal partners. He said, 'It is not good for the man to be alone.'"

"Then why must I be alone?"

"For the same reason I have been. To give myself fully to others, both men and women."

"Father Finbar says the priests in Rome may take wives."

"He also knows, as you and I, that men here take and use women as they would their horses or sheep. They are used and traded. He is at least right in insisting that men be fully consecrated to God, or fully consecrated to their wives. One or the other. In this way, women are no longer the objects of our lusts."

"I have much to learn, and unlearn," Colum said.

"One thing you will learn is that by being single you can travel more freely. And we will begin to travel soon."

Colum turned and broke into a wide grin. "Can you still manage it, Master Gemman?"

"As long as I don't have to walk."

"Where will we go?"

"East, towards Tara."

Colum's heart leaped with the prospect of seeing the magical hill-throne of Erin's kings.

"On the way," added Gemman, "we must rest with Almergin. An old schoolmate of mine." He cleared his throat. "He is a druid."

In A.D. 61, the Roman legions tramped across Britain, stamping out the one force that united the otherwise fractured, feuding tribes — the druids. Since Julius Caesar first described their bloody rituals in Gaul, the Romans reacted with revulsion and ruthlessness.

The retreating diviners, with the armies they advised, fortified themselves on an island near Anglesey. They summoned storms to capsize the pursuing Roman triremes, which dashed to splinters on the rocks in the capricious currents. The sorcerers sent sea beasts to devour the screaming survivors.

But even the Roman augurs, following the moon's phases, foresaw that the tide would turn, in all ways. With engineering ingenuity and Roman resolve, the army forded the shallow divide and planted eagle standards on the beach.

On a nearby hill, the druids danced, an awesome white-robed spectacle, issuing frightful ritual curses. But their brazen insults and bronze hand-sickles were useless against the disciplined cavalry that hacked them to bits. The red-robed riders corralled the confused Celtic soldiers and slaughtered them. Then they trampled the fleeing families, leaving mothers and children in mangled heaps.

Thereafter, the druids dispersed to places beyond the Roman reach — to north Alba, Caledonia, and the kingdoms of Erin.

"They despise all things Latin to this day," concluded Gemman, slouched on his aged steed. "They regard the faith as a subtler Roman invasion."

"Then why will Almergin accept us as guests?"

"He must. It is the Brehon Law. But beyond that, I am of equal rank. He is settled in one place only because he is also chieftain of the valley."

"He will accept you then, but me — look at me." Colum passed his palm over the fuzz of his shorn forehead.

"He won't know you are an oblate for the priesthood," assured Gemman, "despite your appearance. You would be shaved as my apprentice anyway. Still, you must be careful. Almergin can be easily upset."

They followed the snaking turns of the River Boyne, the personification of the old goddess. It led to the path for Almergin's lodge, set on an ancient hill surrounded by ruined earthworks. In the slow ascent, they crossed a fallow field full of upright posts used to align stars and measure their nightly movements. Some bore crude carvings, not to decorate but to count. Other than these, Colum observed no other buildings or fences. He saw only the long wood house with a rickety barn flanked by a long swine-slop outside. All around swished sand-colored grasses, much of it bitten short by the brown-haired sheep bunched near the barn. A black and orange collie, the sheep's keeper, barked at the two travelers.

A hulk of a man in an undyed wool coat and trousers lumbered around the corner. He hauled a heavy stack of fire logs on his thick back.

Colum turned to his teacher. "Shall I ask the servant to tell Master Almergin that we are here?"

Gemman shook his head. "That is Almergin."

The druid dropped his logs and approached the visitors. His pushed-up sleeves displayed whorling blue tattoos on his firm forearms. A bull of a man, he flared his wide nostrils with strong puffs of breath, rippling his shaggy brown mustache. His square, smooth jaw, set in a forward thrust, matched the bony, plated forehead shaven back to the top of his massive head. He had the eye of a hunter who had just heard the bushes rustle.

"Gemman, of course," he said with a broad, upraised hand. "I should have guessed when the winds began to blow from the west."

"Greeting to the Chieftain of the Two Rivers. How fare your sheep?" said Gemman.

"Shedding already. You are just in time. How fare your pupils? Where are they all?"

"Sent home for the winter. This is my only companion, Colum of Clan Conaill."

Colum, assisting Gemman off his mount, nodded politely.

"From so far north?" asked Almergin, eyeing him suspiciously. "Gemman, your fame goes everywhere."

Colum looked for students, servants, farmhands of any sort, but there were none. He tied up the horses himself, untied the packs and bags, and followed the wise men into the house.

The smell stung his sinuses. From the rafters hung branches of aromatic herbs. Dried and tied with sheephair ropes, the leafy clusters swung in the breeze, fanning their fragrance around the room. Fine-fiber sacks of pungent dried pine swung freely. The walls were lined with wax-sealed ceramic jars. Colum guessed the unlabeled containers stored ground plants and packed poultices of every type — apple, barley, barks of all sorts, basil, dandelion, chickweed, thyme, wormwood, and many more. Glass flasks full of raw honey sat on guard-railed shelves.

On a broad oak table, arranged in fastidious order, lay tools and bowls for mixing tinctures, ointments, and liniments. The bronze sickles, small and shiny, could cut and strip plants as well as be used for surgery. The razor-sharp edges had probably removed tumors from men and slit the stomachs of pigeons fed gold dust so that Almergin might study its patterns.

Their host brewed steaming mugs of a minty tea with water from a small kettle on the central fire. "Perfect for travelers," he said through a forced smile. "It reduces swelling."

Colum sipped it and nearly spat.

Almergin cracked a log over his knee and set it in the fire. In the roaring blaze, the bath water in twin buckets bubbled quickly.

"My servant will prepare your bath, old friend," said Almergin with a cough. "I have just what is needed for your aching joints in this damp weather." He leaned out the lodge door and roared, "Maire! Maire! A hot bath at once!" Then to Gemman he said, "A pine extract in the water will overcome your fatigue." He left, barking orders to the servant.

Colum drained his tea in the fire. "Where is he going?"

"He will scrape fresh sap for me," said Gemman.

"He certainly treats you so—" Colum caught his breath as the servant girl entered.

Her sable mane, glossy and thick, tossed wildly around her neck. Her black eyebrows curved like crescent moons in a mysterious mien, daring him to discover their meaning. The smooth, blushed cheeks suggested she was very young, but she filled her nettle-fiber dress with a mature figure. She crossed the room warily on bare feet, the iron anklets of ownership in plain view beneath the hem as she kicked it. When she passed, Colum saw in her stern face the fiery eyes of a filly, tethered but untamed. Her confident stride sent Colum's stomach to his throat.

Over her narrow shoulder, she carried a sturdy pole, which she inserted through the bucket handles. She lifted, then carried the gurgling water to the next room, trailing clouds of steam. Out of sight, the buckets clanked. The water splashed. Gemman said, "Help me up."

Colum assisted his teacher to the tub.

The girl was gone.

■

The next day, Colum awoke long before daybreak. The cycle of daily offices stayed with him. He gently kicked back his covers and stood. Stretching, he almost reached the rafters. The sharp smells were more tolerable, yet he yearned for fresh air. He gathered up the blanket to use as a wrap. He stepped over Gemman, sleeping with a deep snore, and slipped out.

The air was still and cool. Not even the birds chirped. Colum walked towards the barn, his prayerful eyes to the sky. The stars followed their quiet courses in parade across the heavenly vault, a perfect procession of 350 blinking lights set in story-steeped formations. The Hunter. The Boar. The Fishes. The Crown. The Swan. The Bull.

A distant cough startled him. Cloaked in moonlight, Almergin counted the stars and calculated their movements relative to his posts. He slowly unwound a spool of wool yarn, preparing to mark the sunrise from the previous day's position. Colum now noticed the crescent design in the placement of the poles — a sweeping half-circle which Almergin apparently was in the process of completing into a full wheel — an observation tool in homage of the golden sun god and his silver sister, the moon.

As the inky sky rapidly lightened and the purple horizon turned to rose, Colum pressed against the barn wall to observe Almergin. The druid charged across the field to a pole at the far west side, his head low, his cape flapping behind him. The distant hills turned red and then blazed orange as the sun's glowing disc burned its way up, up, breaking free in a blinding climb as though responding to Almergin's ghostly chants. With a sickle, the druid slashed a mark in the pole and hurried towards the barn.

Colum's muscles tightened. He could not return to the lodge without being seen. He slipped into the barn and stood still as a deer behind a pile of wood. Barely a whisper away lay the slave girl on the hay, curled under a twisted woolen cloak. Her oval face was troubled by a dream, and her exposed legs tried to run, but the chain connecting her anklets would never let her.

Almergin entered the barn. Colum held his breath. He heard the clip of a key turn and the clink of the chain.

"Up now. Feed the swine," said Almergin.

Colum heard the thump of Almergin's shoe in her side, a bucket crunch through a bin of acorns, the girl's quick, startled breaths, and the squeak of the door as she left.

Outside the pigs began to grunt. Inside there was an unsettled silence. Then, sniffing.

Almergin's broad nose, sensitive to a thousand herbs, tested the air.

He will think I have used his woman, Colum thought.

The huge man turned, nose lifted, trying to identify the new scent like a dog on a trail.

There must be a scythe on the wall I could use, Colum thought. The pounding pressure of holding his breath pushed at the insides of Colum's eyeballs.

The druid departed, sniffing.

■

The weather turned wet again, troubling Gemman's rheumatic joints. He pressed for a longer stay, and Almergin, mindful of his social obligations, agreed.

In return for lodging, Gemman offered his pupil's services in sheep shearing. But the druid, distrustful of such modern methods, gave him a bronze comb instead with a basket and some orders: "They are already shedding. Gather what you can from the bushes, and give it to Maire. Do it before the rain starts again."

By a prior arrangement with one of his tenants, Almergin walked his animals to another farm. The sheep would graze while they fertilized the ground.

In late afternoon, with a basketful of brown hair-clumps, Colum searched for the slave girl.

She sat under the overhang of the barn. Her left arm was outstretched with a heap of raw fleece hung over it. She pulled small tufts and twisted bits of the loose wool into a long string that wrapped on a wood spindle held in her right hand. With an ancient technique and a deft hand, she fed the yarn through her hard fingers, rubbing with an experienced rhythm. When she saw Colum, she kept on twirling, eyes on the spindle.

Colum approached cautiously, the way a deer nears a snare, smelling food and danger at the same time.

"I am Colum," he said, deciding to stand tall and royal.

"Is it washed?"

"Of Clan Conaill of the Hy Neills."

"If so, then begin to card it."

"Where are you from?"

"The nail-board is over there." She pointed with her chin. She hadn't looked up once. Her eyes were not coy, but frightened. Yet she spun calmly, her wide mouth in a determined pout.

Colum glanced to her feet. The chain was on. She could not run fast or far without being identified.

He sat in the dirt and used the bronze comb to pick out burrs and branches from the raw wool. Working by touch, he looked at her, hoping she would look back. "Why are you afraid of me?" he asked, plucking out a long weed.

His cry caught her attention. He dropped the green stem covered with stinging hairs. Pink welts inflamed his writing hand.

The girl dropped her work and dragged to Colum. She took the hem of her long skirt, wrapped her own hands in the cloth for protection, and grabbed the plant. She snapped the stem open. A pearly juice oozed from the break. Colum pulled away when she put the dripping plant stem near his throbbing hand.

"Hold still," she ordered. She took his hand in hers to steady it and wiped the juice on his palm and fingers. The sting left. The swelling subsided. But Colum felt a new stirring in himself with her touch.

"Nettle juice is also for ulcers," she said, letting him go. She slid back to her seat and resumed her spinning.

Colum turned his hand over, inspecting it, flexing the fingers, examining the spots where she touched. Seeing no stains, he looked into her sapphire eyes.

She averted them quickly, intent on the yarn.

"Thank you," Colum finally said.

She shrugged. "Is it better — Colum?"

"You were listening after all."

She shook her dark hair.

"And your name?" he tried again.

"Maire," she said. "Of Mann." She picked another batch of wool for her arm. "Why are you afraid of me?" she asked.

Colum felt his face coloring. "I do not wish to provoke your master."

She looked at him, surprised, then deeply relieved. "You are not here to use me?"

"No. No, of course not," he sputtered, dropping his eyes to her feet as Finbar had taught him to do. But even the soft slope of her callused soles was too much, and he fixed on a nearby stone. "Why should I?" he said.

"The others do."

She is an amenity for wayfarers, he groaned to himself. *A gift for guests.*

"Do I not please you?"

"You are very pleasant."

The girl set down the spindle. "Then why do you not take me as all the others?"

"I am not like the others," he said, chasing away his temptations.

"You're not?"

"I am just a student traveling with my master. We are here only briefly on the way to Tara."

"Take me."

Her words shocked him, but he quickly realized she was not inviting him to enjoy her body.

"Take me with you," she said, her wet eyes pleading. "I have prayed for so long."

The entreaty pierced his heart, and his passions drained. Colum held up a handful of wool. "I also serve the Good Shepherd who gave His life for the sheep. Do you know Him too?"

Maire began to cry. Colum awkwardly took her hand. She kissed his hand, sending a sparkling sensation up his arm. She held onto him tightly as she spun her story.

"My father owned a villa on the shore," she said. "It was left by the Romans."

Colum imagined its beauty—a noble, pillared home with stone porches overlooking the sea where Saxon and Irish raiders roamed. He could guess Maire's next words.

"The pirates came. I still hear their screams in my dreams. We were all surprised. They killed the men and threw nets over us as we ran away."

"And they brought you here?"

"They put me in the hold with the other things they stole, and they came down sometimes to . . . they came to . . . I tried not to." Her voice dissolved into a labored, painful breathing as she remembered the sailors' abuse.

Colum brushed her hair gently.

"They sold me to Almergin," she said, "for swine and herbs."

"Did he have no one else to care for the animals? He is a chief."

"He needed someone to serve the needs of his warlords," she cried, "who come in the spring for the fertility rites." She put her head to his shoulder, seeking protection.

As he listened, Colum's warm-faced embarrassment changed to a smoldering indignation. "You are not his," he said. "You are Christ's. You have been bought with His blood and sealed by His Spirit."

He searched his mind for a way to free her. But the cost in pigs or cattle for this chattel was forbidding. A runaway could not be protected under the strict Brehon code. Sanctuary, perhaps, at Finnian's great school at Clonard, not far away, offered a possibility. Even so, Gemman may be endangered by a revengeful druid chief.

He suddenly realized he was stroking her long hair as she dried her eyes on his shoulder. They breathed as one, her soft breasts pressed against him.

In the distance, Almergin's collie barked.

Colum stood quickly. "We are truly free only in the Lord," he stammered, brushing his coat as if to remove evidence of the embrace. "We must trust Him. He will find a way to make you free."

He bolted to the lodge, swallowing his tears for her plight, cursing his helplessness and chiding his desires.

■

The next day following morning devotions, Colum made his way back across the barley field to Almergin's lodge. His basket brimmed with bright yellow buttercups. He hadn't noticed them the day before and wondered if they had appeared overnight. He thought they would brighten Maire and that she might use them for a dye. There were far fewer tufts of hair today, but yesterday's combing and gathering had supplied her well.

Her face opened like a flower when he approached, her dark blue eyes smiling and her rough hand quickening its twists of the spindle.

As he watched the bounce of her hair when she leaned into her rhythm, he felt that lightness he remembered from hunting in the high mountains where the thinner air deepened his breaths and the view stole his voice. He broke off his gaze and rebuked himself.

"Can you use these?" he said, setting down the basket as if placing a gift before a queen.

"They're beautiful," she said, "like your singing."

"You heard that?"

"Who couldn't?"

Colum worried that Almergin had heard it as well.

"I didn't hear your words," she said.

"I prayed for you."

"What did you pray?"

Colum paused to see if anyone else might be near. "I prayed one of David's psalms," he said. "'The Lord upholds all who are falling and raises up all who are bowed down.'"

Maire bowed as though repeating the words to herself.

"'The eyes of all are lifted to You in hope,'" Colum continued, "'and You give them their food when it is due. With an open and bountiful hand You give what You will to every living creature.' There is more."

"Will you sing the rest for me?"

He glanced about again for signs of Almergin. "I ought not."

"You are a student of a bard," she laughed, "and you refuse a request for a song?"

He fixed on her fingers, rubbing the sheep hair into long, rough strands. *Finbar knew how easily hands like these could spin a web for the unwary,* Colum thought. He could feel himself becoming captivated again with the captive girl, and to chastise his motives he found his tongue and began to recite an

103

earnest intercession, continuing the psalm he began. "'The Lord is near to all who call upon Him,'" he sang, the Gaelic coming slowly. The Latin was now more familiar. "'He fulfills the desire of all who fear Him. He also hears their cry and saves them.'" Though he watched the gray clouds, he felt Maire's yearning eyes on him. He sublimated his conflict with a louder line, "'The Lord preserves all who love Him, but the wicked He will destroy.'"

From behind the lodge came Almergin's heavy tread and distinctive hack, like a dog trying to dislodge a clump in its throat. His left fist gripped a bronze sickle. He crouched as though ready for a charge.

"Get back to your work," he said to the frightened girl. "And you will practice your songs elsewhere."

"I was helping to pass the time."

"She needs no such help," the big man scowled. "Move along, and speak to her no more."

"I speak to whomever I please," said Colum.

"She is forbidden to speak to others," said Almergin. "If you wish to help her, you will be silent. Now go find your master."

"There is no need," called Gemman, joining them from where the druid emerged. "Colum, come this way at once."

"Master Gemman, he treats her—"

"At once." The bard's serious face drew Colum away. With a reluctant step he left the girl's side, furious with Gemman for standing with the wizard.

Scared into silence, Maire resumed her spinning, her fingers trembling and her eyes downcast.

Almergin studied Colum as he passed, as though trying to probe his thoughts. His hairy nostrils twitched, catching Colum's scent.

Colum walked by him slowly, ignoring the prickling of his arm hairs, which were lifting up as when lightning strikes nearby.

■

After the evening meal, Colum wandered past the buttercup field to the hawthorn thickets. With lyre in hand, he plucked at his heartstrings, singing softly in Gaelic:

From the shore of her birth
*   To the land of red earth*
She came
*   Over the whispering sea*
And the storms of a cruel slavery
*   To find the harbor of my embrace.*

To say I have loved, I
*   Could not well deny*
The same,
*   But beg the Father to bless*
This, our tenderness,
*   Which joined by tears will make her free of this*
*   place.*

The meter was not yet right. As he mouthed a revision, he smelled the tangy oak bark ointment which Gemman rubbed into his old joints.

"Master Gemman?" he called, looking around.

The bard sat on a nearby boulder, his cane across his knees. "What was that you were singing?" he asked. "I have not heard it before."

"It is nothing."

"It is unusual. If only because it rhymes."

Colum picked at the strings absently.

"Will you play it again for me?" said Gemman. It was less a request and more a command.

"I should not," said Colum. "It's not ready. It is rough, incomplete, and—"

"It is dangerous, and you know it," said Gemman. "You are putting her life in danger. And perhaps yours."

"She is already in danger every day. Why don't you care?"

"I must care for you. You are getting too close to her."

"How can you sit by idly?"

"The wizards tried to poison Patrick many times for trying to free their slaves and for lesser things," warned the bard. "Don't think for a moment that Almergin will not try because his slave has broken silence to speak with you."

"Why are you protecting him?"

"I am protecting you," said the old man, shaking.

"I wish to protect the girl."

"You cannot. She belongs to him."

"What happened to your faith?" cried Colum. "The swine belong to him. She belongs to God."

"In Almergin's eyes, they are no different."

"And in yours?"

Gemman sucked on his lips, his fragile hands curled tight on the cane. "There is nothing we can do." He held up a finger to hush Colum's protest. "We leave tomorrow. Prepare the bags. Stay away from the girl."

In the lodge, Colum pressed down his temper and packed the lyre carefully, cushioning it between sweet-smelling sacks of Almergin's herbs.

■

Though the low, black clouds scowled and sent warning spits of rain, Colum secured the saddles on the horses. Angel Wing, restless with the ill-boding wind, whinnied and kicked. Just as he settled the horse, he heard the crying from the lodge.

Maire burst from the lodge door with short, skipping steps, the chattel-chain rattling. She scuffed to him with her hands on her face. She fell to his feet, gripping his ankles and moaning in the folds of his robes. "Colum," she cried, "please don't leave me."

He clasped his hands on her shivering shoulders and raised her up. He grasped for words, but they would not come. "I will speak for you at Tara," he promised, "and I will pray."

She lifted her face and pushed away the tangled black bangs. Her left eye, swollen shut, was as dark as her hair. The ugly purple bruise stained her whole upper cheekbone.

Colum wrapped her in his robes. "Oh, my God."

"I refused him. I told him what you told me. He has me for now, but I belong to God."

Colum caressed her hair to comfort her while he clenched his teeth at the sound of Almergin calling her name from inside.

She clutched at his clothes. "Please take me."

He stroked her cheek gently with his thumb, but Maire flinched and turned to the lodge door.

The bull-like body of Almergin stamped outside. His deep-set eyes glowered. His wide hands were set on his belt near the bronze sickle. "You will release the girl at once," he snorted, advancing towards them.

"*You* will release the girl at once," commanded Colum.

"She is not your business." Almergin reached out to seize her. Colum backed away, tightening his hold on her.

Gemman emerged from the lodge, waving his cane. "Colum! Let her go! We must leave!"

Thunder cleaved the distant clouds.

"Do as your master says," said the druid.

Colum hugged the girl closer. "My master is the Lord of heaven and earth, and in His name I command you to release her."

Almergin pulled the curved blade from his belt and slashed at Colum's face. His other hand snapped out, squeezed Maire's arm white and yanked her from Colum's robes.

Maire's open eye, wide with fright, blinked away the drizzle. She heaved in deep breaths, her mouth gaping in pain from Almergin's hold.

"As you wish," said Almergin, "I release her." He pulled his sickle in a swift stroke across her throat. Maire slumped with a silent scream, her fingers scratching in the wet dirt.

Ablaze with fury, Colum's muscles burned, and his veins bulged a brilliant hue. As he raised his fists, the wind formed a funnel around him, whipping up dust and ripping up grass. He opened his contorted mouth and drew a deep breath.

Gemman spun away and blocked his ears. "No, Colum!" he cried.

"As the soul of the woman went to heaven," Colum bellowed, "so shall the murderer's go to hell!"

Almergin's eyes, swelled with horror, rolled back into his head. Crimson flowed from his nose and filled his ears. With a gargling noise he stumbled backwards, thumped to the grass, jerked, and lay still.

Colum fell upon Maire and wrapped his cloak over her. He prayed in choking cries. He pressed upon her neck and felt her warm life flow through his quivering fingers. He gaped skywards and lifted a loud lament like the howl of a wounded wolf.

■

"We must get you to Clonard," huffed Gemman, "before his allies know of it." He wiped his hands of the wet grave dirt.

He hung the ox-bone shovel in its place. "You will be safe there. It is no matter that your mother is of the royal house of Leinster."

"And you?" replied Colum, his chest hot and sore from sobbing.

"After I escort you to the school, I will go to your family."

"To tell them what has happened?"

"No. I will tell them you were ready for Finnian's school. I will also tell Finbar of Moville."

"And then you will return?"

"No. I will die in Ulster."

Colum looked at him through his grieving tears in astonishment. "Don't say that, Master Gemman. My family will care for you."

"That they will. But it will be too late."

The old bard bowed his head in shame, not sorrow, and turned to leave the barn. Colum dried his own cheek with his sleeve and ran to circle and face the teacher. He grabbed the bard's feeble shoulders and begged with his eyes for an explanation.

"The herbs," whispered Gemman, stooping even lower. "Only Almergin holds the secret of the herbs which hold off the pain."

Colum thought of the bags which cushioned the lyre.

"When that is gone," Gemman said, looking to the horsepacks, "I will also be gone."

"Someone else—"

"There is no one else who knows the blend for my disease. I am his patient. I am his bard." He stepped forward into Colum's embrace, weeping. "I am his foster brother."

6
CLONARD
A.D. 542

 UNDREDS OF HUTS RADIATED
IN PERFECT STRAIGHT SPOKES
from the central church at Clonard. Built in concentric circles,
like ripples in a pond, the timber and turf buildings spread over
the plain beside the River Boyne. A tall, grassy rampart hemmed
the huge settlement, and the wide moat looked like a giant glass
necklace. The terraced fields were specked with men working the
ground without tools.

Finnian's famous school, built twenty-five years before,
today claimed three thousand students. Hundreds of them now
filled the green river bank around Finnian's feet. Men and boys
sat on stones to hear their teacher with a whisper of waterflow
behind them.

Colum and Gemman stopped the horses out of respect as
the abbot prepared to lecture. Colum could hardly believe this
vision of organization could come from the frail figure who
stood on the rocky hill next to the river. Thin and bent as a cornstalk in a drought, the abbot moved his hands in the air as
though trying to grasp a passing thought. When he lectured, it
seemed he had generously allowed others to be present at his
own contemplation. He reflected, paused, and looked about,
waiting for the word to come which would most aptly name
what he sought to understand.

Unable to hear his wisdom from a distance, Colum and Gemman walked their horses over a bridge into the vast monastery to await a personal audience with the teacher.

■

Finnian received the young deacon with the gracious deference due to a prince who could bring his family's wealth and reputation to the school. To host an heir of the Northern Hy Neill in the land of the Southern Hy Neill might be dangerous, but with Colum's own cousin on the throne at Tara, his arrival could only promise influence in both branches of Erin's most tempestuous clan. Who would object, since his mother was of Leinster? And his introduction by a renowned bard of WestMeath impressed Finnian even further.

Colum could not tell if the warm glow in Finnian's wise eyes bespoke his sanctity or his satisfaction at receiving such a prize into his circle. Their words, simple and few, exemplified Finnian's rule — austere, sparse, practical. In a few moments, Colum stood outside in the hot sun, stunned by two strong impressions.

First, he noted Finnian's meagerness. As the abbot had welcomed him to his monastic family, Colum counted the abbot's ribs through the coarse linen. The rope girdled his shriveled waist loosely, as on a tether-post. Shadowed behind the worn spots lay the leeches, feeding on Finnian's sores caused by the constant chafe of the cold iron belt clamped to his hips. Yet he walked without a wince. He spoke without a stutter of discomfort, so well had his disciplined mind transformed the torment to an enviable tranquility. With a transcendent calm and kindness, Finnian invited his new charge to build his bothy by the main church door.

This provoked the second impression. With Gemman standing behind him at a respectful distance, Colum stepped atop a wind-worn stone to claim it. "This is my pillow," he announced, shading his eyes to measure the distance from the church entry.

Gemman noted the remote position with a curious shrug, looking reluctant to correct his pupil. "Do not insult your new teacher," he said softly, pressing his palms towards the ground in a hushing motion. He looked around to see if Finnian were nearby. "It is too far from the door."

"But, Master Gemman," protested Colum, "this is where the church door will be."

"Young prince," said the bard, shaking his head, "up to now everything has come to you easily. But do not expect the church itself to come gliding over the ground to you."

Colum rechecked the distance, shading the glare again to be sure. The faint frame still filled the slope, winking in the sun like long spiderweb threads. The lines followed the shallow, grassy gully where the foundation stones would be laid.

Now certain of it, he strode towards Clonard's oaken gates. Gemman called out, "Now you are further away."

"I'll use the willow-wands we saw by the gate," Colum said. "And I will build around the stone."

■

Stretched out on the stone with the windowless wattle hut covering him, Colum reviewed his tearless parting with Gemman. He had lifted the old bard up to the saddle, his long fingers cupped like a stirrup. When Gemman settled, and he reached down to receive a blessing, Colum folded his hands behind his back. The sweep of Gemman's arm passed the odor of crushed plantain and dill to his upturned nose, and the bard's breath reeked of some unknown poison Almergin had brewed.

Gemman drew back his shaking hand and waved it instead in a regretful farewell. Like a warrior off to a battle he knows he cannot win, yet proud to be called upon for the task, Gemman gripped the reins. "Let the library be your teacher," he said. "It is the finest in Erin."

"Godspeed," said Colum, patting the horse.

"I won't see you again."

"Greet my father and mother."

The old man seemed to search Colum's November-gray eyes for a sign of forgiveness. His expression pleaded for a word that would lighten his burden. But the herbs dammed up Colum's throat, and he firmed his lips.

Colum hoped for a quick parting and an immediate retreat into the order of prayer, labor, and reading to conquer his anger. Secluded in the cell, he had only succeeded in turning the anger against himself for his lack of forgiveness.

He would seek a purging penance from Finnian. Until

assigned a soul-friend, or confessor, he would answer to the abbot. A self-imposed discipline could train him to transcend his self-pity. The purest gold must pass through fire. The slag of sin is siphoned off by self-denial. The sculptor chips away what is not needed to leave a purer form. He could hear the hammer striking against his hard heart.

The striking became insistent. Lifting his forehead from the stone, he followed the outline of a man in the doorless entry. The man tapped the ground with a metal-tipped walking stick.

"Brother Colum?" called the man. The raspy, wet voice awoke him from prayer. The dark figure bent into the bothy and set a cup on the dirt floor. "Water," said the visitor with a nasal sound, as though hoarse with a cold. "It has been almost two days."

Colum's stomach knotted with hunger. He touched his lips, dry and flaked as an old honeycomb. He dared not stand and risk a faint. The ceiling was too low for it anyway. "Bless you," he murmured, his throat tight. He lifted the cup, hands trembling, and moistened his mouth.

The visitor looked too broad to be Finnian. Because of the strong backlight, the stranger looked featureless.

"Are you my soul-friend?" asked Colum.

The man slurped as he inhaled to answer. "No. Just a friend."

The man backed out the doorway, calling to a companion just outside. "Cainnech! The bread."

The light caught his face. The V-shaped mouth, lipless and drooling, split a flat face without eyes or nose. Fleshy dents marked the spots where nature had erred, smooth as calfskin up to the shaven hairline.

Colum dropped the cup with a clatter on the stone pillow. "God help me," he groaned, crossing his forehead. The damp stone assured him that this was no apparition.

The open mouth sucked at the air and spit words. "Don't be afraid. I am Mobhi."

"God bless you," said Colum, pressing his wet fingers to his mouth again. He tasted blood from the cracked lips.

"You must eat soon."

"Two days?"

"Yes. Finnian sent me."

"The offices. I've missed them. Father, forgive me."

"Calm yourself. Eat now." Mobhi moved forward into the wood-woven cell, holding out a bit of barleybread. He held it steady, waiting for Colum to take it. Colum reached for the food, his arms stiff and slow. He nibbled at it, and Mobhi's ribbon lips curved to a smile at the sound.

"Good," said Mobhi. "Get your strength back. Some starve themselves for penance, but Finnian won't allow but a priest to try it."

"I'm sorry," said Colum, washing down the bread with the drops still left in the cup. "I was unaware. Of the time, I mean."

"In prayer, one enters eternity," said Mobhi. "No time exists there."

"But in prayer, I have offended you all."

"There is no wrong in seeking God," said the eyeless man, "but you still need a guide." He slurped in a breath. "Come. Get up. Have more water."

With a firm hand, Mobhi propped Colum in the doorway. On Mobhi's hand signal, a young assistant ran up with a full water cup.

Sandy-haired, with a sallow complexion, the young helper watched Colum with respect. He looked to be Colum's age, but deeper-lined in the face. He guided the cup into Colum's weak hands, kneeling on one knee as though offering Roman wine to a noble.

"Sip it," Mobhi said to Colum when he heard the gulps. "When you are able, you will see your soul-friend."

"Not Father Finnian?"

"No. He is a confessor to kings."

Colum wondered why, then, he should not meet with Finnian rather than be assigned a subordinate. Though Colum wore the tonsure of a deacon, he still could lay a legitimate claim to the brooch of Tara. The great-great-grandson of Niall of the Nine Hostages and the grandson of Fergus, baptized by Patrick, deserved better.

Mobhi held up his thick palm, sensing Colum's complaint. "Father gives you Molaisse of Devenish. Eighty-fifth in descent from Adam, son of the living God. Fifth in line from the royal house of Cashel. Your fellow cousin to King Ainmere of Tara."

Colum brightened at this wise alternative of a mentor of such import. "Where will I find him?"

"Who can tell?" laughed Mobhi, his mouth gaping in a grin. "Can a blind man show you the way?"

"Where is his hut?"

"Molaisse has no hut," said Mobhi, his hand rubbing the soft crater above his mouth. "He wanders. Some say in the body and out. Of course, I have never seen it. Thus God protects me from coveting it."

"Blessed be God," gasped Colum. "As the Spirit took Philip from Gaza to Samaria."

"So they say."

"How shall I find him?"

"If what I hear of you is true," said Mobhi, "you will find him."

Colum guessed his placement of his hut excited such rumors. Had he been presumptuous? Was it truly the church frame, or merely strands of grass spiders? If it would come to pass, the sanctuary would fill with chants like the one that now reached his ear.

Was it just another impression? A triumphant march, broken by blasts from a battle-horn, hung in the air. Colum saw Mobhi cock his head to the sound. Colum suddenly scuffed to his feet. The blood drained from his head, spangling his sight with swirling spots. "They're coming," he blurted in alarm, imagining the armed tribesmen of Almergin seeking the slayer of their chief. They would guiltlessly violate sanctuary, and the helpless monks, without even hoes for weapons, would fall to the vengeful swords as barley to a scythe.

"Easy," said Mobhi. His strong hand snatched Colum's robe and pulled him down. "They are pilgrim brothers. Or a king seeking penance. Or a noble bringing a son for fostering." Mobhi bent his harp-shaped ear in the direction of the procession. "Who is it, Cainnech?"

The student lifted himself up on spindly legs and turned his head side to side like a robin looking for worms. "Sure and it's a chieftain, Master," he said on tiptoe. "Bronze harnesses. Red blankets on the horses. Fat saddlebags. No cattle."

"The harnesses rattle too much," said Mobhi. "He is walking."

114

"It's the armor on the men, Master. They are all on foot, the chief and his men."

"They're searching for me," said Colum, trying to stand again, struggling against Mobhi's tight grip. "Warn the brothers—"

"But the chief is barefoot," observed Cainnech. "He is on a pilgrimage of penance."

"Who is it?" asked Mobhi.

"I cannot tell," answered Cainnech, scanning the procession. "Two priests in white robes lead them. One has a cross, one has a banner. I do not know the design."

"Perhaps you know, Brother Colum," smacked Mobhi. "You would know the colors of the clans."

"He cannot answer," said Cainnech, running past him to the hut's entryway. "He has fainted."

The salted salmon, flat wheaten bread, and stiff mead, left over from the Lord's Day feasting, revived him. Cainnech fed him in a dark corner of the refectory. The other brothers ate silently at the long tables, scratching at the tabletop to request items, waving their scrubbed hands in a host of other signals. Their glances suggested to Colum that they knew of his fast and his favoritism with Finnian.

The looks aggravated his double guilt in knowing he had not worked to provide any of the food, and knowing that many a monk had been left to starve himself into God's presence.

When Cainnech removed his plates, another student with curly, charcoal-colored hair presented Colum with a wet cloth. He bowed, ready with a towel on the other dark-haired arm. Colum took these, crossing the air in thanks with his first three fingers joined.

After prayers and a reading, when he could stand without a wobble, Colum accepted Cainnech's invitation to tour the settlement.

The dark-haired student followed them outside and looked up to Colum. "I am Brendan of Birr," he said. He folded his sturdy fingers in a formal greeting, the tips black with ink.

"Named for the Navigator?" Colum smiled.

The boy brightened at the mention of the famous seafaring monk. "If only I might share his passion for God as well as share his name," said Brendan, the dark eyes lifted. "I can handle a sail, but not for crossing the Western Sea in search of Tir na 'n Og."

"The mouth of hell itself is that way, too," Cainnech said with a trace of apprehension. "The steam in Lough Derg is but a small token of the sulphur-smoke, black as bats, what comes from the pits of Ultima Thule."

They looked towards the West in awe, thinking of the many brothers from Clonard who had ventured out in creaky curraghs to the island the Romans considered the edge of the earth. In that most extreme of places, which even the dauntless Norsemen called Ice-land, one could seek purity and save many souls at the edge of oblivion. "The very sea smokes," reported the monks who returned for recruits, "and the devil sends many storms to discourage us. He hurls mountains from the ocean floor, and they spit fire. But knowing how he hates us there, we stay."

Colum edged between them, clasped their shoulders, and laughed. "Now, brothers, we aren't looking for the way to hell, are we? Quite the other way." He released their shoulders and walked ahead. "For now, just show me the way around Clonard."

They walked the avenues, Colum in the lead, the others huffing to keep up. They passed row upon orderly row of huts. With a cursory look at the stables, kiln, and carpentry shop, Colum headed straight for the Scriptorium and library, confident of access because of Brendan's stained hands.

Inside the hall, rows of rushlights glowed upon the satchels hung on the walls. Brendan elbowed his way ahead, proudly pointing out the precious items as though they were his own. Colum kept note of their positions so he could pore over them later — the *Aeneid*, Aristotle's works, Augustine, even some Plato. Poetry by Severus. Histories by Livy. All the works that Finbar of Moville dreamed of owning. The Psalters and Gospels dominated the collection, some very brown and brittle, sheathed in thick, ornately tooled leather. Many slept in the stone cellar, arranged neatly in stacks reaching up to the main room's floor-planks through which they could hear the coded foot-taps of monks forbidden to speak.

When they finally emerged blinking into the sunlight,

Cainnech noted that the sacristy of the main church contained much more. Gold-covered texts, silver-edged pages, battle-worn books from everywhere on the continent lay in store beside the treasures of La Tene culture — the gold shields, the jewel-encrusted croziers, the finely enameled reliquaries. "You've already noticed the silks of the vestments. And there are many crowns," he said, wide-eyed.

Colum wiped his brow, feeling the bare skin and thinking how a crown would feel. He remembered the silks he had worn as a boy and the bright colors of his father's embroidered cloaks. He lengthened his strides toward the sacristy, the coarse linen scratching at his knees.

Entering the main church, Colum noticed the delicate carvings on the pillars and beams. Interlaced branches, with ribbed leaves and tiny apple-blossom shapes, curled up to the sloped ceiling. Wooden birds perched in the rafters, their hooked beaks open for a kill. Cainnech explained how the designs commemorated the founding of the school. The original apple grove ceded to Finnian after the reluctant landowner was killed in a cattle raid, as Finnian had predicted. When the local warlord came to claim the land, Finnian summoned the falcons to drive him away.

"Will you also show me where Molaisse meets with his children?" Colum asked, perplexed that he should still meet for offices in Finnian's church. Each spiritual director oversaw a separate chapel, as the Brehon code limited the size of church buildings. Though he knew he should find Molaisse's meeting place, he thought it odd that the abbot invited him to build his hut near the central church, and not near Molaisse's.

"Molaisse has no chapel," said Brendan, a stare of wonder in his eyes.

"And you are his only pupil," added Cainnech, opening the sacristy door.

Colum entered the room where the celebrants vested for offices. A muscular monk, his habit hiked up, the sleeves bunched behind his shiny biceps, stood with an upraised ax. Teeth clenched for a mighty blow, he brought the gleaming edge down. Colum fell back, crouched for defense. The curved blade cracked into an upright log, cleaving it cleanly. The perfect halves thumped on the cloth covering the timber floor. The ruddy monk guffawed as he picked up his plane.

"You surprised me," he said, pointing with the plane.

"And me," said Colum, his muscles tensed.

The carpenter squinted at Cainnech. "Nones is still some time away, isn't it? Or has the time passed as in prayer?"

"It is not yet time, Siaran," said Cainnech, his veiny hands hovering around Colum, wanting to help steady him, yet hesitating as if testing the heat of a kettle over a fire.

"Good," said Siaran. He picked up the split wood and inspected it. "Still time to fix this leaking. Have you been sent to help, Cainnech? Why aren't you with your cows? And you, Brendan, with your quills?"

"They are helping me," said Colum.

"So I see. The prince has found his servants already?"

"Or his soldiers," retorted Colum.

Amused, Siaran sized up Colum with his carpenter's eye, the way he measured beams by sight, eyes pinched and piercing. A chariotmaker's son with a rank to rival any noble, he made no sign of deference to the royal-born newcomer. "So yours is the hut built across the way?"

Colum braced for a criticism from one whose whole life was building. "It is."

"It's close to where I'll be building."

Colum returned a knowing smile.

"I marked out the lines today," said Siaran. "The new church narthex will almost reach your door. You might as well be living in the church itself."

Colum didn't hear the last words. Clapping his hands, he had run outside to look, Cainnech and Brendan falling in behind like goslings. They stopped in the doorway as Colum whooped at the sight of the short stakes joined by thin yarn-strings, which measured out the coming church extension. Colum followed the strings along the ground. They matched the silvery lines he had seen with Gemman. When he reached his hut, his hands cupped in prayer, he knelt in praise to the Giver of second sight, who, living in past, present, and future, could see all things and impart to a few a peek over His shoulder.

He returned to the sacristy, thinking of a way to explain his outburst. He paused by the door, hearing Siaran's terse, tense voice. The carpenter was hotly upbraiding his two guides, and

Colum thought it best to stay away. God save him from over-speaking, he prayed, but stopped when he heard his name.

"And why should you be doing his chores for him?" Siaran growled. "Let the abbot decide."

"He is given to Molaisse," Brendan said, trying to calm him. "He must be given to prayer and study."

"Three labors in the day," said Siaran. "Work, prayer, and reading. Even princes work here."

"His work is to pray."

"We all pray. We all work." Siaran clapped the ax in his callused palm. "I see no reason to treat him differently."

"You work with your gift in wood," reasoned Cainnech, "so he should work with his gift of words."

"Then let angels do his work for him if he can summon them," Siaran snapped. "Serve God, not this prince."

"Ask God to forgive you," said Cainnech, sounding grieved. "You are jealous of his gift."

The clink and thud of the auger, plane, and saw followed as Cainnech dumped them before the hard-breathing carpenter. "These are what you sacrificed for God," Cainnech said, "but Colum has sacrificed the scepter of Erin, his by right."

The shuffling sound was Siaran gathering up his tools. "Very well," he said. "Let each work according to his gifts as the apostle says. I build the church with these. He builds with a staff and quill. You build with a grinding stone."

Colum slipped out, twisting the coarse rope belt in his fingers. He was not sure if he should be thankful, or frightened that the favor would fuel his pride.

■

At Nones, Colum evaded Cainnech and Brendan. Separated by his station at the front of the church, he saw their troubled faces in the rear when he turned to follow the procession of the celebrant. Two cantors and a lector, stepping in matched rhythm, reached the altar and bowed at the same moment to the same level. Colum knelt with the others for the silent Asperi Domine. Standing, he listened to the reader's monotonic rendition of *Iube, domne, benedicare* — focused on the priest's brown and green vestments, the colors of earth and burial.

"*Noctem quietam et finem perfectum,*" sang the celebrant to the perfectly pronounced end, the consonants distinct and strongly dental. The lector delivered the short lesson of the day in a rich but remote voice, concentrating on his impeccable timing. "*Fratres, sobrii estote,*" he intoned without stutter or regional accent. As the celebrant responded, singing "*Adiutorium nostrum in nomine Domini,*" Colum heard the singular swish of the monks' arms crossing themselves in unison. Through the Pater Noster, Confiteor (sung on one note), Misereatur, and Indulgentiam, the men beat their breasts, crossed their shoulders, and worked their words with the precision of a legionnaires' drill. Through the three psalms, antiphons and anthems, the proper prayers and the correct credos, Colum followed flawlessly but emptily. The formal, obedient repetition left him uninspired and unable to replace his nagging guilt with the release he usually found in corporate contrition. At this service of the mid-afternoon, commemorating Christ's final convulsion, he felt none of the forgiveness that the sacrifice of the cross had provided. The remembrance of the signs — the darkness, the opening tombs — only reminded him of the shallow graves near Almergin's barn. He tried to see the cross, that instrument of death whereby he might slay his pride. Stroked by Cainnech's and Brendan's admiration, this pride stubbornly withheld him from forgiving Gemman. But all he could image was the circle of stones around the base of the awful beam, holding it upright, covered with the Savior's spilt blood. *Agnus Dei, who takes away the sins of the world, take my pride.* The circle of stones had a familiar shape and pattern. He thought of where he had seen it before, while he bowed for the closing prayers.

With dismissal, he lost himself in the crowd of cowled brethren, stooping to avoid recognition. From the corner of his eye, he spied Cainnech weaving among the men, searching for him. But he joined the barley-field party, silently walking out beyond the ramparts. Why he broke off at the brook, he didn't know; he just followed it until the voices of the singing monks dimmed even to his keen ear.

A circle of mica-flecked boulders slept below a willow, like cows huddled there for shade. He approached them as though expecting them to come alive and roll towards him. The small brown one in the center stirred. It spoke.

"It took you longer than I expected."

Colum genuflected. "Father Molaisse."

The figure, still seated, kept his back to Colum. "What was the object of your fast?" he asked in a gravelly voice. "Or, perhaps, who was the object?"

"I fasted against no one. I meant to pray without ceasing as the Scripture says."

"If you starve, you will cease to pray. Is that why you've come?"

"I came as others do. To pray. To study." He thought of Siaran's rebukes. "And to work."

"'The work of God is to know Him and Jesus Christ whom He has sent,'" Molaisse quoted. He stood. Dwarfish, he equaled Colum's kneeling height. He kept his face turned away. The sheep's hair robe, bleached white by the sun, hung so loosely it seemed a breeze had filled it briefly to raise it and somehow left it hanging in the air. Colum endured the uncomfortable silent wait. His knee dug into the earth. Molaisse prepared to speak, the sound in his throat like an iron wheel on rock.

"Did you touch her?"

Colum felt his cheeks flare. Had Gemman told him? He kept his eyes to the ground as he knew he should have done in her presence. A teardrop darkened the dirt by his knee. "I did," he said. "For her comfort."

Molaisse drew a staff from his robe and held it to his side. The sturdy, short yew-stick, curled at the top like a crozier, was gripped in a white-skinned hand pitted as a hazelnut shell and looking nearly as hard. Colum lowered his eyes again, ready to submit to the stinging strokes on his back.

Molaisse thumped the stick on the ground with the emphases in his words. "There are three gates to hell," he said, lifting the cane. "The eyes which lust." Thud. "The mouth which lets out the sins of our dirty hearts." Thud. "And the thoughts of our prideful minds." Thud. "These must be put to death. Not those who provoke them."

"He killed the girl," Colum said, his fingertips joined in entreaty. "Like he stuck his own swine, he opened her throat." Colum's fingers closed into tight fists. Surely the blows would come now for speaking out, for defending when he must be confessing.

121

"Did you see the swine?"

The question offended him and puzzled him at the same time. He jerked up his head looking for an explanation, but Molaisse's secret face, still turned askance, could offer no clues.

"I said, did you see them? Were they near? Tell me."

"They were not far."

"Did you hear them?"

"I don't remember."

Molaisse sighed. "Then only God knows where they have gone."

"They were penned up."

Molaisse drew the rod back into his robe. "Not the swine," he said.

"What do you mean?"

Molaisse's cowl lifted slightly, as if he were looking for something in the sky. For a moment, Colum feared that the druid might not be dead but transformed into a pig, as the magicians taught they could. Could Almergin have tricked him, as Lug's father escaped his enemies by changing into a pig and joining a herd?

"Read the account of Legion in the Gospel, and you will know," said Molaisse.

Colum crossed his arms across his chest as though protecting himself. In cursing Almergin, what forces had he released? The disembodied, evicted spirits of the man of the Gerasenes begged to be sent into the swine, he recalled. If demons nested in Almergin, where did they fly when their host was destroyed?

"You have learned more from the warlords than from the Lord of Lords," said the mentor. "Now pray with me."

Chin lifted, eyes shut, Colum recited his Misereatur and Confiteor, trailing off as he heard Molaisse's gritty voice interceding. The old master prayed slowly, distinctly, allowing his young charge to imitate him.

"High Priest of all, Cause above all causes, come to my aid, for the multitude of my inveterate faults have hardened my heart. They have bent me, clung to me, pained me, humbled me, maddened me, slain me. Forgive."

Colum joined the mentor's Latin litany, repeating the words which invoked the Lord of Heaven's champions to make war upon his sins.

Propter nomen tuum Domine, propiciaberis peccato meo,
   Break, smite, and war against my many and vast
   sins,
See, summon, and slay them,
   Scatter, slash, and subdue them,
Divide, defeat, and destroy them,
   Bend, wither, and mangle them
Which make my soul bitter and heavy.

Pleading by the womb and paps of Mary, by everyone who touched Christ, by His unique and complete offering, and by every creature on which the Spirit fell from the beginning of time to the end, the penitent monk purified his conscience. He mentally reviewed his farewell to Gemman, envisioning how he could have made it different.

"For every ill I did, for every good I omitted, forgive," he said, still following Molaisse's lead.

"For every evil I did or was done to me, forgive.

"For every good which I did and spoiled, every evil I did and did not redeem, forgive.

"For every provocation, every displeasure which I gave or harbored against God or man, forgive."

The shadow of Molaisse's triple sign of the cross passed through Colum's quivering wet eyelids, though the voice seemed more distant than before. He opened his eyes only after hearing the clear absolution, *"Ego te absolvo ab omnibus censuris et peccatis in nomine Patris et Filii et Spiritus Sanctus."*

But his confessor was out of sight, without even a pathway through the grass to show which way he'd gone.

■

With the faint thump of Siaran's mallet driving in rafter pegs for beat, and the distant rumble of Cainnech and Brendan's grinding stones for melody, Colum moved his pen across the vellum. The gritty juice flowed evenly from the beveled nib, curling in playful flourishes on the eggshell-smooth surface. The lines, straight as harpstrings, sang in quiet celebration:

I wish, O Ancient Eternal King,
*   For a hidden hut in the wild,*
My dwelling.

An all-gray, lithe lark beside it,
*   A clear, cool pool used by the Spirit*
For washing.

Nearby, a wood round about
*   To shelter and nurse the many-voiced birds*
For singing.

And a few men of sense
*   Twice six in the church, fit for every work,*
For praying.

The poetry replaced his vices with contrary goods — dejection with joy, confusion with order, wrath with patience. It worked better than a physical penance to clear his mind and clean his heart. The writing, too, released and concentrated his energy, his accurate pen granting the same satisfaction as an arrow striking a small target.

"More books." An apprentice librarian stooped inside, careful not to drag the satchels whose straps layered his stooped shoulders. He laid them on the packed floor with reverence. "I have an *Aeneid* for you this time," he glowed, like a chief who has raided a prize herd. "You'll see in the Fourth Eclogue how God even revealed to Virgil that His Christ would come. 'Behold the birth of a Boy who shall at last bring the race of iron to an end and bid the golden race spring up all the world over.'" The serious voice and stern, angular jaw disguised his pleasure in finding a pagan witness.

"You seem to know what is in all of them, Comgall."

"I know nothing."

"You remember so much."

"Even a rock can echo." Comgall draped the bookstraps over the pegs which ringed Colum's cell. "These are the Annals. My only copies. I'm still trying to collect them all. To start my school."

He wrinkled his mouth, chastising himself for speaking

too much. Colum guessed he also winced at the sound of his own accent. For all his time in books, Comgall had not yet conquered the telling glottal clicks of his Pictish tongue.

Still his refined royal companion found much to admire in him. Born in the remote colony of DalRiada on Alba, Comgall fought his stigma as an outsider. Raised without the benefit of bards and disadvantaged from the start by his unpoetic language, the determined young man left the loving home of his elderly parents to seek his heritage. Colum drew strength from the intense, self-critical scholar, intrigued by his seafaring stories and impressed by his austerity. Comgall sought him often, urging him to break silence to share the stories which Drummon and Gemman had laced into his memory. In gratitude for finding such a well-trained insider, Comgall guided Colum through the stacks of scrolls and satchels in the huge stone-lined crypts of the Scriptorium. Working without a candle for fear of fire, Comgall felt for the books Colum requested. He kept the books coming, eager to draw more tales from his tall friend, in order to complete or confirm the Annals of Erin. Few others had shown such an avid interest as Colum. "The others say, 'Give us Gospels,'" he clicked with disdain, "and Heaven be praised for them. They say where Christ came from. But no one knows where we came from."

Some believed the island was the refuge of families denied access to Noah's Ark. And after successive invasions, mysterious wizards of the Tuatha de Danaan, the children of the goddess Dana, settled here. Together, Colum and Comgall recited their names, found in the lists of Tara's kings. The genealogies confirmed Colum's own potential ascendancy. "Perhaps you have relatives in the lists," encouraged Colum. The most ancient kings were Pictish, driven out by the heroes of Dana. Comgall shook his head. Colum recalled Erc's hideous fear of the Pictish savages and wondered aloud who might be their king now.

"Brude," said Comgall, exiting with a shrug. "They're all named Brude."

Colum applied his pen to the Annals. The feathered shaft flew across the skins with enthusiasm until he turned to the tale of Dierdre. He dropped the pen in the inkwell, hearing Gemman's one-note chant telling him the story from his native Ulster. He remembered how he'd lain on his bed in the dark, pumping his brain for the words, practicing to give the words back to Gemman at daybreak for correction.

Once when the great bard of King Conor sang to his lord at home, news arrived that the bard's wife had delivered a baby daughter. King Conor asked his druid, Cathbadh, to augur the child's future. The druid covered his face and shook with dismay. He divined that the daughter would become irresistibly beautiful and that the chieftains and champions of Ulster would fight for her glance, causing rivers of blood to flow in the land.

A cry arose from the knights for the child's death. But Conor decreed that the child be raised in seclusion deep in the woods to become his own wife in due time, in order to prevent all jealousies. So the girl Dierdre grew in the care of a nurse, content with her destiny and knowing no man. As predicted, she became beautiful beyond words, rapturous and innocent as the wedding to Conor approached.

But one day, a servant butchered a calf outside the window where Dierdre was watching the falling snow, and as the blood reddened the silvery ground, a raven flew down to peck. Dierdre told her nurse that this vision meant she would marry a man with dark hair, blood-red cheeks and silver-white skin. The nurse, sad to see the young beauty betrothed to an old king, arranged for her to meet a man matching the description. Naisi, a young warrior of Conor's court, fell ravenously in love with her upon seeing her. He summoned his brothers with a call louder than a battlehorn. The youngsters exiled themselves to Alba where they established a powerful chieftaincy from a remote, rocky island.

The tale continued, Colum knew, with vicious battles, Naisi's capture, and Dierdre's sorrowful suicide. He pictured her like Maire, eyes blue as gems, eyebrows blue-black and shiny as a beetle's shell, lips red as berries of the rowan, cheeks pink as a blushing foxglove.

His fist flew up in rage with himself. The inkwell spun against the wall, spattering carbon-juice in a pattern like a bloodstain on a sword-stuck tunic. He crossed himself furiously, the Latin penance a jumble so that all that came out was the Gaelic lament of Naisi, "Ruined by a subtle stroke, my head is bowed, my heart is broke."

Comgall pressed inside. He moved the book away from the overturned inkwell. He hugged the book to his chest and backed out the door, his eyes curious and narrow, his fingers reading the design of the book to determine what had provoked his friend's outcry.

Colum picked up his pen. He regained control, sighed, and said to Comgall's consternation, "Give me Gospels."

■

After so long a time in the Annals, Aristotle, the *Aeneid*, and Augustine's catechisms, he felt soothed by the familiar rhythms of the Gospel. With a newly cut set of white goose quills, small-barreled and comfortably curved for a fine line, he set to work in Mark. Comgall stood nearby, critical, but interrupting only to help him prepare for the offices. After each service, Colum bustled back to the rushlit Scriptorium, bending closer to the skins as the shadows deepened and the other copyists began to drift away, one by one, yawning. When the last book clapped shut and the scribe shuffled off, Colum glanced up. Comgall remained, hunched at prayer or in a slumbering stupor. Colum could not tell. Though his hand cramped, he pushed on, eager to learn anew from the Legion passage, yet unable to jump ahead to it out of sequence. "The measure you give is the measure you get, and still more will be given you," he copied, claiming it as the book's promise to him.

When he reached the calming of the storm on the sea, he shifted his feet on the floorboards, feeling them tilt with the waves. A salty breeze bent his lamp flame, which seemed to grasp at the wick for its life as the fishermen must have grappled for the ropes. He wiped his brow of sweat, cool like spray from a curragh cleaving the foam. The flickering light cast ghostly shadows on the timber walls so they resembled the cliffs of the Gerasenes, pockmarked with the caves of the dead. The open tombs, filled with chattering skulls, gaped at him and moaned as the wind hit their hollows. Go away, they sighed. There is power here, they whispered. We own this place. We own these people.

His pen bore into the page, nearly piercing it. He wiggled his sandal, feeling the cuts of the beach's sharp pebbles. He heard the demons scream, slobber, hiss, struggle, and finally submit, begging to be allowed into the swine. Given leave, the unclean spirits vomited from the man and hungrily infested the pigs. He heard the rumbling hooves, panic impelling them to the cliffs, stampeding, plummeting into the stony surf, squealing in terror. Though the Lord had rebuked the storm and the spirits to stillness, Colum felt no peace. A chill rippled up his spine, deeper than the chill of his wet clothes, at the vision of crossing an angry sea to confront evils on the other side.

The lamp winked out, as though splashed. Colum drew in a deep breath, his lips still reciting the words. By the time of the Matins bell at the lightening of the eastern sky and Comgall's sleepy tapping on his shoulder, he still did not know why Molaisse had directed him to the passage or why he had felt himself in the boat on the sea.

"Comgall, do you smell the salt in the air?" he asked on the way to the church.

"Not in the air so much," he replied. "Just your sweat. Wash yourself well. Father Finnian will not have it in his church."

As he dipped his hands in the pool, the awakening birds began to peep. He thought he heard a sea gull screech among them.

■

Finnian's face was so pale, the brothers wondered if the leeches had sucked him white. Ever smiling, though weak with age and self-mortifying abuses, he drew to himself his most promising students. Chosen for hardiness, scholarship, simplicity, and the ability to carry on his vision, the inner band consisted of Cainnech, Comgall, Siaran, Brendan, and Columcille. After offices, they silently joined the wizened teacher for special instruction. Finnian's tired eyes, fog-white and filmy, looked to the clouds between whispered sentences as though expecting a summons at any moment or a word that would change his plans for his students.

Cainnech was to join Mobhi at Glasnevin, a new school on the eastern seacoast. Mobhi, as an abbot of his own jurisdiction, should ordain his faithful assistant as a priest.

Brendan, following ordination at Clonard, would move to the new settlement of Clonmacnoise to the west. The founder, another Clonard graduate named Kiernaan, had requested of his mentor Finnian an able librarian.

Comgall refused ordination, declaring his intent to retreat to the storm-whipped rocks offshore to more properly prepare himself. Seven monks would join him. Finnian grinned broadly, remembering how he and six others followed the beloved St. Enda to the barren rocks of Aran to purge their worldliness. Some left their bones there.

Colum bowed in quiet tribute to the hermits who would probably succumb to cold and hunger on the bare rocks where not even moss dared to grow.

"And Colum will go to Clonfad," said Finnian, "to be ordained a bishop."

The words fell like a hammer on hot iron; sparks of disappointment pricked Colum's neck. It meant he would serve the countryside under the abbot's authority, away from the solitude and study he loved. It precluded a return to his own clan, serving instead the chieftains of his father's rivals. He had thought of beginning a school near his home, just as Brendan, Siaran, and Cainnech planned to do in their home districts. Cainnech had encouraged him, suggesting Derry near his own place of birth at Dun Geimin. "After all," he said, "your clan owns the land and would sure and spare a bit for a priest with the royal blood of the Northern Hy Neill."

"And with Moville near, we have a source for books," Colum added. He knew exactly which ones to ask for.

But he would not be a priest, free to roam as a filid. He felt choked, humiliated, demoted, and he did not acknowledge the cautious congratulatory smiles of his peers.

Finnian said, "See Molaisse before you go to Clonfad for his blessing." The abbot's curled hand on his shoulder felt like a falcon's grip on a hare.

■

Molaisse had retreated further from Clonard, and, according to the rumor, Colum found him in a cave on a lake island guarded by thickets of thorns. His arms aching from paddling his coracle through the muddy water, scratched as if he'd fought with angry wet cats, he pleaded with his mentor for a reversal of Finnian's decree.

"I cannot change it," croaked Molaisse from the dark. "You must let it change you."

"How so?"

"What would feed the pride of others, robs it from you. Be thankful, and go."

When Colum returned to the mainland shore, Cainnech daubed the bloody scratches with torn strips from his own robe. As Clonfad lay on the road to Glasnevin, Colum and Cainnech walked together. Comgall, seeking a ship and seven kinsmen in Glasnevin, came along. Siaran also sought sea passage to his home.

Colum led the procession toward the sea. With his rusty hair streaming in the wind like a battle-banner and his silver ax bouncing on his shoulder, Colum took to the road with wide strides. He chanted his creed to provide a cadence to their walk, composing a hymn to defiantly declare his station as nearer a bard than a bishop. It was a massive poem, organized according to the letters of the alphabet, beginning with creation and extending to the consummation of history. Without harp or horn, he hurled the words forward for hours:

> *Christo de coelis Domine descendente celsissimo,*
> > *When Christ, the highest Lord, descends from the heavens,*
> *His cross and battle-standard will shine bright,*
> > *And with the two principal lights hidden,*
> *The stars will fall like ripe fruit,*
> > *Burning the earth, a furnace's fire,*
> *Tunc in montium speculus abscondent se exercitus.*
> > *Then the armies will hide in the mountain caves.*

A cloud's shadow passed, and beating his breast, Cainnech checked the sun's position to be sure it was still there.

7

GLASNEVIN

A.D. 545

ISHOP ETCHEN OF CLONFAD
SPAT ON HIS DIRT-CAKED
hands. He gripped the plow arms, shoved forward, and barked
to his tired brown horse. His small eyes, green and glazed like
August acorns, scanned the land he had yet to break.

There was really no hurry. He had no churches or ceme-
teries to consecrate today. No babies to baptize. No annoying
bard and his rowdy party to attend, arriving unannounced and
hungry as they always did. Only the routine rite of ordaining
another deacon from Clonard.

Let him come if he wants the laying on of hands, he thought
as he pulled the reed whip from his belt. *We'll get it over with, and
he can put his hand to a hoe. If he knows how to use one.*

The whip whined. The strike only provoked the horse to
stiffen its legs and pass water, a bilious, foamy yellow.

Etchen skewed his flat nose at the smell. He had the urge
to destroy the bothersome beast and work the ground bare-
handed like the brothers from Clonard who came to him for
their official passage into the priesthood. *Another is due soon, so
says Finnian's messenger,* he thought, rehearsing the words,
*"Ordain him a bishop. He has royal blood in him." That should earn
the respect of the chieftains,* he mused, although who couldn't
claim to have a few drops of kings in him. As though they lis-

tened to bishops anyway. It was the abbots they feared. The abbot could close the door of his school to children. Maybe close the door to heaven with excommunication.

A bishop? "Finnian must like this one," he grumbled. *Enough to keep him on his long leash.*

He stung the horse's rump with the whip again, and the blade ripped the turf. No sooner had he grinned with triumph than a commanding "Whoa!" bellowed from behind him. The horse stopped with a wheeze. Etchen raised the reed.

"Hold your whip!" ordered a tall, tonsured stranger who kicked through the dark dirt to stand by the horse. Three other cowled men ran down the road, apparently calling back their cocky companion.

"Colum!" they yelled.

Etchen shook his reed at the intruder. "How dare you," he growled. "Commanding my horse!"

Colum stroked its sweat-slick neck, his hands working like a doctor's, his face alarmed by the diagnosis. "And how dare you work this poor animal like this?" he said. "He is very sick."

"I'll be the judge of that. I have a field to plow. Step aside, unless you're the one come for ordaining." Etchen's angry stare kept the other three at a distance.

"That can wait," said Colum, still feeling the horse. "Cainnech, some water."

"Stay where you are, boy," warned the bishop. "And you — get away from my horse."

Cainnech looked to Colum for directions. Colum pointed to his feet. Cainnech remained still.

Colum's expert hands, kneading the submissive horse, found the spots he searched for. Head bowed, Colum pressed his palms against the beast and began to pray.

"I said, get away from my horse," Etchen called. He spun the reins around the plow handle and grabbed for Colum's shoulder. Seizing it, he felt a heated tingling shoot up his arm, setting his shoulder to twitching. He struggled, big-eyed, to remove his hand, but it stuck like a burr to wool. His arm hairs uncurled and stood stiff as spines on a chestnut. When Colum removed his hands with a look of relief, the heat dulled, and Etchen pulled his trembling hand to his bosom, inspecting it for blisters.

"Now I am ready for you to lay hands on me," said Colum. "Unless that was it."

The bishop staggered back, hands close to his chest. "Are you the one Finnian sent?" he asked, sounding out of breath.

"I am." Colum knelt in the sod, slowly, one knee at a time, head low, fingers interlocked.

Etchen released the whip. He sputtered while the other three men also dropped to the dirt on their knees. He looked to the horse, straight and sturdy, its once cloudy eyes cleared and its ears perked. Stomach aflutter, Etchen thought of the privileges he would forfeit if the insolent deacon before him became a bishop in Meath. *Why, even the kings of Tara might seek him out,* he groaned, *and I would lose their patronage. Perhaps even lose a position at their banquet table.*

Perspiring, it occurred to him that he still had power to change this dangerous outcome by intoning the ordination of a priest. An honest mistake. How could he tell which of the four Finnian had chosen for bishop? He cautiously extended his hands, smarting from the rush of fire he had absorbed. Braced for a burn, he folded his hands on Colum's head. With a sigh, he felt only the thick, wavy locks behind the shaven line.

When he finished the rite, he looked eagerly for the pained reaction of the new priest's surprise demotion. Drop-jawed, he beheld the joyful face of a man set free.

■

"God willed it," Colum called over his shoulder to his friends on the road. "He takes what was meant for evil and uses it for good."

The smell of the sea filled him with fond memories. He felt most free at sea, and he thought of finding a boat with Comgall to net some fish for Mobhi. It should be easy at Glasnevin, a busy port of entry for the hundreds of hopeful students on their way to Erin's famous schools.

The sky was unusually empty of gulls. The chattering birds clustered on the ground instead, whirling in tight circles. Then he saw the half-eaten carcasses of cows on the roadside with limp sea gulls beside them. Flies swarmed in black clouds at their approach. The salt air became pungent with a putrid odor, stronger than a stagnant pond. As they came closer to

Glasnevin, whatever farmhouse they visited to inquire stood empty and stinking. They fashioned cloth masks to stay the stench and avoided any roaming animals. A pack of black-spotted swine nosed each other across the road, and from a distance Colum tried to see if they bore Almergin's markings.

Comgall dared to say it first. "Fever."

■

Mobhi's mission at Glasnevin occupied an old ring-fort built above the blue bay. Steep, serrated rocks fell away from the stone walls down to the hissing surf. Distant sails shadowed the haze.

The entrygate was flanked by two crackling bonfires which sent up a thick carbon-colored mantle to brood over the stone settlement, dimming the afternoon sunshine. The smoke was supposed to overpower the noxious vapors which carried the fever.

Inside, they found the compound quiet. Chanted psalms drifted from the chapel, though it was not time for offices. A few scruffy dogs, eyes aglow, welcomed them with low growls. But no person welcomed them.

In the round-roofed oratory, Colum discovered the flat-faced abbot, alone and cheerful as usual. Mobhi wore the hair shirt and tight chain of mortification, controlling his hands to avoid swatting the insects.

"Six of our brethren passed into Christ's presence yesterday," he said wistfully, the ribboned lips curled with the happy thought. "In His faithfulness He has afflicted us to humble our pleasures."

"Where are the brothers, Master Mobhi?" asked Colum. "No one greeted us."

"In the church. Waiting for the angels to take them."

"Then I will go there to pray for their healing," said Colum, expecting a wave of dismissal.

Mobhi's hands did not move. "You will not."

"Let me lay hands on them, anoint them with oil, as the apostle says."

"You will not," Mobhi said, more emphatic.

"It is my duty as a priest."

Mobhi tipped his head, as though seeing something

above which no man with eyes could see. "Would you deny them the true love of imitating Christ's suffering? God's gift of sickness chastises the flesh to free our souls. Do you mock God?"

"I also seek to imitate Christ who healed the sick."

Mobhi's chain pinched as he shifted on the cold floor, drawing blood, drawing flies. "God has chosen us to share in the crucified life," he drooled. "How good He is to trust us with this! To count us worthy to bear such a cross!"

His grotesque face aimed at the far wall where a hand-hewn crucifix hung. A gift from one of the seafaring pilgrims from Spain, the painted figure glistened with red stains. Pain was carved into the wooden face. One could feel guilt by confronting it, seeing how comfortable and unmortified one's own life was by comparison.

"Do not touch my children, Brother Colum," said Mobhi. "Those whom God loves most must suffer most."

"No father wishes harm to his children," Colum snapped, gathering his cloak. Mobhi sputtered at the affront, but Colum ran out to the chapel, spurred by the chants of the dying. He secured a scarf around his nose and mouth and kicked open the church door.

Dark, furry shadows scampered into the walls as he ran between the cots up to the altar. He genuflected there, and then pulled the bottle of water from the gold-leafed tabernacle containing the implements for the Eucharist. He prayed a hasty blessing over it as he approached the first cot, wetting his thumb.

The moaning monk held up his quaking hand. "Please," he said, "go away."

Colum dabbed the man's hot forehead. "God of power, by Your word You drive out all weaknesses—"

"Go! Praise Him, I will see Him soon! No!"

"In Your mercy visit Your servant; may the infirmity depart—"

The sick monk swung his arm, knocking the bottle to the stone floor. The water ran in the grooves, which drank it in quickly. With the man's arms raised, Colum saw the swelled carbuncles in the armpit, big as eggs, and the gray-blue blotches on the biceps. Colum rubbed his thumb on the wet stone, picked up the bottle, and moved to the next bed.

"Have you c-come to catch it t-too?" smiled the gray-lipped man, chilled from head to foot. "T-take my clothes when I p-pass, and you will."

Each man refused him. He covered the open-eyed body of one departed brother whose arms lay lined with the scars of blood-letting. As he prayed over the bed, the others urged him to go or in their delirium offered to embrace him and impart the gift.

He left, sickened in spirit. He remembered in the Gospel that the Lord Himself could do no mighty work among His own kin, "and he marveled at their unbelief." Disappointed, he found the pool by the refectory. A glossy film coated the water. Colum held back his dry, cold hands. The gentle warm glow he felt with Etchen's horse had long faded.

■

"Perhaps in the town," he said at the hospitality table with his companions. "Who will care for them with the brothers all sick here?"

"There is no one left, Mobhi says," reported Cainnech. "Many have died. The others have gone to Tara."

"Tara?"

"To seek the druids."

Colum shoved his bowl away. "There is no health in them."

"The people think so."

"There is nothing we can do," Colum sighed. "Not here."

Siaran swabbed his bowl. "Will you go to Tara then?"

He considered it in a wink of thought, weighing the potentials and politics of such a move before Siaran even cleaned his fingers.

A school near the stronghold of kings promised a strong influence. It would shine the truth just as brightly as the rival bonfire Patrick lit there on the eve when Samain and Easter coincided, showing the outraged druids that a new Light that would never go out had come to Erin.

But things were different now. Who of the Southern Hy Neill would grant a northern rival some land? No one.

Would Finnian, thwarted in his plan for his spiritual vassalage and patroned by the dynasties now seated in the Great Synod, offer any support? Doubtful.

"To Derry," he announced, pointing north. "Near the Seat of Ailech." There, he knew, the kings of Ulster would gladly grant a consecrated cousin a space of oaks for a school. And Cainnech's nearby family, though less endowed, might proffer animals. Moville, a morning's sail across the Lough, provided books and seed.

The next day the friends split their separate ways with fond prayers for one another. Colum and Cainnech left together with letters of passage from Mobhi.

Within the week, Mobhi died.

With their teacher gone, the remaining monks who could move escaped to Clonard, their carts harboring, unseen, a pair of onyx-eyed, ebony rats.

8

DERRY

A.D. 559

BBOT COLUMCILLE LEANED ON THE BASE OF A WIND-worn monolith where he liked to sit in the early winter evenings, waiting for the wild ducks to come in from the Foyle River in flapping flocks to feed in the stubbled fields. The wood-pigeons gathered in clumps, cooing, easy to capture. Another time.

The shadows of the mountains deepened on the winding glens. He knew he must shorten his retreat. There was still so much to do before dark.

He uttered a blessing as the wind shifted south, pulsing, it seemed, with the wash of Atlantic breakers to the north. When he pushed his wind-tossed hair from his mouth, he found another gray strand. At thirty-eight, after ten years of founding schools, his head was streaked with distinction.

In his mind, he traversed the Sperrin Range south to the turfed huts of Raphoe. He pictured Cainnech there now, sent as his emissary to settle a minor dispute among the monks. Just a spat, a clash of wills, they reported. Colum had already mounted Angel Wing before Cainnech dissuaded him, eagerly asking to go himself, just this once.

Their granary must be full by now, he mused, *despite the parsimonious chieftain of the plain.* The threat of sending warriors from Fedlimidh MacFergus's household greased his generosity.

He floated downriver in thought, across the midland pastures to the daughter schools of Durrow, Swords, and Kells. By this route, he and Cainnech escaped the plague long ago. The store of inks they brought from Glasnevin launched many a man into an illustrious career. Their abundant herds kept their scribes warm and their Scriptoria well supplied with skins. During his last inspection, the brothers used rare imported aquamarine and crushed silver. But for their inspiration, they looked north to Derry of the Oakwood, where his mind now returned from its wide circuit. *I'll see you all soon, my daughters,* he thought. *Finbar is back from another trip. I'll have new books for you.*

Happily, his tour would coincide with the Great Assembly at Tara. When the mail-shirted messengers arrived in the summer to invite the celebrated abbot of the northern Hy Neill, he accepted. His proud father, boasting his famous son's command over so many soldiers for Christ, promised him a splendid entourage.

The pigeons which pecked at the water's edge fluttered away as he raised a song that bent the marsh rushes:

> *Derry of all my daughters be praised,*
> *Derry of quiet, and of purity,*
> *The welcoming arms of her oaks raised*
> *As my curragh returns from the sea.*
> *Dear is Swords, and dear is Durrow,*
> *Dear as well, Raphoe and Kells,*
> *But the reason I love Derry so*
> *Is for her flocks of white angels*
> *From one end of the wood to the other.*

Perhaps it was only the play of the eastern sun in the oak leaves, as some said. Yet he had refused to fell the sacred trees in order to build the customary sunrise-facing sanctuary. Who would dare destroy the habitations of angels? "What I fear more than death," he told a bewildered Cainnech, "is the sound of an ax in Derry."

So the ash and hickory church faced north, its altar never greeting the new day's sun.

A sliver of sunset struck the monolith's arch, and then the shadows chased it off. The ancient timepiece bade him leave. He stood and watched the marigold sky dim behind the western summit of Mount Grianan where the circular stone citadel of Ulster's kings commanded a fine view. Many a time from its ivied, terraced walls, he had overlooked Lough Swilly and Lough Foyle as far as Moville.

From the thin shapes of the blushing clouds, the tickle of a wishful wind, and the clicking of the first crickets, tomorrow promised a fair sail to Finbar's school.

■

Finbar shook in the straw bed, woolen covers tucked in tightly up to his rippling chins. When he recognized Colum through his rheumy eyes, he stopped heaving and his droll little mouth bent in a bow.

The old mentor's face, always pasty, looked clammy as spoiled cheese. It took on color when he coughed, and then drained.

The attendant brothers, fingers slick from minty ointments, stepped aside.

Colum knelt at the bedside. He kissed the bump on the blanket where he knew the abbot's ring lay. He pulled his sleeve taut in his fist and dabbed the dewy beads of sweat from Finbar's brow.

When the abbot spoke, his breath smelled of stale bilgewater. "Look at you. Famous now," he said with effort. "Schools everywhere. And the stories I hear. Angels? Healings?"

"If true, I have come at a good time."

"Bah, it's nothing," he hacked. "Something I picked up in Constantinople. Besides the books."

"Did you find many, Father?"

"Many?" He started to laugh, but fell into a fit of coughs. When his puffed face paled again, he said, "There are more books in Constantinople than there are people. In libraries that look like temples. And in churches big as mountains. Books everywhere."

"Better than ours?"

"No. And yes. Not as beautiful. No one can match our hand."

Colum recalled Finbar's majestic majuscule that inspired his own careful script. "Did you make copies there?"

"Many. Many. They have better texts. I ruined more sandals on those stone streets, looking for them. Whole collections. Prudentius the Bard. Severus. And all the Greeks, of course. Have you heard of Herodotus? Thucydides? Aeschylus? Sophocles?"

Colum shook his head at each name.

"Even our own tales of the Tuatha de Danaan. Finn McCool. Mananaan, Son of Lir. And the *Tain Bo*. Written down! Imagine!"

Finbar's excitement provoked a trembling that took all the attendants' strength to subdue. They draped cold, wet towels over his pate and steadied his kicking feet. When he controlled his thick tongue again, he complained, "The city has all the pleasures of East and West and all their pestilences too."

"I'll go to the chapel to pray for you," offered Colum.

Finbar's spare eyebrows lowered. He wheezed, "Come closer, my son."

As Colum leaned into the pallet, Finbar fumbled beneath the blanket near his pudgy neck. The abbot withdrew a gold chain with a tiny cross-shaped key. He giggled as he pressed it into Colum's hand.

"When you go," he breathed, "find the cedar box by the altar." The veiny eyes shifted, hiding a secret. "And use this."

The key chain unclasped easily. Colum palmed it, bent his head in respect, and left the snickering, shaking Finbar behind.

■

The cedar box, big as a saddlebag and bright with an oiled finish, hid beneath the altarstone's white cloth. Square, scarred by travel, and bulky as a wooden cheese-wheel, the box slid with a screech on the stone floor. Colum peeked over the table, hoping no one could see his rough and hurried handling. The candlestand he had jammed in the door handles reinforced his privacy.

On his knees, he jiggled the key in the golden lock. The lid clicked open. A leathery smell arose. When he pushed back the hinged cover, he saw the chalk-white coverleaf of a thick manuscript, the bold Latin title in Finbar's unmistakable script:
SANCTI BIBLIA VULGATA JEROME

His finger traced each perfect word in disbelief. He lifted to different pages at random. The words of Abraham, Joseph, and Moses spoke from the cursive letters. Finbar had found the part of God's Testament that preceded the Psalter, a priceless treasure. Not even Clonard boasted of these books.

Penned in the Holy Land, spared by Providence from barbarians, the book radiated the power of God's blessing.

Adding to his astonishment, the box housed the Psalter in Jerome's studious version as well, the fabled standard for accuracy and poetic beauty.

Skimming the lines, he recognized the modest variations from the translation he knew, each choice so visionary, so virtuous, so logical. His memorized lines sounded flat and forced by comparison, plodding at points, arbitrary and obscure at others. But the Vulgate vibrated with life, joyful as a salmon's leap and clear as the brookwater it splashed.

He dropped the lid, snapped the lock, slid the box back into place, and skipped back to the oratory, making mental inventory of the tools he needed for copying.

■

Two brothers blocked Finbar's door.

Colum motioned them aside, but the grim-faced monks refused to part.

"I will see him again," Colum said.

"Father is asleep," they said coldly.

"Wake him."

"We cannot."

"Wake him," Colum commanded.

"We tried," said the guard, "but he does not respond."

From inside came Finbar's fevered moan and a gush of gibberish.

"I must ask him something."

"He can speak to no one now."

As he heard the moan again, Colum's voice turned apologetic. "Of course. He needs rest. I will pray for his recovery in the chapel."

■

Little had changed in the Scriptorium. Colum knew where to find quills and how to fashion their ends and mix batches of ink. He worked at a steady pace, trying not to distract others or draw undue attention. *The abbot of Derry on another errand, that's all*, he thought, projecting the words to the seated copyists. *Nothing unusual about that.*

He chose a broad satchel for loose pages and a volume of Ausonius's poems he never intended to transcribe.

He barred the chapel door as before and spread his materials on the bare altar. He placed the Vulgate Psalter to his left and began the opening lines. At such a steep angle, his pen dragged, and the uneven letters crunched together. No matter. He rebuked his trembling hand and promised himself a more careful copy in Derry. For now, he scratched speedily with minimal doublestrokes or dotting to the hollow capitals, till the rushlight burned to its socket.

He lit another, praying for Finbar.

"Let him stay asleep till I finish."

◼

He emerged for the morning office in the main church, hair stubble and a smile on his face. When he learned Finbar was still abed, unconscious and incoherent, he rushed back to the little chapel.

"How he frets for Father," admired the monks.

Believing this, they left him undisturbed for the whole day. And the next. And the next. Only Jerome and a family of chittering magpies nesting in the walls kept him company.

By darkness, he resupplied his inkhorns and took water from the rain barrels outside. Though hunger gnawed at his belly, he scratched away, switching hands to relieve the cramps, ignoring the ill-formed letters. He vowed to destroy the pages as soon as he produced a more presentable copy. His schools must have the best.

◼

Neither circuit of sun nor of services kept time for him. He paced himself by psalm numbers. Light-headed and heavy-eyed with sleep, he dipped the pen absently. Psalm 105.

The song celebrated the covenant with Abraham, Isaac, and Jacob, and the promise of a new land for their inheritance. Colum wondered again if he should have worked the books of Moses first. He dismissed it, as he had a hundred times through

143

each night, coveting the leisure of studying them at length. A speedy transcription would not do. On the more familiar territory of the Psalter, however, he scrawled freely:

> *A small company it was,*
> *Few in number, strangers in that land,*
> *Roaming from nation to nation,*
> *From one kingdom to another.*

The magpies beat their wings with a clatter, cheeping in fright. Through the timber wall, a man's voice cried in pain. Colum left his pen in the inkhorn and inspected the wall as the cries faded. Close to the floor, he spied a wood slat no bigger than a bread loaf, pushed aside for a peephole. The flapping of the flustered birds echoed inside the wall in a crawlspace big enough for a man.

Short of breath, Colum ran to the altar and packed his tools. He wiped the quill on the inside hem of his smock to hide the stain. *How long have I been watched,* he breathed.

He shuffled the vellum sheets of the Vulgate back into the sweet-smelling box, and then kicked it into its place on the floor. As he slung his satchels over his shoulders, the door rattled. The hinges creaked. The wedged candlestand caught and held. It bounced in the bronze handles with each loud rap, clanking like a chariot's axle.

Colum wrenched it free. The door burst open.

Finbar, eyes wide as an owl on the fly, stamped into his chapel. Behind him stood one of his oratory door guards, his face marred by red scratches and a badly bloodied eye.

The magpies rightly punished the spy, Colum thought. He raised his joined right fingers in blessing. "Father, you are well, as I prayed."

"Well enough to see you sin," the abbot huffed. "Where is my key?"

Colum held it out in his ink-stained fingers.

Finbar snatched it and squeezed it in his fist. "The satchel, too," he said, grasping with the other hand.

Colum pulled back. "These are my books made by my own hand."

"You have stolen them."

144

"They belong to the church of God."

"You covet them for yourself."

"Did you bring back a greedy spirit from the East along with your sickness?"

Finbar fumed. "Who gave you permission?"

"You gave me the key."

"To study it, not to copy it. Give it back."

"Who is the real thief? The one who keeps a sacred book from being known. This is no crown for your treasure room."

"How dare you," the abbot steamed, his face red as an overripe berry. "You have no right to keep it."

"Will you force me?"

Finbar fought down a cough. "Don't think you can threaten me with your father's warriors," he said. "They will listen to what the High King decides."

"He has no part in this."

"He will. At the Assembly." Finbar backed out the door, his fat finger wagging. "Bring your men to Tara, and we will see!"

9

TARA

A.D. 560

HE GREAT HALL OF SYNODS
BUZZED WITH THE DELIBERA-
tions of the lawyers. Bunched together in droop-headed groups near crackling hearths, the solemn men with the black robes and white beards considered the many cases brought for their judgment. At Assembly time, the nobles brought many.

According to the convoluted Brehon code, the wise men imposed fines payable in cows for infractions of every sort. For stealing a needle from an embroideress. For accidental maiming. For inadequate hospitality. One group listed the exact clothes to be provided a deerstalker's son in fosterage.

With their decisions declared and committed to the collective memory, the keepers of the codes drifted to other groups to offer their expertise. Dark Doctors of Letters, colorful poets of various grades, and riddle-rife buffoons made their rounds, consulting where welcomed.

With such help, one group ordered a brooch melted which exceeded the permissible weight. The grim defendants, a goldsmith and an engraver, spat loudly and tramped out with envious backward glances at the gleaming clasp on the High King's cloak.

The Ard-Ri of Erin, Diarmait macCerrbeil, slouched on the sable-draped throne at the far end of the hall, wrapped in the splendid seven colors reserved for royalty. A sour man, he toyed with the heavy brooch of his dubious authority, fingering each garnet and ruby. He wiped his weary eyes while the winter-faced historians around him debated a minute detail of a bygone battle. Overhead, the burnished bronze shields of his southern clan hung dormant and undented. Beneath them, the crossed javelins, unchipped and tarnished only with age, slept in their mounts. Diarmait knew he would only command respect when the weapons were wet with blood. The kings who elected him meant to secure their own positions without interventions from Tara. But the day would come, he vowed. It would come soon.

A battle trumpet blasted a fanfare at the main entry, shaking the shields and setting the pigeons into panic in the smoky rafters. The ceiling banners, once still as bats, ruffled. The hearthfires glowed with the rush of air.

Diarmait bolted upright, his small hands clutching the throne's arms. His warriors emerged from the shadows, their golden hair and silver swords flashing in the firelight.

The lawyer clusters melted away at the approach of Colum of Clan Conaill, clad in a blazing white hooded cloak. With his flaming, flowing hair, he looked to be a cross between a druid and a warrior. *Some said he could lay claim to this very seat,* Diarmait thought. *He took the tonsure instead. A pity.*

With a purposeful, regal gait, Colum led a long entourage of leather-trousered horsemen. They spread behind him like the train of a king's cape. Their loud tunics, splashed with bright pins, were tucked into broad, dagger-filled belts.

High over his ginger head, Colum carried the Vulgate in an exquisitely etched satchel.

Beside him, stormy gray eyes glaring and hair like spun silver shining, stalked his father.

Fedlimidh looked ready for a brawl. His thick eyebrows, salted with age, stretched across his forehead like a helmet brim. He swung his fists rapidly to keep pace with his tall, graceful son. His gold finery clicked in step, the bracelets, earrings, and buckles announcing his noble station. His cloth trousers, heavy with Eithne's embroidery, swished in rhythm with the squeak of his steerhide leg strappings. Diarmait noted the odd half-smile on his bearded, battered face. He had seen one like it before, on another chief who had just slain a rival and sliced off his rings.

Diarmait realized the procession lacked drummers; it was the pounding of his own heart he heard. He repressed the urge to stand, locking his knees. *The Ard-Ri pays no homage to a northern underking,* he groused. *Especially if it concerns the petty dispute of a common monk.*

Colum raised his arm, halting his troops. He listened for the jewelry to settle, and then boomed, "Cousin, we come to defend the name of—"

"You will wait your turn," announced Diarmait.

"—our clan and the Word of God—"

"And you will speak when allowed."

Colum drew a breath but held it. His jugular stood out, an angry purple.

"Next case." Diarmait pointed lazily to a nearby judge. "Yours."

The aged judge poked his chest, questioning, confused. Diarmait encouraged him again, knowing he had not shown interest in cases all day.

"It concerns a bee sting," said the hoary-headed judge, hesitant.

Colum bristled. "You will make us wait for a bee sting?" he shouted.

Diarmait ignored him. "Tell me everything," he said coolly to the judge who now stood in the open space of the court.

The old man beckoned to his peers and the plaintiff, a donkey-faced poet of the Fourth Grade. They stood with him, nervous.

The judge outlined the case of the stung victim and the responsible roadside beekeeper. He cited the lengthy precedents of the Brehon for fines which governed such suits. But Diarmait heard none of it. He was enjoying Fedlimidh's smoldering frustration. He studied the son's insulted impatience.

The judge droned on. The bee case, as such, held no interest for Diarmait. Nor had he concern for a bickering about books. His advisors, briefing him in advance, had urged him to dismiss the book dispute to church elders. Ignore the fine foreign treasures offered by this Finbar, they had pleaded. Avoid confrontation during the Assembly. The Northern Hy Neills would welcome an adverse decision, they had warned, giving them an excuse for war.

But they use anything as an excuse for war, Diarmait had reminded them. Let them come. Let them remember that the southern branch of Niall's descendants hold Tara. Let them see that the rightful heirs of the goddess Dana are rooted here as firmly as the oaks.

The judge finished. "What is your decision, O king?"

"Give him what the law allows. Two cows." He waved his hand as if shooing a gnat.

"Next case." He feigned a yawn. "Bring the next plaintiff, Finbar of Moville."

A company of elderly brehons broke from the wall and entered the open court under the hot glare of Colum and his father. The lawyers held the tottering Finbar by the elbows. Though frail, pale, and weak from the trip, Finbar never removed his gaze from the throne. He searched Diarmait for any sign of duplicity, any hint of deviation from their agreement.

"And the defendant," called the king, "Colum of Derry and Durrow."

Colum marched forward, strong and radiant. When he met Finbar, a fire kindled in his eyes.

"I am aware of the details of your case," said Diarmait, rubbing his rings. "The issue is simple. As to every cow belongs its calf, so to every book belongs its copy."

Colum stood dumbfounded with rage. He gasped like a thrown rider with the breath knocked out. His eyes glinted silver. He stormed forward in protest. "It is a wrong judgment," he thundered, "and you shall be punished for it!"

Fedlimidh bolted to his son's side, gripping his arm. They looked at each other as though in sudden recognition. Colum took his father's other arm, and they stood locked together in an alliance of fury.

Fedlimidh raised his son's hand as high as he could. "You have seen it yourselves," he shouted to his warriors, "how they insult the men of Ulster. Their blood be on their own heads!"

Diarmait began to perspire. At his signal, a guard slipped out for reinforcements. Diarmait felt for the bronze blade hidden in his sleeve.

But Colum had already thrown down the satchel and marched with his father through his cheering men out the door.

■

Fedlimidh felt no need to remain for the Assembly. He had what he came for. As soon as the horses were properly watered and rested, he would depart, sending swifter messengers ahead with the summons to war. There was no need to best the Meathmen on the chariot course. As cheers from the first heats reached him along with the rattle of iron wheels on cinders, he thought, *Let them race. The real test will be in combat.*

He squeezed his solid fists together, grateful to the spirits of Tara's Hill for turning his son's heart to his proper destiny. His chest swelled with the fresh memory of Crimthann's forceful grip, the oneness he sensed with him in that moment before Diarmait's throne. *The wolf will mangle that weasel,* he thought, *if he is not turned by his timid friend.*

All the way back to their tents, the skinny one called Cainnech had buzzed about his son like a troublesome fly. "'Anyone angry with his brother is guilty before the court,'" the whiner had spouted from Scripture. "'Love your enemies, says the Lord.'" Crimthann wisely ignored him. How could he love his enemies? Could his son betray the teaching of his own father? Smite your enemies at the proper time, no sooner; leave no one to strike back. It was his own father's teaching, and his father's before him. How could his son rule as king otherwise?

He reconsidered his strength against the south. His cousin Cadoc, eager for sport, would join. But Cadoc's men might scatter at the first fatal blow, accustomed to taking cattle rather than heads. Cadoc may have mocked him for being the ceremonial keeper of the clan's chessmen. But the game taught him good lessons. Position yourself. Be patient. Wait for your enemy's mistakes. Then attack.

He counted his allies, knights and rooks assiduously collected over the years for this moment. And bishops? Could the abbeys Crimthann controlled in the south be compelled to join the struggle? Take up arms for their abbot? Or refuse the sacraments to southern warriors? Ah, that would put fear in them. *I must ask Crimthann about it,* he resolved.

Rising with a crack in his back, Fedlimidh swatted aside the tent flap and raced for his son's tent.

When he saw the cowardly cleric inside, nervous as a chipmunk and still nagging his son, Fedlimidh sniffed with disapproval. He was tempted to dismiss the man if Crimthann lacked the sense to do so. But he controlled himself, staring Cainnech away instead.

Colum, tying up his saddlebags, wore a pleased expression as though relieved of a stone in his shoe. He secured his ax with rawhide strips to the pack, and then scraped the edge with his fingernail to test it. A thin white flake fell away.

"We leave at daybreak, Father?"

"We do."

"What do the scouts say?"

Fedlimidh, distrusting Cainnech, lied. "Nothing yet. They return with us." The scouts' information reported Diarmait's weak resolve and unreliable resources. The northern Hy Neill could overcome the less confident, more numerous, yet more divided south. "Still, we must be on our guard," said Fedlimidh. "They may try to prevent our leaving. Or try to take hostages."

A chariot rumbled outside. It rattled up to the tent. A horse snorted wetly; it had been driven hard.

Fedlimidh drew his dagger as the guards at the door struggled with the intruder.

"Save me, Father!" the driver cried from outside. His hands tore at the tent flaps while the warriors restrained him.

"Let him come," called Colum.

Fedlimidh glared at him. He suspected a ruse. "Be careful, Crimthann."

The sweaty, dust-covered driver stumbled in and fell at Colum's feet. It was a boy, a beardless fifteen, no more. "Save me," he cried in his newly cracked voice.

Colum knelt down to him. "Save you from what?" he asked quietly.

Fedlimidh frowned while the boy told his story. Just a hurly game, he explained. He had played as hard as the others. In a swinging tangle he cracked a man's skull, and the man lay still. Chased off the court by vengeful relatives of the dead player, the boy hijacked a chariot from the nearby racetrack and whipped the horse here. "They will kill me," he finished.

Through the sobs, Fedlimidh recognized the boy's accent. "He is a man of Connaught. We have nothing to do with Connaughta."

"He has come for sanctuary, Father. I cannot deny him."

"You must."

"We will bring him to the church." Colum started to raise up the boy.

"The kings of Connaught despise us!"

"I'm sorry, Father." Colum lifted the boy, brushed him off, spoke words of solace, led him outside, and asked his name. Curnan, youngest son of Aidh, King of Connaught, locked onto Colum's arm.

Fedlimidh nearly spat. Protect an enemy against an enemy? His mind reeled with the contradiction, the foolishness, so that he sputtered in protest, unable to voice his outrage. Colum already hurried across the meadow towards the cube-shaped church stuck on the same hill as the druid stones.

Fedlimidh ordered the warriors to strike camp at once. He might need the advantage of an early mobilization under the cover of darkness. Then he chased Colum, cursing the Connaughta boy under his hot breath. He hoped there was still time to persuade his son to leave the offender to his fate. Let him submit to the Brehon code. No, there could be no invoking the law. Though it had played into his own plans, it had betrayed his son's suit.

He caught up to them at the door. "How long must you keep him?" he barked, following them inside.

"I don't know."

"But we leave before dawn."

"Not any more." Colum touched a candle to a fat-soaked torch. It bloomed into flame.

"You have chosen a poor place for a battle with Diarmait, my son," said Fedlimidh. "Do you expect to hold off his men from inside?"

"He will not violate sanctuary."

Fedlimidh turned his head at the thumping of approaching hoofbeats. "I am not so sure."

The clinking told him a sizable guard in mail shirts had stopped outside.

The prince of Connaught panted in fear. Colum steadied

his shaking shoulders, reassuring, "If he enters God's house, he will be cursed."

The doors split open with a double kick. A cloud of dust spilled into the room. A phalanx of pikemen, lances lowered, rushed at the altar. Astonished beyond words, Colum raised his palm.

"The High King of Heaven will not allow—"

The stub end of a pike caught his chin, clapping shut his jaw, and he tumbled backwards against the altar. The soldiers seized their prey. They dragged him outside on his knees.

Colum recovered, spit blood, and ran to the door after them. Fedlimidh intercepted him to hold him back, but Colum's momentum pulled him outside.

A circle of mounted archers, bows at the ready, hemmed the church.

Diarmait sat astride a handsome stallion, its ceremonial blankets dimmed with dust. He stroked his high, dark chin, amused.

"Are you now an ally of Connaught?" he asked Fedlimidh with a sneer. "And would you, an abbot, protect a murderer?"

The boy knelt on the grass, gasping, his arms firmly gripped from behind.

"He is in sanctuary," growled Colum. "The penalty is high for one who breaks it."

Diarmait's face hardened. "The penalty is high for one who kills a Meathman." He snapped his fingers. A muscular warrior, his face obscured by the long nosepiece on his helmet, drove a sword through the boy's back. The crimson point ripped through the chest. Eyes popping, the Connaughta crashed to his face.

"Two times we have met," Diarmait called to Colum. "May there not be a third."

■

Diarmait rode to the camp in the honeyglow of the early morning. In the moist turf, torn where the tentpegs had been pulled, a score of abandoned stone-banked fires smoldered with purple peat smoke.

Diarmait chuckled at his triumph, reveling in Fedlimidh's retreat. The scrambled hoofprints suggested a hasty departure.

No doubt his stomachless son, humiliated by the court and the boy charioteer's execution, had convinced him to withdraw. No wonder Fedlimidh left his seats empty at the banquet hall. A pity. Diarmait reserved one more scheme for his northern rival—that when the trumpet blew and the marshall took the guests to their ranked places beneath their shields, Fedlimidh would find his among the chessplayers and jesters.

The hoofmarks lengthened as they reached the Slige Asal, the northwesterly road of the five avenues that converged at Tara. With a boarhunter's instinct, he studied the prints to guess how long ago they were made.

The ground was churned up at the foot of a knoll, indicating several horses had veered off sharply from the group. Puzzled, Diarmait spurred his stallion to follow the tracks. He bid his guard of pikemen to gallop behind. Diarmait ground his corn-colored teeth as he realized where he headed. The tracks narrowed to a single file through a hedge which circled an age-less oak grove. He spanked his horse with the flat of his sword. Over the pummel of the hooves and the hiss of leaves as he tore through the hedge, he listened for any hint of his rival's lingering.

He jerked up his hard-breathing horse and stared at the tree. The mighty oak, with a name no one could remember, had shaded eons of secret ceremonies insuring Tara's power. The charred limbs with the deep rope grooves had hung countless wicker cages of criminals, burnt as offerings to guarantee sons to the reigning line. Its guttered bark served as an astringent to staunch the childbirth bleeding as new kings entered the world.

But now the great tree bowed on its side, its twisted arms dismembered. The split trunk, with huge splinters like spears pointing up where it had cracked and fell, showed the chip-wounds of a furious ax.

Diarmait faced his somber guards. He gnashed his teeth. He thrust his swordpoint north.

10
CULDREVNE

A.D. 561

OLUM SCALED THE STEEP BLUFFS, CLIMBING THROUGH pasture painted with the orange blossoms of hinds-foot trefoil and sun-yellow tormentil. Near the top, grass gave way to rock where the heath-spotted orchis, a delicately fragrant orchid, showed palely through the heather.

From here he could see Sligo Bay, placid Lough Gill to the east, the sharp peaks in the north, and directly below, the strawberry-strewn Plain of Culdrevne.

On opposing hills, the armies camped, their countless fires burning columns of bluish haze over the knolls. The smoke knit a gloomy canopy over the valley, a pall over those who would give their lives in battle.

Colum heard the smiths at their anvils, beating iron swords to a fearsome cutting edge, tempering them till they rang. Young apprentices blew the furnaces white-hot while the sparks flew. Wagons unloaded wood for the carpenters who cut spear shafts and chariot spokes. He discerned the songs of the shieldweavers who stretched hides over wicker frames. Archers strung their bows. Slingers picked their stones and tested them in the pockets of their fat-softened thongs.

On the nearest hill, bright clan-banners waved in the wind of the bay, surrounded by scores of lean-tos and tents. The

Ulstermen, in an uneasy alliance with the forces of Connaught, held the same high ground but with a grassy gap between them, a no-man's land, a testimony to their ancient animosity. How often Colum had heard Drummon rehearse their heroic war against each other recorded in the epic *Tain Bo*. CuChulainn repulsed the invaders from Connaught, defeating the legendary evil Queen Maeve. Even today, his men exaggerated her powers beyond all bounds, some believing that her spirit mated with the ruling High King of Tara.

"We go to war with Maeve again," they said. "But now even Connaught is against her."

King Aidh of Connaught, sworn to avenge his son's death at Diarmait's hand, grudgingly agreed to fight alongside Fedlimidh. Colum knew he must pray that they did not turn upon each other in the pitch of battle.

Choosing a rounded rock for his kneeler, he began his entreaty from the Psalms. He regretted that he could only remember the Old Latin. Soon he would have the Vulgate again. He wrung his mind to recall Jerome's phrasing, but the rapid transcription never stuck. He slapped his palms together, sulked, and recited reluctantly:

> *Certa, Domine, contra certantes mecum,*
> *Strive, O Lord, with those who strive against me,*
> *Fight against those who fight me.*
> *Grasp shield and buckler,*
> *Rise up and help me.*
> *Disgrace be on those who seek my life,*
> *May those who plan to hurt me retreat in dismay.*
> *May they be like chaff before the wind,*
> *Driven by the angel of the Lord.*

He prayed and fasted all night. Early on, when the sun dimmed and the darkness of men's hearts prompted hidden deeds, he had been distracted by the echoes of drunken songs and the laughter of loose women. But as the campfires ebbed and Venus appeared in the low sky, there came only the yips of wild dogs foraging and the brush of wind off the water. With no fire to warm him, Colum chattered and curled himself tighter. He recited his psalm again.

The Morning Star brightened, swooped lower, and rushed towards him, fast as a slinger's stone. What first seemed a shooting star became a glowing blue ball, flying like a lit catapult's missile. The intense flare enveloped him with a sudden gale that blew off his hood. Even with his hands pressed over his eyes, he saw a shimmering whiteness. The chill of night left him, yet he shook. The balm of a summer night washed over him as he lowered his hands. The warm wind gusted, flattening his tunic against his body. A sweetness deeper than the wild white roses filled him.

Through the flickering glare, he discerned a vague human shape. When it moved, blue rays flashed from the limbs, and when the outline of the six massive wings unfurled, the air whistled in his ears. Colum fell on his face.

"You will have a great victory," came a male voice, clear and commanding. The bushes tossed with the blast of his words. "And you will have a terrible loss since you have asked for so worldly a thing."

"What does my Lord require of me?"

"A terrible loss," repeated the voice.

The wings wrapped into a ball, whipping the heather. The light condensed around it, a pulsating aura, and the sparkling sphere shot away like lightning into the eastern sky.

◼

When he reached the camp, the men were already astir, clasping their shirts and buckling their trousers. They cinched saddles and clipped bridles on the horses. The great beasts stamped, sensitive to the serious mood.

Colum's nose itched from the stink of the dungfires, and his eyes burned from sleeplessness and the blinding vision. His heart ached with the angel's bittersweet promise. Yet when he saw the weapon-laden men of Ulster, he straightened and greeted them, his apprehension gone.

With helmets under their brawny, braceleted arms, quivers on their backs, pikes in their palms, and swords at their sides, the men streamed from their leathern shelters towards the crest of the hill, the center of camp. They converged on the golden bonfire crackling there. Each man stooped to pick up a stone on the way. Colum bent to a blackened campfire and chose a blood-red rock, charred on one side.

At the summit, on a stilt-raised throne of ash frame and willowweave, presided Fedlimidh. His multicolored cloaks dazzled in the fire's glow. He wore his hunting helmet, a pointed brass cap with enameled trim and menacing antlers. To one side stood his reluctant, pouting partner, Aidh of Connaught, counting his warriors. They looked wary and suspicious, like rats watching encircling hawks, as if expecting to be set upon by the more boisterous Ulstermen.

The warriors gathered in their loud tunics and fine tooled leathers. Preferring silken tops, they looked better prepared for a banquet than a battle, except for their limed hair, stiff and spiked. Their eyelids, painted black, stood out against the chalky white of their hair. Silver torques, inlaid with coral, ends adorned with toothy animal heads, circled their throats. Their bronze sleeve fasteners and fibulas glittered with opaque rock crystals.

To Fedlimidh's other side stood a warrior oddly bereft of such gaudy decorations. His treelike arms folded over a barreled chest, Drummon inspected the troops.

He looked older, of course, the hair silver on his strong, bare shoulders. The lines around his roving eyes were as deep and numerous as the engravings on his helmet. His waist, taut as ever, fit into a thick belt. Beside his prize dagger shone his pennywhistle.

When he saw Colum's face high over the heads of the soldiers, his eyes showed the same mischievous gleam as when playing the tunes of the banquet hall.

Fedlimidh motioned to his son to stand by him. Colum assumed the position of the prince, between the kings. Drummon eyed him proudly, welcoming him to the inner circle.

Through the morning mist, Colum watched the men of Meath maneuvering on their hillside, lining up like rows of short pines.

Fedlimidh stood up on the small footstool that projected from his seat. Colum heard the crick in his father's back as he drew his sword. It slid soundlessly from its soft boarskin sheath. The chieftain held the hilt against his chest.

The men filed past the kings and the white-robed prince, each dropping his stone at Fedlimidh's feet as a pledge of bravery. The pile grew to a mound, then a hill, as the stones clicked into place. When the men returned later to reclaim their stones, the casualties could easily be counted.

The procession moved to the rhythm of Colum's Gaelic prayers. He crossed his finger in the air in blessing.

His arm froze as Cadoc swaggered past. A fanged boarhead fit over his fleshy face. The cruel grin on the beast matched his own. The stiff bristles looked plucked from his own pointy mustache. He held up his stubby hands. Ten rings, mounted with orange and aqua gems, clicked as he wagged his fingers. He spit on his right pinky and slid off the ring. He tossed it into the stone pile.

"I must make room for Diarmait's ring," he gloated. "You can keep this one, Fedlimidh, if he doesn't get yours first."

Colum gestured the blessing, more as a signal to move on. His prayer became louder. The men repeated the words. The marching chant grew in volume and pitch to a chorus of frenzied shouts. The warriors beat their swords against their limed shields in unison, a fearsome rhythm punching clouds of white dust into the air. The deafening roar joined the discordant trumpeting of the animal-headed canyxes which called the chariots into position. The horses, decked with gorgeous caparisons, snorted angry bursts of steam. The barefoot drivers reined them into rows. They jerked the jingling harnesses just as they did at Assembly races.

Fedlimidh's freshly-washed stallion was led to the throne. The chieftain clenched his jaw against the pain of his rheumatism, aggravated by the early dampness. He slipped his naked foot into the iron stirrup and leaned into the saddle. When he lifted his antlered head, a cheer erupted from the warriors. Even Cadoc's rustlers raised a salute, hooting with anticipation. Emboldened, the men leaped and hopped, mocking battle by slashing their swords and bumping each other's shields.

Fedlimidh locked onto his son, and then looked to the bluffs. Colum knew that with his gleaming figure prominent on the heights, hurling the terrifying words of satire, the men would be spurred to victory. As he dashed away, the charge imminent with the men's hysteria nearly peaking, he heard their shrill insults:

"As many as hailstones will be your cloven skulls!"
"As big as the hills will be the heaps of your bowels!"

"Your pieces will fit through a sieve!"

From the other hill, Colum heard the Gaelic spells of Diarmait's white-faced druids invoking powers to bind the urine in the bodies of the enemy and their horses. They jumped and jeered, their black robes beating like bat wings. Huffing as he scratched up the steep hill, Colum breathed a bard's counter-curses, grateful finally for Gemman's training.

When he fell upon the summit, his lungs ached. His thighs burned. Below, skittish horses pranced sideways and kicked. The deft riders, form-fit to their muscular mounts, leaned them back into line.

Colum crossed himself. Sweat drops pearled on his fingers. The shouts subsided as Fedlimidh guided his horse to the front. His sword was down. *When will he go?* Colum wondered, head throbbing. Then he noticed the position of his father's antlers, spread side to side. He was watching the bluff for a signal.

Colum stood, chest high. He shot his arms outward, a great white cross.

Fedlimidh smacked his horse's sleek rump, and it bolted forward. Horns bellowed. Hooves drummed the ground.

In reply, the Meathmen screeched like crows, stripped naked, and rushed headlong.

From each side, the tramping horses strained at their bits, flecks of white foam spraying from their mouths. Their manes whipped like long grass in a storm. Their thundering hooves churned up chunks of turf. The riders, two to a horse, one to steer, one to slash, urged them ahead.

The first whistle of arrows pierced the clouds of dirt. Some thudded off shields, some found flesh that bloomed into red.

Colum mounted his prayer rock, arms straight out. From the new vantage, he saw beyond the scraggly bushes on the adjoining bluff. Finbar of Moville stood there in alba vestments, hands over his head in prayer for Diarmait's men.

Colum's hands curled into fists. He rained curses upon the nude men of Meath, his lips peeled back like a wolf's. The taunts turned Finbar's head. The old man seemed to shake with the words, as if caught by an unexpected wave while standing in a boat. He regained composure, his eyes fixed on the plain.

When Colum saw the object of Finbar's stare, his eyes

watered in anger. High on a pole swayed the enameled satchel of the Vulgate. A trio of monks processed down the hill with it, measuring the tread of the talisman into battle.

The buzz of slings filled the air. Thongs whirred with outstretched arms, flinging a deadly hailstorm of pebbles. They clattered on wood and metal. Horsemen toppled with screams into the brook dividing the valley, where the armies splashed and began their riotous slaughter.

Chariots crashed. Heavy wheels splintered and flew. The drivers, their javelins spent, leaped into the conflict on foot. Swords sang, helmets crunched, cuirasses creaked, and shields cracked till the brook ran red with blood. Limbs dropped to the mud where the tangled heaps of the wounded lay shuddering. Terrified horses, their masters slumped, stampeded.

Above a thousand deadly duels, the impartial sun burned its way higher to its midway point, a dull, unblinking white eye on the melee below. The diffused gray light could not burn off the stubborn mist. Instead, columns of cloud poured atop the Meathmen's hill. The vapor wrapped around it like a white cloak, and Colum realized with a sting in his stomach that the shroud was a druid's fence, conjured to conceal an attack.

Finbar waved his arms slowly, upholding the spell of the sorcerers.

Colum looked up for the Morning Star to descend, to rain fire, to roll over the enemy. But the shouting cloud advanced. Diverted by this danger, Colum lost sight of the sacred book. His eye jumped from standard to standard. But it was gone.

His fists high and his chest full, he cried over the plain in a voice that sheared the din of battle. The booming baritone sent Finbar's palms flying to his ears, as Colum intoned:

> *"My druid, may He be with me,*
> *Is the Son of God, and Truth with Purity."*

The boats in the bay rocked in their slips. The blackberry bramble and heather bent westward. With indignant alarms, gulls retreated into their cliffside holes. Colum's hair lifted like flames in the warm wind of the Morning Star, and he widened his stance to brace himself against the familiar gust. The fog in the valley churned like potato soup stirred in a cauldron. The wind whooshed across the plain, spinning upturned iron wheels and flinging loose shields into the sky. The druids' mist swirled and evaporated, revealing a cadre of confused warriors armed with swords and hawthorn branches. They threw down the now-worthless charms and milled about, dazed.

Fedlimidh's horsemen charged into the wispy remains of the cloud, axes high. Colum turned his face away from the carnage.

Finbar crumpled to the ground, his head buried beneath his hands.

The victors exulted with wild whoops. The vanquished southerners scattered.

Colum dropped his heavy arms and stumbled down the rocky path, craning to glimpse the book-pole.

Overhead, the carrion birds circled in a wide black wreath, swooping in for their spoils. The trees, suddenly alive with ravens, rustled with their hunger. Dark flocks launched with a loud flutter, landing on the bodies that no longer twitched.

Amid the groans of men and the cackle of crows, Colum plodded through the field. The bloody mud sucked at his sandals as he searched for the book. But when he saw the ravens alight on a dead man's head, pecking to steal his soul, he shooed them off and knelt by the body. He dipped his fingers in a puddle and rapidly anointed the dirty forehead while the ravens scolded him.

"*Per istem sanctum unctionem indulgent tibi Dominus quidquid deliquisti amen,*" he muttered. He followed the moans of men, repeating the hurried prayer in the plural. He waved his hand over piles of bodies where the crows fed, chasing them away.

He nearly tripped on a bent-over body, half swallowed by the mud. A boarshead helmet lay next to it with an evil grin, daring the dead man with the fingerless hands to retrieve it. It was Cadoc. His rings had been sliced off.

From the victors' hill came the rhythmic drumming of swords on shields and a joyous chant to the one who led them. He dropped his eyes when he heard their song, "Crim-thann, Crim-thann."

"Crimthann," croaked a voice behind him. "They want you."

Colum whirled about to see Drummon, pressing himself up by one hand. The champion's other hand gripped the hilt of a sword protruding from his side. Blood oozed from the wound over his mud-spattered body. It was his pressure on the hilt that kept the gash closed.

"It's all right," he coughed, rolling up against a tilted wagon wheel. "No, don't try to pull it out. I would have to gather my bowels in my arms like CuChulainn."

"If I dress it—"

"Like CuChulainn," he grunted. He tried to plant his heels into the ground to slide himself up, but the wet dirt squished away.

"Stand me up," he said. He pinched his lips into a determined smile. "I will face my enemies on foot."

"Rest while I get—"

"Stand me up," Drummon repeated, kicking. His bare feet slid in the sanguine mud.

Colum braced the warrior's wet armpits and hoisted him up higher on the wheel. Drummon, pleased, burst into laughter. His side shuddered and spurt a dark liquid. Tears overflowed onto his shaded cheeks.

"Listen to them," he said, his eyes distant. "Your father will be pleased. You will be king now." He clutched his side, and a ghastly pallor clouded his worn visage. His breathing shallowed, became forced, as he sang in short bursts:

> O Cu of grand feats, Unfairly I'm slain!
> Thy guilt clings to me; My blood falls on thee!
> My ribs' armor bursts, My heart is all gore;
> I battled not well, I'm smitten, O Cu!

He flinched, and then assumed a stoic grin. "You remember those lines, eh? Remember this: CuChulainn died because he broke an oath. But I have kept mine. They will make you ki—"

He gagged, and his eyes widened in a fear Colum had never seen in him. "His horse bid him farewell," Drummon said, his eyes roving the plain peppered with ravens. "Where is my horse, Crimthann?" His voice became desperate. "My horse! Crimthann!"

"Crim-thann, Crim-thann!" His cries joined those of the warriors.

163

"Colum, Crimthann, Colum, Crimthann!"

A chorus of voices raised his names, but he could see no one alive around him. Only the scavenger birds, flying into the frowning sky, called as they wrested the spirits of men from earth. The woeful voices echoed in his mind, fading as the birds flew away.

"Colum, don't let them take me!"

"Save me, Colum!"

"Not yet! Not yet!"

"No! Not to there!"

"I am burning!"

"I have sinned! I am sorry!"

"I am sorry!"

It was his own voice, added to the anguished cries which spun in his head, a dizzy maelstrom of moans. His vision blurred with tears as the crows buzzed him with taunts. "See how many you sent to hell! Hell! Hell!" they cawed.

"Do you hear them, Drummon?" he cried, wetting his fingers for unction. "I won't let them take you."

Drummon stared back, the pupils dark and empty.

Colum tore at his red hair and stepped back. His mouth contorted in grief. He retched as the smell of loosened bowels rose into his flared nostrils. His white smock, stained with blotches of Drummon's blood, stuck to his wet skin. He could not shake it loose though he pulled at it over and over. He turned and ran off the field, the sound of his name diminishing in his ears. He vaulted corpses and thought of the stones that would remain in the huge counting pile. He ran until he could no longer hear the laughter of the crows.

■

He cleaned the coracle at the edge of the reedy, shallow waters of Lower Lough Erne. In the wet season, Colum had longer to row through plant-thickened water to reach Molaisse's island retreat of Devenish.

After two hours of pulling against the prevailing northwest wind, he began to wonder if the island had disappeared as its mystical patron was wont to do. But a low green mound, its grass and trees growing down to the water, loomed ahead like a huge turtle surfacing from the weeds.

Colum moored the basketlike boat among the cow lilies tangled in the floating alder roots near a low stone dock. The wading birds, probing in the branches of half-drowned trees, stiffened and watched him anxiously.

He hurried through a grove of twisted hawthorn trees, their wrinkled roots overground and coiling in patterns like the interlaced lines of his manuscripts.

A curlew flapped up, frightened by the tall, loping visitor, giving its high bubbling call. Swallows circled and dipped, drawn to the insects scurrying away from his steps in the moist, luxuriant grass. On the summit, safe from flooding, sat the stone huts, looking like snails asleep in the gray-gold sun.

He approached the center hut, a pitch-roofed oratory without windows. He knelt outside the doorless entry, prostrate, penitent, poised for the words of his confessor to come from the darkness within. Despite the absence of smoke from the ceiling vent, he did not doubt Molaisse sat inside, expecting him. Molaisse would know from the curlew's call and from the subtle shift in the wind from the flight of the sparrows.

He felt the stare of his stern mentor and waited for the invitation to speak. Perhaps it would never come, and he would accept a penance of silence for having spoken and prayed so impetuously, so selfishly. But that would be the least severe of the possibilities. For if Molaisse emulated Finnian's rigorous rule, his terms could be extreme.

Still he prepared to hear it, technically accountable to no one, yet driven to seek the counsel of his teacher. How could he return to Derry and hold the chalice with blood on his hands? He mourned like David, who murdered Uriah to claim a beautiful woman for himself. He had murdered thousands to claim a beautiful book. Using the ancient king's confession, he repeated:

> *Miserere mei, Deus, secundum misericordiam tuam,*
> *Be gracious to me, O God, in Thy true love,*
> *In the fullness of Thy mercy blot out my misdeeds.*
> *Wash away all my guilt and cleanse me from my*
> *sin.*
> *For well I know my misdeeds,*
> *And my sins confront me all the day long.*

"Does the Psalter bring you peace now, when it first brought you to war?" came the gritty voice from inside.

Colum peered in, seeing only the shadow of Molaisse's yew-stick.

"You have heard of it," he said, not surprised.

"Who has not heard of the Battle of the Book," Molaisse replied, "or of the synod called for at Tailte in Meath to excommunicate you for it?"

Colum buried his face in his hands. "Can they do such a thing?"

"Finbar has many friends. But so do you." He shifted inside, mumbling, as though rehearsing what to say. "I have sent Brendan of Birr to intervene and plead for you."

"What can he say? One against so many in the land of my father's enemies?"

"He will say what I instructed him to say."

Colum waited breathlessly to hear the instructions, but Molaisse mumbled again. Colum wondered if he might be praying even as they conversed to avoid anger against his former student, or praying for mercy in meting out a punishment.

Colum whispered his own prayer, beating his breast:

> Cor mundum crea mihi, Deus,
>> Create a pure heart in me, O God,
> And give me a new and steadfast spirit.
>> I will teach transgressors the ways that lead to Thee,
> And sinners shall return to Thee again.
>> O Lord God, my deliverer, save me from bloodshed.

"Is this the penance you truly request?" interrupted Molaisse, sounding hopeful.

"I will do what you say."

"You will do what God says."

He felt slapped. "How can I hear His voice again?" Colum pleaded. "I only hear the voices of the dead."

"Do you remember where you ended the copy of Finbar's book?"

Colum crinkled his brow. Puzzled, he struggled to find a connection. Was Molaisse suggesting that the Psalms themselves prescribed his penance? He wrested the memory from the

166

recesses of his spinning mind and recited the verses he had scribbled before the alarm of the magpies in Finbar's chapel. Somehow he recalled the rich Vulgate version:

> *Cum essent numero pauci,*
> *A small company it was,*
> *Few in number, strangers in that land.*
> *Roaming from nation to nation,*
> *From one kingdom to another.*

The grim conclusion, now clear as quartz crystals and just as sharp, stabbed his heart with grief. He covered his eyes and whispered, "You instructed Brendan to say I would enter exile."

"In exchange for rescinding excommunication," Molaisse said. "Do not weep, my son. See how God has spoken to you through your own hand and mouth. You will journey to other kingdoms as a stranger to teach wanderers the way to the true God who forgives sin, even a sin as great as yours. You will go to claim as many souls for Christ as were lost on the field of battle."

Colum's throat constricted. He fought a stinging in the back of his eyes as the sentence was passed. Regret rippled through him and overwhelmed him. He shuddered uncontrollably like the skewered men on the Plain of Culdrevne. His stomach squeezed, and he felt himself dying to an old self. The dread penance hung on him like a millstone, and he bent forward on his elbows under its weight.

Molaisse's rumbling voice swaddled him as he emerged slowly from the labor of his rebirth. "It is a good thing for the proud to fall into an open and manifest sin, and so become displeasing to themselves. When Peter wept and reproached himself, he was healthier than when he boasted. The psalmist says, 'Fill their faces with shame, and they shall seek Thy name.'"

Colum steadied himself and asked meekly, "Where will I go?"

"You must go until you can no longer see your homeland," said Molaisse. His voice cracked, not with the normal roughness, but in a pang of sadness for his countryman. "You must not see it, not even from a mountaintop. And your feet may never again touch the soil of your native land."

Molaisse cleared his throat, a grinding sound like stone on

dried corn kernels. Though it was normally his way of changing mood or subject, Colum thought Molaisse choked back tears.

With the terms of the penance pronounced, it was time for the penitent to accept the sentence or abdicate his ordination. Yet Molaisse refused to yield to his student's choice, rehearsing his final charge to him with muted mumbles.

Colum rubbed his eyes and concentrated on the dim outline of his soul-friend. He could not sense from Molaisse's unseen expression or position what further requirements he would impose. Humbly, he kept silence, but in his mind he roamed the rough coastline and visualized the green sea. He was steering the wicker wherry with a full sail. He pictured the provisions wrapped in waterproof skins. He thought of Comgall leaving Erin in a ship headed north from Glasnevin. He longed to visit him to seek his comfort and direction, but he groaned to think it would be under the cloud of exile. Could Comgall receive him?

Molaisse tapped his yew-stick, a signal he was ready to speak. "God makes even the wrath of men to praise Him," he said. "And though He may be displeased with your temper, it may come to fulfil His purposes. As you consider where He would lead you, your own kinsmen of DalRiada settled on the edge of Alba need you." His voice turned bitter. "King Brude of the Picts makes war against them. He has taken many heads. And many Christian women for the pleasure of his men."

Colum lifted his head at the mention of the foreign colony. His pulse quickened. "Comgall," he whispered.

"I have seen Comgall," reassured Molaisse. "He has come to me to request prayer and provisions. What he really needs is you."

"After all this, you send me to battle?" Colum asked, incredulous.

"Yours is a spiritual war. But for a member of the royal line to visit DalRiada would encourage them. You are one of them. They are pressed to the sea, but they must not be crushed. You must help them to stay. And to survive." He lowered his voice to a more serious tone. "Then you will go to King Brude and present to him the King of Kings. In this way you may save your people. And meet your penance."

"Why should he receive me?"

"Perhaps he will listen to one born to be High King of Erin."

The title shot through him like a hot spear. He thought of his father, probably confused, embarrassed, pressed by his men to explain how the one they sought to exalt to the throne of Tara humiliated himself by running away. Yet in Molaisse's proposition, there appeared a higher purpose to his privileged bloodline.

He wrinkled his brow in concern over the colonists, people of his own northern tribe now threatened with extinction by the savages whom Finbar feared. With a grimace, he blocked from his thoughts any scenes of atrocities that might ignite his anger. He began to plan a route. Construct a ship in his mind. Outfit and rig it. Select a crew. Consider his approach to a powerful foreign king. What language to learn, what to say. His mind raced with the complexity of bringing the Word to men who ripped open rib cages with their hands.

In his deliberation, he forgot Molaisse waited for him to accept the judgment or not. He paused, folding his hands close to his forehead, taking care to shape his reply in the words of the psalm which so aptly prophesied his destiny.

"'O God,'" he quoted, "'grant me a willing spirit to uphold me. Open my lips that my mouth may proclaim Thy praise.'" He glanced north. "In Alba."

11

BRUDE

A.D. 556

NVISIBLE EXCEPT WHEN CROSSING THE CLOUDED moon, the crows croaked overhead in the indigo sky of Alba, their cries piercing the predawn blackness.

Far below, the Pictish villagers stood in concentric circles outside the boundary of tall, upright totems which ringed the sacred slaughter-stone. Weathered brown skulls necklaced the poles, their empty eyes witness to many a ritual to satisfy the ancient powers.

Broichan the druid, robed in white with a flower garland, checked the horizon. The knife must strike at the first break of sunlight.

He drew a long, patient breath and exhaled slowly through his curved, beaklike nose. The steam rose in front of his deep-set eyes. He scanned the vista over the River Ness aligned to a distant, flame-shaped menhir which helped him calculate the movements of the sun god and moon goddess.

With similar sun-marks scattered over a fifty-mile arc of the Hebrides, Broichan calculated this night as the autumnal equinox. Equal day, equal night. A time between. In his long ship, he had felt the pull of the moon on the tides. By his precise counting of her fickle phases, he knew she would favor the upcoming expedition.

But there was a sacrifice to make to the sun first.

He breathed in and out again with the controlled, deliberate manner he used for everything, especially for measuring the skies. He looked relieved that the inconsistent lunar cycle met his predictions. At least the sun, the Life-Giver, was regular. Punctual. Exact.

He smiled as the sky colored to magentas and violets. The crows called again. Three of them. A good omen.

"Brude, prepare the stakes," he called calmly to his young student.

Brude MacMaelchon cowered beyond the birch totems, clutching white-knuckled to the sharpened markers. Each dawn, his bulging eyes measured the sun's rising at its appointed place, a different spot each day. He marked the important positions as Broichan instructed, noting where the sun reached the northerly extreme in summer and the deep south point in winter. Now he was marking the midway point for the first day of fall.

It would be the first day of his reign as king of the northern Picts. Buck-toothed and barely fifteen, he picked at his smooth cleft chin, searching for beard hairs while waiting for the sun.

As the sky lightened and the scintillating stars began to blink out, the moon set over the distant promontory of the mull. The upper rim showed in the notch as it dipped behind the purple hills in its sloping path.

But Brude was not watching it.

Behind his white-robed teacher squatted two black-haired druidesses, each holding a goose with its bill tied shut. The nude women, streaked with blue clay and scarred with tattoos everywhere, also watched for the first fingers of the sun god climbing over the edge of the earth. Brude followed the black-and-blue etchings in their skin — fanciful birds across their shoulders, fearsome beasts down their narrow backs, flowering vines laced down their legs, flaming suns circling their breasts. When the women moved, their tattoos came alive. Brude watched the designs dance on Ainu, the taller woman, who cradled her goose on one knee and calmed it with a kissing noise. Brude stirred with the sound and the sight of her thick-lipped, generous mouth.

"Place the stake there," ordered Broichan.

Brude snapped away from Ainu and scurried to the spot. He blew on his hands and pounded the point into the sod.

"Bring the king," ordered Broichan.

The villagers shuffled. Muted whispers sounded like crinkled cornstalks in a winter breeze. Coughs and hacks rose here and there. The geese struggled. Like so many other animals confiscated by the druids, they would be given to welcome a new season. Some were slain to bring rain, to repulse invaders, to increase harvest.

But this year, the ground yielded gourds, not grain. Even the potatoes failed. A diet of eels and gulls from Loch Ness kept the people alive. But sunken cheeks and groaning bellies testified to the resistance of the soil. Without invoking the proper forces, they would soon be eating the horses and the dogs. Broichan, the Wise One, Knower of the Sun's Secrets, had made this plain. The signs were unmistakable.

So the king must die.

This ancient way of the People of the Long Night sent the king to the Otherworld to personally plead for the restoration of the tribe's fortunes. As the gods would have it, the druid's foster son, Brude, was ready to assume the chair of power, being at the end of his formal training. A time between.

No longer a boy, not yet a man, Brude stood chattering from the September chill and from the dread anticipation of the knife's plunge. His knees wobbled when he watched the druidesses stand, ogling their sensuous sway.

The murmur of the crowd tore his eyes away. The king walked through the crowd, the people flowing from his path like water before a prow. Most eyes closed in respect, but Brude's eyes popped like a frightened rabbit's. The king glanced his way, and Brude lowered his head, because the king must die.

The chieftain came to stand before Broichan on the round stone embedded in the earth. Tall, unafraid, looking straight ahead, the king reminded Brude of his own father far away in Anglesey. Maelchon, Dragon of the South Islands, agreed to this fosterage under Broichan with a view to extending his grip on the North Islands. Brude shivered with the realization that the kingship would pass to him in just a few moments, far earlier than he had thought. For the king must die.

The king allowed two warriors to strip his cloak and strap

his wrists behind his naked back. He stood sturdy as a megalith, his broad frame outlined by the blood-red sky, now brightening to pink. A round silver medallion, etched with the unending lines of eternity, caught the light and glowed against the king's chest.

Broichan swung his knife hand in a slow circle, signifying the cycle of life and rebirth. His throaty chant joined the song of the crows:

> By Belanos, by fire-of-sun,
>   Spilling life from the horizon,
> By Macha whose messengers circle overhead,
>   Spilling life, the royal red,
> Though he die, the essence fly
>   To plead our case among the dead.

The druid's circular swing sped up. Brude's breathing sped up with it. The first glint of sunlight flashed on the blade as it drilled into the king's abdomen.

The king dropped to his knees. His eyes shut hard as the bowels spilled to the stone. Brude snapped his eyes closed, squeezing out tears which traced silver streaks over his gaunt cheeks. There was now only the sound of the throttled geese, flapping briefly in the struggle on the stone as Broichan sliced their bellies open. When Brude dared to blink away the stinging tears and look again, Broichan was poking the entrails with his hazel-wood staff, comparing them thoughtfully with the king's. The gold dust he had fed them sparkled in faint round patterns, draining off in the stone's spokelike grooves.

Broichan led the druidesses in a sunwise circuit of the convulsing king. Broichan studied his jerking motions. When the spasms stopped, Broichan bent down to the lifeless chest. He fingered the medallion. He followed the intricate lines with his pointed fingernails before yanking it free from the neck. Flanked by the druidesses, Ainu and Dana, their blue lips curved into crescent smiles, Broichan approached Brude.

Shaking, Brude stepped forward and stooped. His foster father tied the medallion around his thin neck, and then cawed to the crowd, "The gods have spoken. Brude MacMaelchon is king."

■

As the orange sun neared the end of its daily circuit, Brude resisted a return to the stone circle for the sunset measuring. He knew that Broichan, always fastidious, would not excuse any tardiness. Still he leaned listlessly on the rough timber rampart of his hillside fortress overlooking the rugged beauty of the hills which ringed Inverness, a wilderness of fragrant spruce and larch. He sniffed it in and sensed a fishy odor from the snaking flow of the River Ness below. The wide waterway linked a chain of firths and lakes, visible for many leagues, which connected the North Sea and the far-west Atlantic. His bulging eye traced the silvery water route through the hills and hollows of the Great Glen that split the Pictish kingdoms. How long a trip it had been from Wales to the Caledonian capital ten years before when his Pictish mother's tartaned warriors guided him to his foreign fosterage.

His mother's corn-complexioned champion, Baru, guarded him from a distance. Visible from the corner of Brude's puffy eye, Baru paced at his post like a caged bear. His veins wrapped around his muscles like ropes. His fair hair hung long, loose, and lice-ridden. His woolly skirt looked as if it had come from a mammoth, the hairs bushy and crimped. Like the rest of his stern, silent troop, he went barefoot and half-naked in all seasons, exposing a fearsome menagerie of tattooed beasts, purple-black with red eyes.

Baru gripped a small, square wood shield with a lead boss over the handles. His stone-tipped spear, weighted to the ground with a knob at the butt end, would be banged tonight at the bonfires with a terrible noise. Brude hoped the heavy spear would also keep the dead king's champion in check and discourage him from usurping his new position. He worried even though Broichan had the spells and Baru had the spears to secure his power.

He rolled his eyes, uneasy. Turning to the dark loch, he watched fishermen dock their tarred coracles among the craggy cliffs that dropped directly into the lake from the ramparts above. It was a formidable fall, dizzying, and he turned from the sight of men hurrying to ascend in time for the bonfires.

Brude rubbed the silver medallion lying on his hairless

chest. The tattoos of manhood stained his skin a dark blue, making the medallion appear brighter. At last he wore the emblem owed him through his mother's line. Though thin, it felt heavy, and he could not tell if its warmth was from his own finger's friction on it or the life of the former king still throbbing within it.

His stomach jumped as he realized he stood in shadow. The sun! He mustn't miss the measurements. He spun around, cheeks sunken with dread, making his swollen eyes bulge all the more.

Broichan stood there, facing him.

Baru, spear ready, watched the wizard suspiciously. He could say nothing to warn Brude of his approach since no one could speak before a druid without punishment.

"What do you see, Brude?" came the druid's liquid voice.

Brude caught his breath and tensed. He had heard no sound of his foster father's entry, no squeak of plank or tread of step. He feared he'd been watched a long time. Perhaps the magician could vaporize, transport, and re-form as the villagers said. Or enter the bodies of wolves and birds and even the pines which formed the very walls. *I am late,* he thought, *and he's come to fetch me.*

"Look at me when I speak to you, Brude. You are a man now," said the ArchDruid.

"I see nothing, Father," said Brude.

"Nothing?" Broichan arched his velvety eyebrows. "I don't think so. You see the past."

"As clearly as you see the future, Father."

"They are the same." The druid joined Brude at the wall. He stood a full head over the teenaged king. Baru followed him with low-browed eyes, his hammerlike fists tight on the spear shaft.

Broichan leaned on his hazel staff, a more powerful weapon. He looked between the pointed stakes over the darkening valley. "Do you grieve for him, the king?"

"No," said Brude, uncertain.

"Do you fear for yourself?"

"No, Father."

"Why not?"

Brude's palms dampened, but he tried to look confident. "Because you have done all required to please the powers of earth and underearth." He looked at the medallion, polished to a high gloss by his day-long rubbing. "And the king pleads for us. He was brave."

"He did not fear death, Brude," said Broichan, checking the sky. "Nor will you."

Brude's throat went suddenly dry as old straw.

"Our life does not end," continued Broichan. "It changes. It returns. It passes between the worlds easily, and the end is always a beginning." He bent forward on the staff and bore into Brude's wide eyes. The boy's brow broke into beads of nervous sweat. He felt that at any moment the druid might disembody and enter him through his dilating pupils, bringing a cadre of spirits with him to build nests in his innermost parts, anchored and intertwined around his deepest fears, never to be extracted.

"Let us go to the Stone," said Broichan.

Brude followed his foster father down the plank steps to the spacious courtyard. Baru trailed them, the thump of the spear heavy on the steps. The sound turned the heads of men and women piling dry willow branches into carts.

A squatting woman with her wide skirt bundled up finished passing water and stared at the new king with a frown. Goats with bells clattered out from the wretched cottages mortared to the fortress walls. Children in goatskins chased them around the upright stone slabs posted around the central well. The eyes of the bulls, boars, snakes, and sea beasts carved into the stones seemed to study him.

At the gates, a party of druids waited, hands tucked in their droopy sleeves. Barefoot and bareheaded, the shaven foreheads dotted with tattoos, they fell in behind Broichan and Brude, whispering ancient chants to Balor, the one-eyed god of darkness. The druidesses, wrapped in white wool, carried crackling torches.

Baru stopped at the gate, forbidden to witness the secrets of the Stone Circle. Grim-faced and snorting, he ordered the gate shut. The guards grunted and pushed until the iron bolts thudded into place.

Brude heard the clank of the gate behind him and bit his fingers. In the woods near the cliffs, with only druids and their willow-wands for weapons, Brude jerked his head towards any unusual sound. When he reached the Stone, he gathered his sharp marking-sticks and held them like knives.

He watched for Broichan's instructions. Only the Wise One knew the exact time, for magic worked in the in-between. Between day and night, wake and sleep, life and death.

Brude watched the golden sunrays fall on the brown blood spots, while Broichan dropped a limestone chip into a nearby hole. By keeping tally of the nights, he ordered the calendar, regulating the times of harvests and sowings. By counting the moon shapes, he predicted the neap tides of the quarter phase and spring tides of the new and full. At winter solstice, with sun and moon in line, especially high tides would threaten the fishermen, seal hunters, and raiders. No one else could predict the motions of the capricious currents. Only Broichan knew. Brude squinted at the sky, searching for lucky stars, but he did not know which to look for. Only Broichan knew.

"Now," Broichan cawed, "over there."

Brude planted the stake, again a diameter and a half from the previous day's mark.

Broichan rubbed his clean chin with a thoughtful pout as a pattern took obvious form. A rectangle of stakes for the sun-moon lines distorted to a pushed-over parallelogram, crossing the circle of sunrise stakes.

The ArchDruid considered this for a moment. Then, with the others of his retinue, he raised an incantation to the orange disc as it bedded below the horizon. Brude rubbed his palms, thinking of Broichan's pout. Had he misplaced the markers? He kept his eye on the circle of stakes. Perfect, precise, ethereal, eternal, the circle enclosed the maximum area for a fixed length of boundary. The radius marked off six chords, being the curve of the apex of a right triangle, the perimeter of six touching equilaterals, with all sectors of the perimeter having equal curvature. Broichan's teaching echoed in his head; the circle was a hymn to the sun's divine symmetry.

But the moon reminded Brude of life's irregularities. It did not follow a single path, he remembered, but oscillated side to side. Moving from extreme north to extreme south in two weeks compared to the sun's six months, it edged farther north and south each year, repeating a horizon-skimming pattern every nineteen years — the sacred moonswing. Brude tried to count by sight the number of counting-holes filled with white limestone chips. The magical kiss of the moon upon earth was near. A few more years, a few more holes — he shuddered. What could it portend? He could not tell. His training only took him to the edge of the ancient secrets. Only Broichan knew.

With the ceremonies complete, Broichan turned to other sidereal interests — measuring Sirius-rise and locating the Five Wanderers. As dusk turned to dark, Broichan motioned Brude back to the fortress to prepare for the bonfires. The druidesses led the way, torches high.

"Tonight you will truly be king," Broichan said. "Your mother would be pleased."

Brude fingered his medallion. "Am I not king now?"

"You must have more than the medallion on your chest. You must have men under your feet. When the chieftains hear that you rule Inverness, they will find a relative to claim the kingship. A cousin, perhaps, with no foreign father, as yours is."

Brude heard disdain in the voice. He avoided Broichan's eyes and asked, "What must I do?"

"Attack and subdue them before they attack you."

"But I am my mother's oldest son!" Brude whined. "How dare they challenge me."

"But they will. So you must have hostages to secure your claim. It is not enough to have the name of the king, Brude."

"Hostages from where?"

"Everywhere from the Orkneys in the north to DalRiada in the south. From anyone who may not acknowledge you."

"But the men of DalRiada are so far away. They are no threat to us."

Broichan glared at him. "They are the worst threat of all," he hissed.

When they reached the pathway along the cliffs leading to the fortress, Broichan stopped and pointed south with his hazel-stick.

"If you ignore the invaders of DalRiada, they will grow and drive a wedge between you and your mother, between north and south. You cannot allow it. The intruders must be subdued."

"Why do you call them invaders, Father? They have been there for over a hundred years."

Broichan pulled up his hood. "They must be rooted out like thistles."

"But they speak our language," he clicked, "and they have Wise Ones, like yourself."

Broichan jabbed his stick into the dirt so hard it nearly snapped. "They are imposters. They wear the hair and robes of Wise Ones, but have no knowledge of the powers of the sun or moon."

Brude, startled by his sternness, lowered his head. DalRiada was a subject that somehow crossed his foster father. Brude wondered why. His own father, Maelchon of Anglesey, had friendly relations with the DalRiads for many years. Being so near, Maelchon had even allowed the priests of the god Christos to teach Brude's Saxon cousins. Could his father have been so wrong?

Broichan edged closer to him, making no sound on the gravel. "You have learned history well, my son," said the druid, "but there are other things to learn if you wish to prosper the clan." The wizard spoke in a more secretive tone. "Nothing is free. In everything, there is an exchange. Life for life. The grass dies to give life to the cow. The cow dies to give life to the king. The king dies to give life to the tribe, for his rank equals the power of many. His buried body gives life to the herbs. The herbs are burned, and their life is released in exchange for the future to be revealed. If you were in training to be a der-wydd, you would share the sacred knowledge of the balance of forces to make the proper exchanges. But even as king, you must make these exchanges. Do you understand?"

Brude's mind raced. He felt he had angered his foster father on the matter of DalRiada. It was not a good way to begin his reign. It was a good way to shorten it. He looked south over his shoulder as they reached the stockade, the dark, pointed timbers looking like the bared teeth of a cornered carnivore. "Life for life," he said. "I will call a council of war at once."

Broichan smiled. "You will do well as king."

■

Brude shifted his sore buttocks on the oaken throne of the council chamber. The wolf's head slipped down again over his eyes, and he tried hard not to sneeze from the oiled hairs which fell into his face. The teeth dug into his scalp. The stiff fur piece bunched behind his back, and the fierce claws, draped over his shoulders, itched his chest. As he pushed the jaw of the wolf higher on his brow, he saw the last of the warriors leave the room. They carried the druidesses' torches to light the bonfire and begin the night-long frenzy for raiding. The cattle and goats would pass between the blazes, then the warriors caked with clay dyed with blue woad. Already there were shouts and hoots outside as Baru led the men in curses and insults against the king of Orkney. The thick spear butts began to thump on the shields, mustering the men and matching Brude's heartbeat.

Two lights, bunches of twisted flax soaked in tallow, flickered on the wall. Broichan glided through the smoke to face Brude's seat. Ainu and Dana materialized behind the ArchDruid as if conjured from the smoke. Their white cloaks shimmered with patterns from the fireglow. Brude averted their coy looks and fixed on his foster father. Broichan looked deep in thought, weighing options, calculating.

"You spoke well," he said. "In three days, you will have a good store of meat and hostages from Orkney as pledges of fealty. Then you will warn the kings of Dinwall, Elgin, and DalRiada to volunteer hostages for your court. You will give them privileges, and they will enter my schooling. You will specify a tribute. If payment should fail, you will behead the hostages."

Brude paled. "If they refuse to send any?"

Broichan arched a brow. "We take them, of course," he said, scratching his hooked nose. "Now go to the fires. I go to the oak grove to raise a favorable wind. The tides are already with us."

He pivoted and passed between the women who closed rank and followed him to the door as if in tow. They padded across the room soundlessly on their bare callused feet. At the door, Ainu turned abruptly and locked her cloudy green eyes with Brude's. She licked her blue lips hungrily, and then slipped out into the hall behind Broichan. Brude felt a tightening between his legs, not of desire but of fear.

■

With the fires long faded, Brude tossed sleeplessly beneath the sealskins. The drumming, chanting, bleating, and lowing reverberated in his colorless dreams.

The bolt to his chamber clicked. Brude rose on his elbows with a start. He tried to blink away his bad dream, but still he saw a dark spectral shape in the room.

Ainu the druidess stood in the moon-blue light, two mistletoe clusters in her hands.

"Why are you here?" Brude whispered after a deep, dry swallow.

"Broichan sent me," she said in an oily voice.

"What for? Is it time for the sunrise measure?"

"You need not do it anymore."

Ainu slithered out of her gown like a serpent shedding its skin. Brude quaked as she pulled his covers down and lay the small berried branches by his bare hips.

"Don't be afraid," she purred. "This night you are wed to the earth through me."

She pressed her pointed fingernails into his chest as a cat steadies its prey.

Brude gulped for air and fainted.

■

He awakened to the bitter smell of crushed mistletoe. A soft light filled the bedchamber like a mist, and as he rubbed the sleep from his swollen eyes, he trembled. The prickly leaves convinced him that Ainu's visit was real. He examined his body, checking for scars. Just a few light scratches from the leaves and the sharp fingernails. Had he breathed his essence into her mouth without meaning to? Were their spirits merged? Had she taken a part of him as hostage so that he was now, more than before, subject to the wizards? He cursed himself for losing consciousness, and then chilled as he heard the thump of Baru's spear outside.

The champion kicked open the door and advanced to the bed, two helmeted warriors close behind. They pulled Brude from the sealskins and propped the shivering boy upright. Wide-eyed, Brude choked on his words to plead for his life. But as he gawked at their sheathed swords, they dressed him in battle gear which they had brought, working with such a steady precision that they seemed under orders. Before Brude found his voice, they laced on his leather cuirass, strapped on shin guards, buckled a sword belt, clipped on a scabbard, and pressed a bronze helmet a size too large on his head.

181

The pungent smell of the horses in the courtyard fully awakened him. The warriors hoisted their king onto a mare's back. Brude's quivering legs slipped against the beast's silky sides. The horse, sensing his awkwardness, stamped and tossed its head, but whispering warriors calmed her, and Brude held on.

The fat iron bolts of the front gates squeaked through their latches, pulled by brawny men with the arms of seasoned blacksmiths. They pushed with loud grunts, muscles strained and bulging. The heavy plank doors yawned open.

Baru came alongside the king and motioned him forward. Brude kicked his heels into the mare's side. In passing through the gates to the outside, he left the smells of cooking fat and waste and drank in the fresh pine and heather. A cottony mist hugged the Highland mountain tops.

Far below in the dark water bobbed several ships, their high prows carved into angry serpents' heads. Iron lances and leather shields lined the tar-smeared sides, and the oars stuck out over the water like stiff millipedes' legs. When Brude came into the view of the sailors, and the soldiers around him raised their swords, the beach resounded with cheers. Bug-eyed, Brude wondered how the ships could have been prepared so quickly overnight, armed and provisioned for a raid.

Broichan, he thought. *He had planned this for a long time. He had measured the tides and even provided the wind.* A cool breeze whistled under his helmet.

Brude watched the men splash into the boats, unlock the oar handles, and man the riggings. As they stamped on the decks, Brude's heart drummed with the rhythm. He felt a new confidence, and he sat up higher in the saddle, careful not to slip. *Perhaps Broichan sent Ainu after all,* he mused, *to put a bold spirit in me.*

At the draw of his sword, he would send the ships carving their way through the choppy bay. Pumped by battle frenzy, pulled by the smell of women, pushed by a druid's breath, the men would kill for him and charge the walls of determined defenders. All he had to do was raise his arm, and the king of Orkney would be humbled, and all the Great Glen west to the Isle of Skye would know that Brude rules. The rush of excitement made him slightly faint, but he gripped the reins and lowered a shaking hand to the sword hilt. *Where is Broichan? Didn't he want to see me deliver my first order as king? Is he at the Stone Circle, still working to raise the wind?*

Brude squeezed his hand over the cold iron handle, pulled, and jabbed at the clouds. The roar of the raiders hurt his ears. He kept the arm up while the boats pushed off and the oars dipped in unison. The yardarms loosened their leathern sails.

When the ships were lost in the glare of the green sea, Brude lowered his aching arm. He replaced the sword, missing the scabbard twice. He tugged at the reins, and to his delight the great beast turned about. He grinned as the warriors followed his cue and circled round to face the fortress.

Brude's arm, at first numb, now burned with pins and needles. He frowned in discomfort and whimpered to himself softly. *Where was Broichan? Why didn't he watch me? After all the years of teaching and prompting, why couldn't he be there to see me do something right? Why couldn't he see me act like a king? Did he have to stay at the Stone Circle for so long?*

From his mount, he could peer through the bramble and see the birch pillars, Broichan's celestial clock. No, Broichan was not to be seen with the two druidesses there. Brude saw only three crows pecking at the head of yesterday's king, which had now joined the other skulls clicking in the wind.

12
DUNADD
A.D. 563

HE SUN DID NOT RISE EASTER MORNING. A SOMBER SKY wept over the chapel of Derry where Abbot Columcille led the monks in observing their most solemn feast. The pure alb vestments, the bright white of the cross-shaped patens, the shining linens and laces, the banks of lily-scented candles, and the daisy-filled baskets failed to cheer the men. For their beloved abbot had chosen Easter for exile.

He tried to encourage them in the homily, his voice low and comforting. "Our most blessed day celebrates a rising, not a dying," he said, "a beginning, not an end."

But in the meal that followed, rich with sweetmeats and honeybreads, even he tasted only ashes and gall.

He left the mead untouched and circulated among the tables. He gave long, silent hugs and lock-handed squeezes to his men. He whispered his last exhortations and endearments at each table in turn, his sleeves dark with their tears. His lips trembled when he prayed with his palms on their heads, but the voice was calm and deep.

Looking on in silence, mouthing the same psalms, sat twelve men appointed to accompany him in imitation of Christ's mission. They dressed for travel in bad weather — white tunics overlaid with long garments of milk-colored wool, tightly woven for waterproofing, with large hoods. The Derrymen were barefoot, but the travelers wore shoes of hide, suitable for rocky shores.

Colum recruited each man for the special skill he could bring to the mission. The leather bags at their feet contained the implements of their trade, soon to be packed with the other provisions in the boat. Colum glanced up at each in turn and bade the brothers to uphold them in prayer.

Baithene, the abbot's scholarly foster son, carried the knives to shape quills, while his brother Cobthach bore the only sword.

Ernan, Colum's uncle, knew the sea lanes of the Hebrides and the paths of migratory birds.

Diormit, a personal attendant, guarded the gilded chalice, a thick-stemmed cup with interlacing ribbon designs delicately carved into the rim. He had once joked about how close his name sounded to Diarmait, deposed king of Tara. But the tormented look he received from the abbot rebuked him, and he never mentioned it again.

Rus and Fechno, sons of Rodan and cousins of the abbot, held the bags of corn seed from Durrow, that school's parting gift.

Luguid the miller was keeper of the cauldrons.

Scandal the smith packed thongs, hammer, and fireflints.

Echoid and Tochannu, a king's son, brought skills in herding and husbandry, being handy with hides and skins.

One duty remained. Colum ended his rounds with Cainnech. The thin monk, yellow-faced as a scarecrow, cast his eyes down, refusing to acknowledge the moment.

Without a word, Colum tugged off his ring, lifted Cainnech's unresisting hand, and slipped the ring over his knotty knuckle.

The watching brothers bowed their heads in Cainnech's direction, recognizing Colum's choice.

Cainnech stood, his palms together, the joined thumbs pressed against his pointed nose. He tried to smile.

"Brothers," he said, clearing his throat, "God Almighty called Father Abraham out of his country away from his kin to go to a place, he knew not where. By faith, Abraham obeyed. By faith, he settled in an alien land, which God promised to give him. So by faith, Father Columcille goes to an alien land," the thin voice stumbled but continued, "where God will give him many souls."

The refectory door creaked open. A tall brother entered

discreetly and shook from his cloak the tiny crystals of drizzle beaded on the wool. He pulled back his hood, his carrot-colored hair tussled by the stiff breeze on the lough.

Colum looked up, wet-eyed. "Is it time, Grilaan?"

The freckled man nodded. "The clouds are breaking up."

Colum hoped for the reassuring gap-toothed smile he remembered from their boyhood, but Grilaan's mouth was set in a severe line. He was aware of the import of his message.

The abbot glanced to Cainnech, bidding him to go on.

"I am finished," said Cainnech.

Colum gathered up his bulky book bags over his shoulders. He kissed his right forefinger and touched the little square chrysmal which hung from his neck, containing a blessed Host from the morning service and a pinch of soil. "It is time then," he said.

The men processed out, donning hoods against the light rain. In single file, they followed the abbot over the riverside path leading to the lough, joining his determined call-and-answer song.

"*Qui descendant mare in navibus*, others there are who go to sea in ships."

"And make their living on the wide waters."

"These men have seen the acts of the Lord."

"And His marvelous doings in the deep."

"They were glad that all was calm."

"As He guided them to the harbor they desired."

■

In the long, freshly-caulked curragh, a large-muscled monk tightened the leather straps which laced the hardened hides to the gunwale. His white habit, hiked around the waist while he worked, sparkled with raindrops. The boat swayed with the incoming wash, and he steadied himself on the oak mast stepped in the middle of the rowseats.

"Is it ready, Siaran?" called the abbot from the stone dock.

The curly haired carpenter slapped the mast. "I've never made a better."

He offered a hand, but the experienced abbot let himself into the boat. When his foot left Erin's soil, a loud lamentation arose from the men. They knelt on the rocks, unashamed of their open grief. Some gathered up the stones he had touched and clasped them closely. Colum kept his back to them, not quite ready to say his final farewell. He feigned a check of the supplies as the crewmen took their places at the oars. His eyes filled while counting items of husbandry, fishhooks, the two sacks of barley and oats, the two goatskin bottles with milk and water, wax-coated wood tablets, and a box of metal graibs. Satisfied, he told the men to cover the cargo and secure bags under the seats.

Grilaan unwound the rigging of the quadrangular sail which was bound to a high yardarm. With the sail pulled up, Colum thought the mast looked like a giant cross he was carrying to the Picts.

Grilaan handed Colum the halyard cords which would let the leather sail fall and drive the boat forward. Colum tugged the hemp ropes. The sail fell and filled. The curragh jerked ahead.

Colum positioned the sail on the lee side, trimming to the wind at his back. The sighing breezes snapped the sail, and the slanting drizzle speckled it with dark spots. The oars dipped and pulled. The curragh creaked out to open water.

Colum made fast the ropes, with a finger on them to sense the windshifts, and then he turned in farewell to Derry. He crossed the air and lifted his chin for the men weeping on the dock, but he bowed when he saw Cainnech prostrate on the stones.

The wicker wherry foamed through the low whitecaps. Overhead the gulls mourned. Swift gannets hovering over the boat swooped by in salute, unlike the gulls, making no sound. Crying kittiwakes beat low over the water towards their nesting young in the clefts high above the sea. Colum followed their flight up the steep ledges, savoring each sight and smell. Burrowing rabbits scurried into frozen formation, paws up, as he passed. The deep green grasses waved to him, and the first yellow blooms winked from crops of spiky gorse bushes. At the crest of the cliff, another creature bade him good-bye.

Angel Wing, old but hardy, drooped his head to the ground. It was not just any horse feeding; he knew from the distinctive swish of the tail. And he knew from the figure astride the beast, a bent woman in a flowing white cape.

Eithne stretched out her arms and called, but the words melted in the wind. Colum tried to call out, but his throat clogged with regret. Although in his winter visit he had exchanged all the words necessary, seeing her now made him yearn for the feel of her fox-pelt hair and the stroke of her wrinkled hands on his head.

Through the drizzle, he saw that she was not alone. From behind, another horse appeared, its husky rider erect and proud. The wide antlers of his helmet stood out against the glare of the gray sky.

Colum choked and spun his face forward. The sting of the breaking spray over the prow felt as hot as the salty tears burning his cheeks.

The oars plunged and pulled in hard strokes to reach the golden clearing ahead where the sunrays pointed the way to the Atlantic. His sea legs steady, bending with the tug of each slap of wood in water, Colum looked aft and vented his anguish in a tight-throated dirge. The words poured out loudly as his chest heaved to the beat of the oars:

> How swift the speed of my curragh,
>> Its stern turned upon Derry.
> I grieve at my errand over the noble sea,
>> Sailing to Alba of the ravens.
> Large is the tear of my soft gray eye
>> When I look back to Erin.
> There is a gray eye
>> Which looks back and gazes,
> It shall never again see
>> Erin's men, Erin's women.

The figures on the clifftop faded from sight. Colum swallowed hard and worked the ropes as if they were a horse's reins.

The curragh cut across the choppy lough, passing Moville and slicing into the open sea while the stony clouds above rolled back like the round rock of the empty Easter tomb.

■

Colum leaned his elbows on the cold drystone wall ringing the king's terrace at DunAdd, capital of DalRiada. He looked over the precipitous crags to the serpentine River Add flowing into the Sound of Jura. The water, rippled by wind and slashed by diving ducks, foamed at the edges.

"Look down, Diormit," he called to his attendant. "The boat is a mere sliver from up here."

Diormit waddled closer to the wall, his out-turned feet reluctant. "Please, Father, the heights, they scare me so."

Colum smiled with understanding and turned back to the vista. "As you wish," he said. "But how will you get along in God's heaven which is much higher?"

"I'll keep my eyes on God's throne," said Diormit.

Colum shared his chuckle, and then breathed deeply. His chest filled like a sail in a summer breeze, light and free. He leaned back in a relaxing stretch. Above and all around him in a sky blue as the Virgin's cloak busy birds rode the fresh May winds. Fulmars, razorbills, and guillemots noisily tended their nests in the cliffs of the Kintyre coastline. From the crevices and ledges, a clamor arose of herring gulls, gannets, petrels, and oystercatchers as the crying, crowded birds protected their tiny territories. Some dashed from their holes, black streaks diving to the ice-blue waters, hunting for fish. Colum's white robes fluttered in the wind like the gulls' wings, and he lifted his arms to imitate them. The floating gulls laughed with Diormit.

"Would you be one of them and fly?" asked the servant.

"Straight to Erin if I could."

The gulls waved their wings, looking as though they'd dipped them in ink; then they steered away to steal eggs from unguarded nests. Colum waved back to them.

"I think they're the same ones that escorted us up the sound," he said.

"They all look the same to me, Father."

"Perhaps their ancestors guided Fergus when he came here." He studied the stone citadel carved into the huge rocks. "They say Fergus had seawater for blood, and I can't think of any other reason he'd want to come here."

He measured the steep gray rocks which leaped abruptly from the waters below. Fergus MorMacErc and his small band of Irish settlers had made the whole mountain an impenetrable dun sixty years before. Fergus chose his site well, Colum observed. The craggy heights culminated in twin tops. The north cone looked bare as a sharply bent knee. But this south peak, a high hog-backed ridge, featured mosses and grasses sprinkled with broom and bluebells, with clusters of larch and pine.

The stone fortress, accessible only by a winding path of steps cut into the cliff, mounted two rocky outcrops. The upper cliffs were crowded with houses made of fragrant Caledonian pine. The resins and smoke of the curing houses competed with the fishy stink of the bird colonies.

The lower cliffs were walled as a keep, with three connected but separately defended forts. The patrolling warriors, as alert and evenly spaced as the cliffbirds lining the ledges, enjoyed a fine view of the flat approaches across the peninsula. From the Sound of Jura, across the moors to Loch Fyne, an enemy would be exposed. The only attackers today were the brown goats pulling at the scurvy grass. The thick-leafed succulent padded the lowest ramparts, and Colum thought the stubborn plant would be the only thing capable of scaling the thick walls. *Fergus knew back then how savage the Picts could be,* he mused. *They still are. It is why the king wishes me to stay.*

He looked longingly to the distant gray shadows of Erin's Antrim Range. *Fergus chose to come here,* he sighed. *How could he leave the clover-green pastures, the tall oaks, the music of the swans?* The chattering birds led his eyes back to the guano-spattered cliffs. Despite the rugged majesty of the Alban peaks, clothed in ermine clouds and perfumed at their feet with patches of primrose, DunAdd and its land looked barren to him. He shook off the despondency as he heard Comgall's sandals slapping on the stones behind him.

"Father, it's Brother Comgall," said Diormit gently as if waking him.

Colum brushed his windblown hair behind his ears and turned with a smile. "You're back sooner than I expected."

Comgall panted from the long climb. "The king is here to see you as you asked." His inquisitive face, lined with worry, searched Colum's eyes.

"Then show him in," said Colum. The wind played again with his copper hair, and he grinned to suppose the outdoor terrace to be his oratory.

"Have you decided?" asked Comgall, holding his chest.

"I'm sorry, Comgall, I can only tell the king. Please call him."

"You've decided not to stay, haven't you? I should have known when you arrived with twelve and not twelvescore men."

"Call my cousin, Comgall," said Colum. "He is waiting."

Comgall's face fell, disappointed that his old friend would not entrust his thoughts in advance. Colum stood tall, smiling and silent, aware of the protocol of positioning when negotiating. No matter how close their friendship, he must bypass Comgall and speak to his host as one king to another.

Comgall disappeared down the stone steps and returned quickly with a party of brown-cloaked warriors who attended the Fifth King of DalRiada.

The king kicked his long cape as he mounted the terrace and approached his cousin from Erin. The glossy otterskins fringing the neck and hems of his garments rustled with his dignified strides. His tunic, bright with royal colors, sported fine ribbon designs. A thin gold headband and noble's torque announced his kingship and kinship with Ulster's ruling clans. He wore a glad face beneath his frosted hair.

"Cousin Columcille, tell me what you have decided." They embraced, and the king bent his berry lips to Colum's upraised ringless knuckles.

"Walk with me," said Colum, pivoting. The king followed.

Comgall and Diormit folded their hands in prayer for opposite outcomes.

"I cannot stay," said Colum, watching the gulls. "And I cannot lead your men against the Picts."

The king shook his head. "We are your kinsmen," he protested. "Everyone has lost a family member. To have a son of the Hy Neill go before them would give them new courage."

"But, Cousin, I do plan to go before them. I plan to go into Pictland with my own men."

The king huffed. "Are you still so proud, you think you can save DalRiada by yourself? Twelve monks against all the Picts?"

Colum placed a calming hand on the king's shoulder. "Not twelve," he said. "I was thinking of taking only three."

"Three!" It was almost a shout.

"To Brude's capital."

"You are no longer proud, you are mad. Brude is very powerful, and he hates men of Erin."

"God is more powerful, and He loves men of Pictland."

The king's mouth turned down in a lemony look. "You never saw the mutilated bodies. Or heard the cries of our daughters being carried away in the night. You never collected the heads of friends to give them proper burial. And you want to go to Brude and tell him his sins are forgiven?" The voice broiled. "Do you expect him to let you approach freely? Give up his druids who have gotten him victory over all of Alba?" His pleasant face, now pained, flared a troubled crimson.

"I will not abandon you, my cousin," Colum reassured, "and I will not let my people of DalRiada be wiped out. God willing, I hope to bring many of Brude's people into the kingdom of God. But what I also propose to you is a diplomatic mission. To secure our borders. Free our women."

The king considered this with a suspicious frown, scratching his hot neck. "Why should he listen to you? He has nothing to gain from meeting you, except perhaps another hostage. And a royal one at that. You realize the danger of it?"

"There is more danger for you if I do not go," said Colum. "And I believe he has much to gain. I will offer him the gospel of peace. Along with seed, tools, and teaching to improve his farming and husbandry. Comgall tells me these have been lean years. That the Picts have raided as much for food as they have for captives and treasures."

"That's true," admitted the king. "And what they don't take, they burn."

Colum remembered seeing the blackened fields. "If they raid so much for food, it may be a sign that their farms are still in trouble. Brude will have less faith in his druids, and he may be more open to negotiating."

Colum could see the king struggling with the idea, rearranging his hopes that the royal-born monk would inspire his men in battle.

"Cousin," said Colum, stopping at the north wall and staring into the green-gray hills, "God has called me to preach to the Picts. I will go with or without your blessing. I will go on your behalf, or only for the sake of the High King of Heaven. I will go with twelve or three or alone with God, but I will go." He let the wind dry his eyes, and then turned his face, serene yet stern, to the king.

The king paused, squeezed his eyes, and asked, "What do you need?"

"I need a lonely place to seek God and prepare my mission, a place by the border of Brude's lands, but secure. It must be on the sea within reach of DunAdd for supplies. And near timber for a school. And I need books from Comgall's library."

The DalRiad ruler looked over the Hebridean archipelago. "I can give you an island," he said. "You'll have to ask Comgall for the books."

When they returned to where Comgall and Diormit prayed, they announced their decisions. Comgall gasped with astonishment while Diormit bowed in thanksgiving.

"Surely you've read how even the great Ninian failed in Pictland," Comgall said. "Those are not men; they are animals."

"Then you will help me tame them," said Colum. "I need you to teach me more about them. Their history. Their ways. Their language."

Comgall whitened with shock. "Their language?" he clicked. "But there is nothing written in it, just a few carvings in stones. Pictures of beasts, such as they themselves are."

"Then how will I speak to Brude if you don't teach me? In pictures? Or have you forgotten it all?"

"No, it's that I . . . well, I . . . ," he pinched his lips, embarrassed by the bastardized Pictish accent that flavored his Gaelic. "The language is very difficult to learn."

"By God's help, you will be a good teacher," encouraged Colum.

"But if you are leaving, where will we meet for lessons?"

Colum turned to the king for the answer.

The king pointed over the wall, tracing a map in the air. "The portion of Riada follows the coast north to the Isle of Mull at the mouth of Loch Linnhe. Your Uncle Ernan will know the way. Anyplace up to there is easily within our reach and close to the Great Glen leading to Brude's lands."

The king counted on his ringed fingers as he continued, "The first island you'll reach is Islay at the mouth of the sound. Take the north shore, if you wish, but there are other colonists there. North of that, you will find Oronsay and Colonsay. Mostly bird colonies, but a few farmers. Good land at the base of the heights."

"Can you see Erin from them?" asked Colum.

The king shrugged. "Perhaps on a clear day."

Colum ignored the homesick pang creeping into his abdomen. "Is there any other place, further north?"

"There's Mull, but it is crowded with seal-keepers."

Comgall raised a curious eyebrow. "There's Hy," he offered, his Pictish throat slurring the "Ee" of the Gaelic name. "An old graveyard island of the Picts. A few fisherfolk. In late summer, the she-bears of Mull swim there to hibernate. They can be very fierce when they cub in spring. There would be many this time of year."

"We shall see," said Colum.

"There is something else the bears protect on Hy," added Comgall. "The Sun-Circles of the druids."

∎

Colum's curragh rose and fell in the swell along the wildly serrated coastline of Kintyre. The sea, blue and bubbly, swished against the sides of the boat as it cut south past the bird-filled fiords and heathery hills. Sweet sphagnum moss and bunches of bluebell graced the grass down to the water where the wild goats fed. The black-headed gulls and the gannets gathered again, calling out directions and disagreeing with one another.

On Islay, the mild breezes ruffled the unusual palms and figs just sprouting on the pebble beaches. When Colum noticed the salmon nets and lobster creels draping the black boulders of the foreshore, he signaled to move on to the next site.

At Oronsay, a small rise of torrichon sandstone, the black swans welcomed him with loud trumpets. Encouraged by this sign, he ascended the central hill, stepping through the cheerful magnolia, blood-drop emlet, and rock samphire. The south horizon stretched in a wide blue arc with nothing on it but the glare of the sun. Hopeful, he climbed an ancient standing stone, toppled at the top.

The dim hills of Erin lay low on the sea.

Their sloping shadows looked no smaller from Colonsay. As Colum waded back to the boat, his robes bunched in his fists at the waist, he called to his crestfallen companions.

"To Hy."

13

HY

A.D. 563

N PENTECOST EVE, THE TWELFTH OF MAY, THEY grounded the boat on a beach steeply terraced by the unending siege of Atlantic breakers. The waves rolled up with a noise of distant thunder, pounding colonies of white-shelled creatures into banks of fine ivory pebbles. As the waters fell back, they left slopes of many colors — fragments of white marble, silver mica, red feldspar, and crystalline quartzes of violet, green, and pink — all polished by the surf to resemble a shore of tiny jewels.

Some wondered aloud if Pictish pirates hid their booty here on Hy. "For the ghosts of the graves and the bears of the caves would sure and keep people away," someone said.

After securing the boat to boulders of rose-red granite, they inspected their landing. The sheltered east side of Hy provided a few low bushes and a tree here and there. On higher ground, a spongy turf littered with rocks and flecked with wildflowers angled upward to a group of hills. Fulmars and puffins dived into burrows to protect their young as the black-headed gulls announced the arrival of strangers.

Across the narrow straits lay Mull, a rocky mass of mountains, scruffy moor, and deeply indented coves where the wild eider ducks and waterhen built their floating nests. They held the promise of quills and meat in plenty. Yet the men postponed their prayers of thanksgiving until the abbot ascended the heights.

With a stiff walking-stick, a capula, in hand, Colum hiked up the irregular land alone, eyes fixed on the highest point. He reached it in minutes.

An ancient cairn, a barrel-shaped pile of stones, sat on the summit in the midst of wind-worn gravemarkers. He stepped up on the loose rocks, remembering the minute difference in view caused by a similar vantage on Oronsay. He firmed his footing and saw the whole length of the Inner Hebrides from Islay to Skye.

The sea stretched out blue, lavender, and green in uneven patterns, bright with the high springtime sun. Just north, the neighboring island of Staffa rode the sea like a tall, gray ship.

Hy itself, purpled by heather and haloed with white sand, showed patches of pasture in the midsection. The rolling grassland, fertile with lime, could support sheep or crops, especially the sheltered north shore. Clumps of rock to the west could be huts of fisherfolk, he guessed. He shielded his eyes and peered long and hard over the southern sea.

The horizon showed a smooth line. Erin was gone.

He turned away, his back to his homeland, and cradled his face in his hands. When his eyes cleared and he lifted his tear-streaked chin, he noticed threads of black smoke rising from the landing site. *Have they begun a fire already?* he wondered.

He picked his way down through the boulders and peat-haggs. The boggy patches suggested the presence of underground water, feeding the small ponds in the hollows. He noted the holly, crushable for ink, and the yellow flags and buttercups, suitable for coloring. The honk of seals echoed from the offshore skerries, and he thought he heard splashes of trout or otters. He counted the flat stones, refuse of a long-ago glacier, needed for the men's mortarless cells. He would spare the occasional tree, importing timber from Mull. And he would burn none of it, harvesting peat instead.

What then, he puzzled, *are my men burning on the beach?*

The dark smoke coiled from two torches held by a pair of strangers dressed in undyed wool robes. The greeters engaged in lively talk with the newcomers, using the torches to point south. They also held high bishops' croziers, carved from oak and capped with shiny brass. Both men, shaven ear to ear, spoke a plodding Gaelic.

Diormit kicked through the sand towards Colum, waving both arms and wearing a troubled face.

"Father," he hailed, "these be bishops of the isles. They say to go home. The people already believe."

"Believe what?" asked Colum skeptically, brushing past him to meet the tonsured strangers.

"The faith is already here," said one, a thin man with skin pockmarked as driftwood and a voice as dry and cracked. He motioned with the snapping torch, as he had before with the twelve. "There is no need for you to settle here. Go, while the weather holds and the wind is favorable."

His partner, an older man with bent shoulders and winter-white hair, agreed in a deep, authoritative voice. "There is enough light left in the day to reach Islay. The villagers there will receive you to their hearths and show you proper hospitality. We are poor and have nothing to offer to so many."

Colum studied their smooth scalps. On the newly shaven foreheads, pink with irritation, light V shapes remained where their druid's forelocks once fell.

"You are imposters," Colum said, loud enough for all his men to hear. "Liars and imposters posing as bishops."

The thin man smiled, unruffled. "No, you are imposters posing as Wise Ones, with your white robes and cut hair. You cannot fool our people. As we said, the faith is already here. A faith more ancient and powerful than yours."

"Your power, such as it is, comes from demons, who disguise themselves as you do. I bring the power of God."

The older man nodded and spoke as though correcting a well-meaning child. "You are not the first, you know. Others like you have come and gone. They told us the same thing. But the powers are strong on Hy. They could not overcome it, nor understand it. I advise you to leave."

Colum stepped forward to a place where the footing felt more secure. The wizards widened their pupils, realizing his great height. "I understand it well," said Colum, boring into their eyes, "as I understand that God has authority over all the forces of earth, seen and unseen, which He placed in His creation. He has revealed true power through the teaching and wonders of His Son."

The old one, unimpressed, replied, "So you speak of miracles. We deny such things. Even magic is the restoring of the balance of natural forces. Rearranging them for harmony. It is a principle of nature you can see and measure like the circuit of sun and moon."

He dragged his crozier through the sand to scratch out a circle. "Nature is balanced and perfect like the circle," he said. "Miracles contradict nature."

Colum lifted his walking-stick and slashed a cross through the circle. "Miracles intersect nature: they do not contradict it."

The thin druid eyed the Celtic cross severely. "Miracles interfere with nature," he said dryly. "They violate nature. Her laws are fixed and secret, and we discover them. We do not seek to break them."

"God does not break His laws. He accelerates them and reverses them, and He has laws we do not know."

"We know the earth's secrets, not you."

"Your magic secrets are for your own gain and power over others. But God's works are open to all and are signs of His goodness, as when He raised Jesus Christ from the dead."

The thin man put on a look of boredom. "We have heard all this before. Your words are empty. The others who came before you had to leave because they spoke of this God who raises the dead, but they could not even heal our people who were yet living. For that, they come to us."

Over the edge of the moor, a group of curious fisherfolk appeared. They kept their distance, trying to see what newcomers would challenge the ghosts of the graveyards and the she-bears of the caves. Among the onlookers stood two men shouldering a heavy pole connected to a wide but shallow basket used for sorting fish. They let it down gently with a third man guiding the ropes. The basket held no fish, but a young woman. Her brown hair was cut short to prevent knotting. Her head and withered arms twitched in spastic jerks, and her uncontrolled tongue licked and uttered helpless garble. Her legs, bony and thin as a new colt's but horribly undersized for her body, bunched beneath her.

The thin wizard noticed Colum's interest in her. "The ones before you did nothing. Perhaps you would like to try?"

"You have been powerless to help her?" challenged Colum.

"Herbs do no miracles."

With a heavy heart, Colum listened to the girl's thick-tongued moans. Her short twisted limbs slapped at the basket's sides. The two carriers held it in place.

"Who is she?" asked Colum.

The older one answered. "It is Eileen. A fisherman's girl. She hangs near his nets by the sea. She it was who saw your ship and cried out."

Colum tightened his grip on the walking-stick. "Bring her to me."

The old wizard motioned to the two basket-bearers to carry their charge forward to the beach. Then he turned to Colum, bending his neck back to look in his eyes. "Perhaps you can also multiply her father's fish as you monks say Christos did once."

"I will," Colum said to the surprised druid, watching the men lift the basket. "Because God will make her able to go fishing with her father."

The attendants guided the basket to a resting spot. Colum pushed the ropes away, knelt, and observed the girl. Her bright hazel eyes rolled. They looked afraid, then ashamed, then imprisoned. Her open mouth sucked at the air, trying to talk, but the stubborn tongue refused to obey, and a frustrated hack emerged instead.

"Step aside," he said to the druids. "I will be alone with her."

"Of course," said the thin one. "Every magician has his secrets."

He followed the older one up the bank to where the people stood. The torches trailed a dark, acrid cloud.

Colum touched Eileen's arm. She pulled away violently and cried out.

The other men shied away, and someone whispered it was the voice of a devil in her.

Colum pushed his palm to the ground, and the men knelt in the sand, crossing their foreheads and hearts.

He gripped the girl's arm, and rather than forcing it still, he followed its jerking movements. "Eileen, I'm here to help you," he said close to her ear.

Her legs quaked. The basket squeaked. Colum steadied it

with his free hand. "I'm going to pray for you, Eileen. It may hurt or feel very warm, but it will get better. Do you understand?"

The hopeful eyes glanced up. Was it a "yes"? A spasm? Could she even speak Gaelic? *God does,* he thought, and he began his prayer. Within minutes, a tingle in his finger tickled and pricked like pine needles. His hand warmed. His arm went hollow with a pleasing flow through it from his shoulder to palm. He closed his eyes in great peace. The girl's thrashing increased, but Colum held her fast, his hand heated as though held to coals on a damp night. He heard snapping noises, the sound of bones straightening.

When his hand cooled and he opened his eyes, the girl looked more frightened and gnarled than before. Embarrassed tears squeezed from her roaming eyes. The snapping, it seemed, was only the breaking of reeds in the basket as she shook.

The two attendants, stone-faced, lifted the basket pole and trudged away. The basket swung beneath, and Colum heard soft crying in it. The people turned and left with murmurs. The thin druid pointed his torch south again.

"Go home," he called. "Your God can do nothing here, for magic is strong on Hy. Even if you wish to stay, you know well the price nature requires."

The words sent a sick feeling through Colum, adding to his dismay over Eileen. The seafaring Gaels' long tradition of human sacrifice to secure a new settlement made him wince in disgust. "We will never do such a thing." He shook his fist.

"Then you know the island will not allow you to stay. Like the others." The druids disappeared over the ridge.

The point was not lost on the monks, who knew the old ways well. "Who will it be?" they whispered among themselves before their abbot rebuked them.

"We will offer a sacrifice of thanksgiving as the psalmist says," he ordered. "Then we will make shelters."

Recalling the terrain from his survey on the summit, Colum chose a site further up the eastern shore for their shelter. With the tide out, they pulled onto the beach near arable slopes of gentle green machair.

Colum assigned spaces for the brethren's huts. They would form an irregular circle around a grassy knoll where his own cell would preside. The men collected stones for hut foundations, lugging the rocks in bags on their backs. Any stone with grave markings was left untouched. At sunset, with a few mortarless walls serving as windbreakers for the night, they broke for the vespers of Pentecost Eve, ending their holiest season. Afterwards, they feasted on salted fish and drank fresh water from a cool stream.

"Tomorrow we'll have fresh flounder," promised Grilaan.

■

Within several days, the beehive huts took shape, with stone corbels jutting from the sides to support sod roofs. Each cell had a hole in the top for peat smoke, closed by a flat rock. As yet without straw or bundled cornstalks, the men slept on stone slabs.

Colum summoned his men to offices with a handbell, using the beach as his chapel and a block of eroded gneiss for an altar until a wood church could be built.

From his split-level cell on the hill, Colum planned the outlay of the settlement's other structures. Within earthen ramparts, they would raise a simple refectory and commonhouse. A library and guesthouse. A kiln and smithy near the stream that emptied into the bay, and perhaps a mill powered by the flowing water. Nearby, the docks would anchor the fishing boats and barges to ferry goods between Hy and Mull, trading grain and fish.

The thought of fish turned his mind to Eileen. The sinking emptiness he felt over her returned. Why did God's power abandon him? Didn't he feel the warmth? How did he sin, or what did he lack, or what had he missed, bringing shame on himself and the gospel? Before raising Jairus's daughter, he recalled, the Lord sent away the unbelieving mourners. Was it the presence of the unbelieving wizards that hindered him? Or his own men? Or was the magic on Hy as great as the druids claimed?

He crossed himself and recited the penitential psalms for even posing such a question.

There must be some sin in me blocking His power, he thought. He searched his heart, but found nothing unconfessed. He prayed again for Eileen, hoping she could forgive him for making her endure yet another demeaning spectacle.

The second challenge of the druids troubled him no less. Each man had volunteered to be the sacrifice, if necessary, by seeking a lonely place to enter God's presence by starvation and exposure. But the abbot refused each one. "Let this be your sacrifice: that each continue his work as unto the Lord and not as unto men. As the apostle says, 'Offer your bodies as a living sacrifice, dedicated and fit for His acceptance, which is your reasonable worship.'"

But he knew talk persisted about who was to die.

While he pondered, he heard Siaran's shouts across the narrow straits, coming from the red granite shores of Mull. He stood up, though not fully because of the low ceiling, and looked sunriseward through the doorless entry.

The carpenter was ordering groups of men around a ship, successfully trading barley seed for a load of wattles and wood. *He will need many more logs for the church,* Colum thought. The friendly contact meant that arrangements would come for milk and seal — necessary for hides, lamp oil, and meat. Then they could have proper Sabbaths and hospitality feasts. For now, the flounder would do, and Grilaan was out in his coracle again, making his daily catch of them.

Colum stepped outside, knelt, and then stretched skyward. His lower back complained, and he felt that he must escape his quarters more often. His father's spinal troubles might finally be developing in him at mid-life. The vigorous carrying of stones certainly did not help the aching, though the work kept him trim.

Also, the air felt damper than before prayer time. He remembered how his father could predict rain by the crimp in his back, and sure enough, a storm was brewing in the west. A horde of low brown clouds, looking like a pack of dogs on the prowl, crept across the darkening sea. Streams of rain flew over the water, bright as burnished swords with the morning sunrays on them. They slashed the north shore of the island and passed in a few minutes, leaving a rainbow and a cloverlike scent. But behind them, a line of fiercer clouds, ripped by lightning, growled with thunder and moved stealthily closer.

A few men who had been meditating in the hills scurried

back to their stone huts. Colum saw Siaran and the natives of Mull run into the rocks.

Colum rushed to the shore and mounted a boulder. The wind whipped up whitecaps as the angry clouds snarled and stalked nearer.

Grilaan's coracle was nowhere to be seen. The abbot cupped his mouth and called Grilaan's name. The rocks of Mull threw the name back, and the rolling clouds answered with a crack of lightning.

The sea heaved and crashed onto the rocks. The sky trembled, and the fulmars fled into their holes. Gulls shrieked a warning, but Colum bonded to the rock like a barnacle, rebuking the wind.

The rain lashed the island again in leaden gray curtains, obscuring the sea. The force of the downpour pressed Colum to a knee as he prayed in great cries for Grilaan.

He spied a dark shape riding the Atlantic rollers. The waves threw it onto the beach in a shock of spray as if coughing it up, and then receded with a splash of milky foam. Half of Grilaan's wicker coracle, smashed and strangled with seaweed, tumbled in the wash. A shoe fell out and filled with wet sand. It sank out of sight as the next wave claimed it.

Soaked and shaking, Colum struggled up the slope against the howling gale. Rain slapped his face, mocking him. He fell into his cell, hands clasped in beseeching. "Let him come back," he begged. *Do not let the island have its tribute,* he thought. *Not like this.*

The sky flashed and roared like a she-bear, turning the cell white and rattling its stones. A human shadow fell across the wall through the doorway.

"Grilaan!" Colum cried. "Thank God!" He hurried to his feet and embraced the dripping wet head.

The hair felt short. The face tilted up.

It was Eileen.

"Thank you," she sobbed, hugging him back with long, normal arms.

■

Colum folded the brown vestments, the color of earth and burial, after the mass for the dead. For twenty months, on the date of Grilaan's passing, he offered this memorial and called a fast regardless of the day. The holy food of the Eucharist, a leavenless barleybread, would be his stomach's only satisfaction today, and as it was a Thursday his body had a third consecutive day of denial yet to come.

He re-dressed in the white tunica and the undyed wool overcloak he had woven himself. With Diormit close behind, holding the used Communion cloths for laundering, he left the wooden sacristy of Hy's church and enjoyed the frisky wind outside. The sky and sea shone a Persian blue, like the crushed gemstone that illuminated his best Psalters. A good day for sailing.

He sighed with concern for the men going fishing, facing the temptation of their catch on a fast day. On the stony beach, the fishermonks crossed the saving sign over their pitched coracles as they did with every tool, invoking Grilaan's aid before paddling into the sound. Some had already rounded the bend on their way to join the islanders who shared in the day's catch and, because of Eileen, shared in the faith.

The seals barked from Mull, and for a moment it sounded like a chant from Hy's former druids. How could it be? He shook his head. With the conversion of the islanders, the magicians had retired to the mainland to cast their spells and send a warning through the Great Glen which cut through Caledonia all the way to Brude's capital. They left behind only the strange granite gravemarkers, the roughly hewn sunstones, and a spoken curse. But these sounds were, indeed, only seals welcoming travelers.

It was no longer unusual for the harbor to be cluttered with incoming boats. Colum watched from his hilltop hut as the brothers assigned to the task received the visitors.

A chieftain of DalRiada, dressed in penitential white but still sporting a gold torque and headband, kissed the sand. A poet stripped his colors and sang a psalm aloud. Pilgrims seeking the famous abbot's touch or his teaching followed down the plank. A few dipped bottles in the water to take home for baptizing their babies. The waters of Hy, or Ioua, as the Gaels called it, or Iona, as the Latins mispronounced it, could work healings, they believed.

Colum counted the new arrivals. The settlement was nearing its limit of threescore and fifty souls, as he had calculated from the island's food-producing capacity. Soon he would have to turn inquirers away except for temporary guests.

Surveying the grounds, he planned the newcomers' tasks. For the sake of a chieftain of DalRiada and his bard, he would forego the fast and set out a hospitable feast of seal and beer. But like any other newcomers, they would build their own wattle-and-daub dwellings alongside warriors, pig farmers, bakers and chariotmakers, without respect to rank. He decided they should further prove their earnestness by stacking stones for the thick ramparts which hemmed the huts dotting the turf, where all the other penitents and pupils studied and slept on stones in imitation of the abbot.

Satisfied that the new guests were well cared for, he took his place on the stone in his hut and began to write:

> That I might search the books of all
> That might be good for my soul,
> At times to belovèd Heaven kneeling,
> At times psalmsinging,
> At times contemplating Heaven's King,
> Holy the Chief.

A little crowd of white-robed novices pressed at the door, genuflecting, eager to see the abbot work the graceful curves of his script. A pair of working brethren passed by on their way to the fields, seeking his blessing on their hoes. He crossed the *signum salutare* with the pen still in his hand and turned back to his poetry.

> That I might work without compulsion,
> That would be delightful.
> At times bent to the rocks, duilise plucking,
> At times fishing,
> At times bent toward the poor, giving
> Or alone in my cell.

A group of senior brethren knelt outside on the stone path, awaiting permission to enter. When he bade them come, they laid newly completed books at his feet for inspection. Colum's critical eye and finger traced the prickmarks and wedged strokes of Severus's *Life of Martin of Tours,* a Latin Josephus, and a personal favorite, the *Gospel Harmony of Juvencus* in hexameters. With his nodded approval, the scribes departed with their books. They bade a blessing to Diormit, who stood there whittling new quills and mixing fresh ink with a pestle.

A briny seabreeze flapped Colum's parchments, and he looked up. He heard the boats bumping in the bay and the whisper of the waters curling on the shore.

"Diormit," he called, "I will be on the sea. To Hinba." He rose, genuflected at the door, and left his attendant there stirring ink as he descended to the docks with long, eager steps.

On the sea he felt totally free and totally dependent. He blessed the One Who Walked the Waves for each shift of salt-sweet wind and for each purple seaweed patch. He asked to be borne along by His mercies as his little boat coasted on the sea, blown by His breath and steered by the twin oars of Scripture and reason. On the broad moor of blue with heathery foam, he listened for God in the creaking of gulls and in the clicking of the rowlocks. He pulled for Hinba of the Garvellahs, a craggy, lumpy mass of rocks that looked like they had tumbled off the peaks of the nearby Nevis Mountains.

In the harsh shelter of the lime-coated cliffs he prayed. The cave-dwelling cormorants cried out with him and seemed to carry his pleas into the sky.

Could he not stay at Hy where there was so much work yet to do? Why must he traverse the Great Glen to bargain with King Brude when all the other kings came to him at Hy?

As he walked the beach and the sand ground under his feet, the sound reminded him of Molaisse's gravelly voice. Could not the penance be fulfilled by founding schools on the islands? There was already the nunnery at Tiree where Eileen studied and other settlements soon to begin.

He scolded himself for preferring the comfort and routine of the settlement to his call. He raised his hands and his eyes to the fleecy clouds, like wandering sheep, like wandering thoughts. The closer his mind came to the heights of the Most High Shepherd, the more his feet felt like the stringy moss rooted in the rocks. The more he tried to see the great Throne with the white-winged seraphs, the more he imaged Brude's throne with ravens perched on it. Torn between two worlds, he unclasped his hands, breaking the connection.

He filled a vial with seawater. He hiked inland to the hermitage, a crude stone hut with a garland of ling and with heather growing in thick tufts on the roof. He laid out his writing tools, mixed a carbon ink from fire cinders, and drafted letters to his schools. Permissions, penances, and personal notes flowed from his hand onto separate sheets to be carried to Erin by the sailors from Derry.

When he finished, he interceded for the men of his choice to visit Pictland. *Diormit, of course. Though slow of foot, his prayers fly faster to heaven than any other,* he thought.

Cainnech and Comgall, who speak their strange, unlearnable language.

His prayer turned to Lugne Mocu-min, a young Derryman without fear, and to his nephew Drostan, a fine sailor with a heron's sense of direction.

> *A small company it was,*
> *few in number, strangers in that land,*
> *roaming from nation to nation,*
> *from one kingdom to another.*

He prayed on to the next verses, claiming their promises:

> *But He let no one ill-treat them!*
> *For their sake He admonished kings!*
> *"Touch not My anointed servants!*
> *Do My prophets no harm!"*

Thus assured of safety in Brude's court, he remembered leading a larger entourage before a different king. He pictured Tara's Great Hall with its pennants and shields. He felt the High King's throne under his own cloak and the clasp of kingship on his chest. Suddenly he felt the warmth of the chrysmal hanging there and the hardness of the stone seat.

He left the chapel for the boat, chastened, challenged, his

head full of the many chores and many checks to be done before the journey. With a few mighty strokes, he was out to sea again, guided by the gulls who mewed out his name.

With the wind at his back, he knew he would return in time to wash the field-workers' feet before the evening meal. *The Lord Himself did so on the eve of His death,* he thought.

He looked across the waters to the wild woods of Alba. The trees rimmed the hills like the palisades of a great fortress.

14

GLEN MOR

A.D. 565

ONG BEFORE THE GRAY LIGHT OF DAWN CAME TO ALBA, the birds had word of it in the woods. Throughout the Great Glen, from Loch Linnhe and the cormorant caves of Mull, across the Caledonian channels to the bluffs of Moray Firth, the scattered twitters built to a full chorus to welcome the sun. From the oystercatchers, with their long orange beaks looking like swords heated for the anvil, to the timid sparrows of the Highland hills, a many-voiced song awakened the world. Facing east, Colum joined their chants with his arms upraised like wings, bidding the Sun of Righteousness, the light of Christ, to come.

He saw the high points blaze into gold, and then watched the sunshine spread down like poured honey to the dew-drenched glen where the wild roses waved in greeting. The coming of the light was to him the Creation all over again, a daily miracle.

The sleep caked in his eyelashes. He wiped them clean, careful not to smudge the eyelids, painted black in the Pictish custom. He missed his bell to call the sleeping brothers to Prime, but he heard the men stirring and continued in private:

> *I arise today*
> *Might of God for my piloting,*

> Eye of God for my foresight,
>   Ear of God for my hearing,
> Word of God for my utterance,
>   Shield of God for my protection
> Against snares of demons,
>   Against allures of vices,
> Against any, far or near,
>   Who wish me ill.

Diormit and Comgall uncurled beneath their bundled cloaks like moles in a hovel, muttering the same prayer. Their voices echoed in the overturned boat which was their shelter.

Drostan sneezed under his mantle and emptied his nose on the ground with a finger pressed to each nostril.

Lugne Mocu-min, perched nearby on the nightwatch, cocked his pointed face towards the sound. He stretched his athletic frame and rubbed his clear, quick eyes, glad for his turn at guard to be ending. He leaped up with a push on his staff, accustomed to using it to guide sheep or dig up soil, but ready to beat away weasels or Picts.

Cainnech sat up straight, eyes wide and circular as the whooping gray herons calling from Loch Linnhe. He shook off his dreams, threw his wrap over his shoulders, and stumbled to Colum's side.

When by sound Colum accounted five sets of knees pressed to the stones, he began the morning office.

"*Tu es vita et virtus,*" he sang, hushing the birds,

> You are life and goodness.
>   *Tu es adjutor in tribulationibus,*
> our help in trouble,
>   *Tu es defensor animarum nostrarum,*
> defender of our souls,
>   *Deus Israel in omnibus qui regnas.*

After prayer, Lugne blew up the fire he had begun and banked. Around its warmth, the men reviewed their progress while munching hard cheese. By way of the slender chain of lakes stretching northwestward, they had paddled and portaged in good time through the pathless wilds of Alba's spine.

"We'll see farms or villages soon," said Comgall, hands to the fire.

"And they will see us," worried Cainnech with his arms tucked under.

Comgall pointed to his shaven forehead. "We need not fear. They will take us for druids."

"And if they hear us speak our own tongue?" asked Diormit.

"They will take it for spells. Even if there are roving bands about, they will pause when they see the white wool on our backs and the long sticks in our hands. It is bad luck to rob a traveling druid. Who can tell what his stick may do? One could have his insides changed to eels which crawl out of him."

Diormit pursed his lips as Colum gave the order to push ahead. They doused the fire, passed water, and turned over the boat, propped up by its short paddles. Shallow-keeled and newly caulked, the curragh fit six men seated in pairs beside leather rowlocks that served as handles for carrying. By these, they lowered the boat into the cold river. The wickerwork squeaked, and the tarred, hard hides braced like skin in a winter spray as they stepped in and leaned into the oars. With the mast and sail assembly rolled up between their legs on the floor, they launched into the thin steamy fog, ears tuned to the slap of ripples on rocks and wading of stilt-legged birds along the stony shores. In the muddy water, Diormit spotted a few eels shimmying near the surface, long and gray like spilt intestines, and he turned away from them in disgust.

Where the waters became marshy, thick with rushes and flies, they put in to shore. After lifting out the boat, they rubbed water off its sides, as if squeezing a horse's hide after a washing.

With loads on their backs and straps dug into their palms, they crossed the sunny meadows. The boat swayed and swished in the grass with their coordinated step. Colum adjusted his long strides to Diormit's short waddles and Drostan's short breath.

They paused to watch the red deer romping on the misted hills. Mild-mannered, some of the waist-high does wandered near to their outstretched hands. With large, trusting eyes, a deer pushed its black, wet nose into Colum's leather-smelling palms.

"At least the Pict's ancient relatives are friendly," he said.

"Send them ahead to speak well of us to those who are yet human," said Cainnech.

A pair of crows flapped up from a birch tree. Cawing to each other, they swooped upriver.

"It seems there are other messengers speaking of us," Colum said.

They kicked through ragwort, bracken, and long-stemmed hairy-cap moss with glad orange heads. Near the river rocks where the dragonflies danced, Colum bent to a low plant with tiny wine-red tubes for petals. The glistening tendrils, tipped with sticky blood-red drops, secreted a sweet smell. A zig-zagging bee tested the tendrils and alighted inside, its legs busy and searching. In a wink, the tendrils closed over the insect like fingers clutching a prize. The bee shook and buzzed, stinging in fury. Its six spiny legs pulled in vain at the gluey dew. The interlocked tendrils held until the bee exhausted itself and lay still. The glenside sundew's juices began their slow digestion.

The men took new notice of their surroundings. The meadow and stream were flanked by rows of pine, tall and wet with sap. The bee buzzed a warning.

"I smell smoke." Cainnech pecked his beak into the north wind. "Wood smoke. Sweet, like pine."

"And perhaps as sticky," said Diormit.

Colum took his boatstrap in hand. "To the water. Over there, it looks deep enough."

Diormit, despite the rest, breathed more quickly.

Farther ahead, they saw the cottony smoke, tumbling from a stone chimney set in a turf-covered mound. The low hill overlooked a grassy slope to the river where a wharf, made of logs and with a tilted roof, protected birch canoes and pitched paddleboats.

A bent, bare-chested old farmer with his three young lads dug with bone shovels near the mound, weeding a turnip patch. His goats saw the visitors first and pulled at their tethers, bleating. When the man and his boys raised their eyes, they gripped their shovels like clubs and came to the wharf. With a face shrunken from lack of teeth and a suspicious eye that spun like a wheel, the farmer weighed the handle in his hard hands.

Colum pulled the boat alongside the fishing boats, grabbed a dock post and hoisted himself up. The farmer, seeing the towering figure and the high staff, motioned for his boys to get behind him. His rolling eye measured the staff's size, weight, and position, as a warrior assessing an opponent's blade.

Colum pointed the staff low and away from his side, a gesture of greeting. "I am Colum of Hy," he said in clear Pictish. "What is your name?"

The farmer firmed his stance.

Comgall stepped from the boat and on tiptoe spoke in Colum's ear. "He may not want to tell you, as knowing a man's name gives power over him."

"Then he must be surprised I gave him mine so easily."

Cainnech hurried to his side, looking disappointed that Comgall had offered advice first. "Let's go on from here. We can see that we're not welcome."

Colum turned back to the farmer. "Will you share a meal with me?"

The farmer looked thunderstruck. Then he burst into a toothless smile.

"Comgall," said Colum, worried, "did I ask the right question? Or did I ask him to eat me?"

"You said it rightly. Perhaps he is surprised that a Wise One would dine with a peasant."

The old man beckoned him up the hill to the mound-house.

"Diormit," Colum called with relief, "bring the barley-bread and cheese." He patted Comgall on the back and loped up the slope, not noticing Cainnech's jealous frown.

■

Torlec the farmer, a widower, added wood to his bluish hearthfire while Colum broke the unleavened bread. Torlec's eye rolled when he watched the visitors cross their portions before eating. Comgall explained that they signed not to ward off poisons, but to honor the One God who makes bread to grow from the earth which He created.

"Who, then, is the god of turnips and potatoes?" Torlec asked. "For they do not grow as well as before."

Colum spoke a slow Pictish. "There is one God who made the earth and the heavens," he said, his tongue contorting. "In His book He says He made every plant and its seed."

"This god speaks?"

"We, His servants, have brought you His words in a book, along with some seed."

Torlec narrowed his eye, peering closer and studying them. "You are not like the others who came."

"There have been others like us?" asked Comgall.

"They looked like you," said the farmer. He moved his finger past their fire-lit faces. "And they took what they pleased, even my geese, and went their way north. They also said they were of Hy."

He spoke more quickly as his anger rekindled, and Comgall translated in haste to keep up with him. Colum nodded and assured him, "They were of Hy. But no longer."

He turned to Lugne and said in Gaelic, "Bring the barley seed."

"Isn't it too late for planting, Father?" asked Diormit.

"Didn't you see the lads clearing the ground outside, Diormit? Growing nothing but weeds? I'd say it is a good time."

Colum held the bread and the seed in the sealskin bag side by side. He offered Torlec help in planting and instruction in the August harvest and milling, "when we return this way about then."

"And this, did you learn from God's book?" asked Torlec.

"No, from our fathers."

"Then what does God talk about in His book?"

Colum opened his satchel. He slid out the leather-bound Gospel, opening to the first page in his own handwriting. "Let me tell you," he said.

■

Through the day, working with their bare hands as at Clonard, Colum and the men loosened dirt, dug furrows, and dropped seed. Colum and Lugne taught Torlec to sow it for proper cross-pollination and root binding.

But Comgall kept his distance, his muscles tense and his dark eyes alert, as Cainnech explained their technique to the Pict.

Colum worked the soil towards him. "Stay near me," he said in his ear. "Help me to speak with him. He is so open."

"He is too open," gruffed Comgall. "He received us too

quickly, especially after what happened to him before. He fears us and will agree to anything to be rid of us."

"That may be, but it still gives us opportunity."

"Or gives him opportunity."

"Do you think he means us harm?"

Comgall bashed a chunk of loam with his heel. "How do we really know the priests of Hy are gone? As he welcomed us, he welcomed them, and perhaps they are merely across the river. Or in the woods keeping to themselves as they like to do. Perhaps he is under instruction to keep watch for us and send for them when we come."

"God keeps watch for us, too. And we will post a watch as always. Even if he means us ill, we still have time to change his heart."

"If he has one."

◼

Twice, when the shadows were right, the men stopped for singing the offices while Torlec watched. From the way Torlec turned askance, Colum could tell the Latin verses sounded magical, forbidden. When the fish leaped in the river after their psalm, he saw that Torlec took note of it.

At Vespers, the white-robed Wise Ones faced the setting sun in the manner of wizards. At their meal, Torlec said he hoped their words would be effective not only to raise the sun again but to raise the crops as well. Then the villagers might return to their fields.

When the sky glowed red, Torlec showed them the plots which his relatives had abandoned. Rude, half-buried huts of the hamlet nestled beside the banks of the stream that bubbled down to the loch. They crossed on stones and bade good night to their host. Comgall suggested they sleep in separate quarters. But Colum insisted they make their lodging in what used to be a barn.

Diormit tore away cobwebs from a corner and lay down.

The others found their spots and, yawning, settled for the night.

Colum leaned against the gospel-satchel next to Diormit, the babbling stream tickling his ears, and he said to the bleary-eyed servant, "Diormit, it is good there is such clear water nearby. I believe Torlec will be baptized before we leave tomorrow."

Diormit answered with a snore. The others, too, tasted their first sleep. The curled-up lumps rose and fell with slow breathing.

Colum folded his arms behind his neck and watched the sky through the holes in the roof until he could see the first stars peek out. He listened to the woods coming alive in the dark — hares nosing for food, beetles foraging, woodmice burrowing, owls swooping from branches to snatch them screaming, foxes on the hunt, weasels, maybe wolves. He squirmed, uneasy, and sat up. He felt more awake as he heard every whisper of leaves, distant growl, and splash of water.

Water. The boat. Up to now, it had always been in sight. Could he be slack about it now in the midst of a people so recently at war with his own? What if Comgall was right about Torlec and the priests of Hy? They could easily know of their sojourn at Torlec's. They had ways of knowing such things, not the least of which were their Latin songs in the fields, announcing their presence.

He patted Diormit to awaken him, and then shook Comgall and the others. "Quick," he ordered, lifting them by the arms. "Get out to the boat. Diormit, wake up. Go at once and bring it to a nearer hut." He hustled them outside. "That hut over there. Drostan, stay by me."

He brushed off Diormit's back and pushed him to follow the other three who were already hopping the rocks across the stream in the watery moonlight.

When the round shadow of the boat, lugged by the four companions, came to view, Colum breathed his thanks. He directed the men to store it upright in a nearby shelter.

Afterwards, the men returned to sleep without questions or complaints. Lugne, staff in hand, stayed with the boat.

Colum hugged his capula closer as the temperature dropped. Or was it a chill of foreboding?

He thought of the boat, light and seaworthy, turned about and entering the straits under a full sail:

> This were pleasant, O Son of God,
> with wondrous coursing
> To fare across the swelling torrent
> back to Ireland.

To Eolarg's plain, past Benevanagh,
    across Loch Feval
And there to hear the swans in chorus
    chanting music.

And when my boat, the Derag Druchtach,
    at last made harbor
In Port na Ferag, the joyful sea gulls
    would sound a welcome.

I ever long for the land of Ireland
    where I had power,
An exile now in midst of strangers,
    sad and tearful.

Woe that journey forced upon me
    O King of Secrets,
Would to God I'd never gone there,
    to Culdrevne.

The words flowed through him like the water in the stream, and he wished for a pen to release them onto a fresh absorbent surface. But the writing tools were packed securely, and without ink or lamp, he longed for the comfort of his Scriptoria.

Well it is for son of Dimma
    in his cloister,
And happy I but were I hearing
    with him in Durrow.

The wind that plays us music
    in the elm-trees,
And sudden cry of startled blackbird,
    wing a-beating.

And listen early in Ros Grencha
    to stags a-belling,
And when cuckoo, at brink of summer,
    joins in chorus.

The sounds vanished from his imaginary hearing. The noises of the forest quieted. Was it due to the curtain of cloud now drawing across the moon? He felt suddenly very alone.

He thought of old Torlec asleep in his weem. *How ready he seemed,* Colum thought. *His soul is tilled by the plow of the Spirit.* Would all the Picts be so prepared? Surely it was a divine prompting that led the farmer to overcome his hostile reluctance to invite the strangers to his fire.

Fire.

Colum inhaled through his flared nose. A mossy smoke scented the still air even though Torlec's hearth should be banked for the night. Did he arise so early with the moon so high?

He heard the goats whine, and the sky looked lighter, a dull, dirty orange.

He poked Diormit with his staff. Diormit awoke with a start and said, "Fire." His forehead was damp.

"It is not a dream, Diormit," said Colum, rising. "Come outside."

They stepped into a brownish haze lit by the gourd-yellow flames licking from Torlec's weem and wharf. The roof of the mound, consumed with fire, caved into a charred heap. The chimney spat fire as though through a dragon's angry nose, and the glowing sky swallowed the smoke.

Footsteps rushed behind Colum. He whirled and raised his staff.

A frightened goat bleated at him and ran off into the wild.

"Father," wept Diormit, "those boys! And the farmer!"

Colum restrained him from running toward the flames. "They are gone," he said. "Stay on this side of the stream."

Lugne stumbled out of the boat shed, coughing. "God a-mercy, what is it?"

Diormit clasped his hands in grief and helplessness. "The farmer's hearth!" he cried. "Rekindled while he slept! A terrible accident."

Colum watched the boats, loose and blazing on the water, their rope-ties burning like wicks. They sank in hissing puffs of steam. "We are meant to think it was," he said.

■

218

When morning broke, Colum sprinkled the smoking remains of Torlec's dwelling with water from the stream he had blessed. Circling the collapsed hut, he concluded the last rites with the voices of the others joined to his. Comgall muttered under his breath, disapproving, as Colum dipped into the bowl again. The droplets sizzled on the smoldering stones which entombed Torlec and his sons, and Colum felt his own heart hot with indignation. Anger snarled deeply in his soul, and he recited the prayers of the dead loud enough to drown it out.

"Be angry, but sin not," he chastised himself. "They will use it. To go back in fear or to go forward in anger would equally suit their purpose."

"*In saecula saculorum*, amen," he finished aloud. *Have I come so far into Pictland,* he cried inside, *not to save men but to cause more to be killed?*

In the boat, Diormit cut the somber silence. "Even if it was an accident, it sure and was a sign to us."

"Given by whom?" asked Comgall with a sour face. "By God or by demons?"

"Why be reminded by either that we are unwelcome here?" asked Cainnech. "Unless we were so encouraged by Torlec's response and so open to pride."

"It was a warning," said Colum, "but not of God or spirits." He looked upriver towards Loch Ness. "Someone else knows we are here."

■

They sailed Loch Oich and portaged to Loch Ness, a tiring climb made pleasant by the fragrant azaleas. A wildcat howled in the woods, and Diormit quickened his flat-footed pace. Lugne set his falconlike face forward. When he twitched his head, he looked as though he were spotting a place to strike. Cainnech aimed his eyes to the grass, searching for signs of other travelers.

Colum read the clouds for weather changes. He pointed out the pine martens and the soft golden-eyed ducks, whom he fancied as angelic guides. He looked beyond the lochs over the pine-thatched hills into the future.

Cainnech's earthbound observation brought his vision back to the stone-strewn beach. "I see huts over there," he said with his neck stretched like a swan's. "A small village."

219

On a far bank poked into the water, thin lines of smoke snaked into the sky over meager dwellings. Colum ordered the boat into the water, aimed for the houses. The men stepped through the rubble of rocks on the shore, waded into the cold water with their lips pressed against the shivers, stored their backpacks, and pushed off. The murky waters sucked at the oars as though tasting them.

Through the lick of the waves, Colum heard a mournful song. He leaned into the wind. "What is it?"

Comgall cupped his ear. "A trick of the breeze?"

Drostan shook his head. "It sounds like a funeral, Uncle."

"The boats are all grounded," Colum observed.

"It is not a good sign," replied Drostan.

When they reached the sandy banks, the wailing stopped. A circle of villagers stared at the incoming boat. As Colum and the men disembarked and walked up the beach, they noticed long streaks of fresh blood in the sand, leading to where the villagers stood. The people watched them, and then looked beyond them to the lake as though watching for more boats. Mothers pulled their children away. Through the gaps in the group, Colum saw a newly dug hole, man-length. Beside the soft piles of dirt lay a corpse.

The male body, though wrapped in bloodstained cloths, showed rows of deep red punctures and puffed, purply gashes, as though savagely bitten. Fingers were missing, and the stumps looked shredded and blue, as from a desperate fight with a hungry shark.

When they heard a plunk of the lake water, the villagers sucked their knuckles and squinted past the visitors. But when Colum swiveled, he saw only ripples.

A short village man, dressed in plain homespun with an odor of stale sweat, barefoot, ringless, and unevenly whiskered, stepped out of the huddled group. His cheeks moved as if the words struggled to escape from his mouth. Yet without permission from a Wise One, he could not allow it.

Colum raised his palm and lowered his staff. "I am Colum of the island called Hy. I bring you peace in your time of sorrow."

"Have you come for the burial?" croaked the man. "To help my brother pass to the Otherworld?"

Comgall translated the thick dialect, and then added in a low voice, "He thinks we are druids."

Colum noted the dark brows of the Picts, lowered in fear, anger, or suspicion. The women pulled at their baggy sleeves to veil their faces. The men locked their sad eyes on him. Judging by their awed expressions and squat statures, Colum guessed they had never seen a man so tall as himself.

He spoke with a measured calm. "We are servants of the One God who made the world and the Otherworld and all that lives in them. Tell me, what happened to this man?"

The leader ground his molars. "Do you not know? Did you not send the sea beast yourselves?"

The lake rippled again with circles of bubbles. A mother hugged her children's faces into her dress.

Colum shook his head. "Please, why are your people so afraid of the lake?"

"You truly do not know?" asked the leader, confused.

The buriers came forward, chattering and clicking. Comgall and Cainnech pieced together their stories.

The victim, while swimming across the wide lake to retrieve his drifting boat, had been seized by a water beast, "bigger than an ox with a serpent's neck and head," "with a long snout," "making an awful noise like splitting wood," by various accounts. The men launched their boat for a rescue, but only in time to retrieve the mangled remains with their fishhooks.

"We left his boat. The beast is still out there."

Colum looked over the ominous waters. "We shall fetch the boat."

Diormit waddled forward, hands pressed to his cheeks. "Father, mightn't it be that the sea beast was sent for us, and this poor soul spoiled its evil plan against us? Its appetite will not be slacked, but whet for prey."

"Fear is a greater monster," said Colum. "It will devour us more quickly."

"I will get the boat," said Lugne, stripping his robe with one swoop, leaving the tunic. He raced to the water and plunged in, disappearing into the darkness. The water closed over him, and he was gone.

"Now the lake itself has swallowed him!" gasped Diormit.

The people inched forward, watching the still surface. The bubbles from the dive popped, and there was a nervous silence. But Lugne emerged, stroking, many yards offshore. He

221

blew a spout and pulled with powerful arms towards the lost boat which bumped the opposite beach.

Diormit hurried to the monks' curragh and began to haul it up on the beach, asking for help and scolding Lugne for the scare while urging him to hurry. Suddenly he dropped the rim and retched.

The brown water around his feet crawled with eels. Colored a sickly yellow-gray, they tumbled and weaved like baby snakes just hatched. Diormit kicked them away, his teeth gnashing, and splashed up to dry land, stamping his feet.

"Where did they come from?" he groaned.

"They always come before the sea beast," said the Pictish leader gravely. "It drags them up from the pit beneath the lake where it lives."

A broad patch in the lake foamed and whirled as if stirred from the bottom. Lugne, halfway across, took no notice of it.

From a bubbling eddy, not threescore yards from him, a small head punched into the air. It resembled a horsehead, muscular but flatter, its snout spitting water with a sharp bark like a dog. The head dived, followed by a wide-ridged back like an overturned boat, toad-colored. It sped towards Lugne, carving a long wake. Lugne, troubled by the wash, took a mouthful and coughed.

Diormit hopped, shouted, and pointed. But Lugne swam on.

The head broke water again and snorted, diving below with its needle-toothed jaws cracked open. The humps appeared behind again, like the coils of a snake bunched up and prepared to spring. The villagers howled with terror and covered their faces. A few turned to their huts and ran. Cainnech fell to his knees, his face long with fright. Drostan bowed his head, and Comgall gripped Colum's tense arm, breathing, "God have mercy."

Colum broke the grip and ran into the lake up to his knees. The shock of the icy water pulled his breath deeper than he intended. He signed the air with his staff and shouted, "No further!"

His trumpeting voice blew up a spray. The Picts bent over and covered their ears at the blast. His men winced as the psalmist's words whistled over the water like spears:

King of Old,
   Mighty warrior,
Thou didst cleave the sea monster in two,
   Thou didst crush Leviathan's head!

The sea beast yelped, twisted, and lunged past Lugne at a mere staff-length. Its bulbous body sank in a great splash and welter of foam. Lugne, sucked under for a moment, bobbed up spitting, and then paddled his arms to escape the whirlpool of the beast's descent. He splashed with high kicks as the waters gurgled and spun. The maelstrom shallowed and slowed to great circles of ripples, and the hissing bubbles dissipated. The eels, too, had gone. A few flip-flapped on the stones where Diormit had shaken them out of his robe.

When the water calmed and Lugne reached the boat, Diormit's agitated leaping became a dance arm in arm with Drostan. Cainnech jumped up, his face split with a smile. He threw open his spindly arms and hugged the breath out of Comgall. Colum whooped and swung his staff like a hurly player after a score.

The Picts ventured back to the beach, whispering and pointing to Lugne, who stood in the lost boat on the other shore, turning its prow.

When he crossed safely, crunched ashore and stepped on land, they crowded him, seeking to touch him.

The whiskered leader, short of breath, looked up to Colum. "You have a powerful magic."

"We have a powerful God."

"You do," agreed the man. "But a sea beast must be summoned. If you did not call it up, who did?"

15

BROICHAN

A.D. 565

ROICHAN FOLLOWED THE CURVED SAIL OF THE MOON as it scudded across the sea of stars. He aligned his piercing eye to the long avenue of stones radiating from the sun-circle. The ancient menhirs marked the farthest north and south positions of the moon's wobbly trek and pointed with pleasing accuracy to the azimuth of the moon at its lowest declination. At that point, the moon in its full phase, when rising at sunset, would ride so low at midnight it would seem to roll on the distant flat stone altar affixed due south of the sun-circle. Then Broichan would drop a nineteenth stone into the counting holes to mark the year of the sacred moonswing, and it would not return to the spot for another nineteen sun-years. When the moon was framed by the two upright pillars flanking the flat stone, Broichan would make an offering to aid in its ascent.

Ainu the druidess gripped the whittled star-markers. On a clear night like this one, Broichan measured the degrees of descent for the Twelve Great Signs — The Balance, The Bear, The Archer, and the others seasonally visible. As the Sphere of Fixed Stars turned and the twinkling dots approached the horizon, Broichan snapped orders for her to place the stakes.

Ainu planted them with a rock used for a hammer. Her tatooed hands looked black against the ground, and only the

white fingertips with the pointed nails showed clearly, tight on
the rock like ring points holding a gem in place. She bashed the
heads of the stakes with white-fingernailed resentment. *This is
work for an apprentice, not a priestess,* she hissed to herself as the
rock thudded. With Brude enthroned and with no new apprentices appointed until the moonswing, the task fell to her. With
each order she hurried to the next spot, grim-lipped, and
pounded the points in as though through Broichan's sleeping
chest.

Dana strung the sheephair twine between stakes for measuring the latitudinal deviations. When Ainu heard Broichan
compliment her on the twining, she grumped. She considered
that chore to be far easier.

The hooded men watched, their arms folded into their
sleeves against the chill. They traded whispers, memorizing the
courses of the 356 stars, measuring their chords and arcs of
deviance and, Ainu thought, studying the curves of her body as
she jumped with each bark from Broichan.

By the time the crows warned of the royal sun's rebirth
and the raven sky turned to gull gray, Ainu subdued the anger
throbbing in her neck. *The moonswing portends a great change,* she
thought, seeing the flat stone begin to glow a dull blue like her
dyed lips. As the goddess of night becomes ascendant in the sky,
so a woman shall be in Brude's house, she purposed, her full
mouth taking the shape of the grinning moon.

Broichan called for the sun-stakes, sounding like the large
crows circling above, bits of night refusing to die. He corrected
her placements twice, making her squat until the posts fit his
preconceived pattern precisely.

Then she waited, tense and expectant. At the first golden
glint of dawn, she poised over the last alignment spot.

"Now," said Broichan.

She drove the wood dagger into the dirt with the sound
of crunching bone.

In his stone-cold chambers, Broichan poked the embers of
a dying fire with his staff. "More wood," he said to Ainu, with his
coal-black eyes deep in thought.

She bent her long legs in submission to the log pile. Dana

lifted the chainmail skirt of the stone hearth for Ainu to insert the log. *Just as she lifts her own skirt for Broichan to use her,* she thought. She stabbed the log into the cinders.

As ashes and smoke jumped up the flue, Ainu felt a warm flush through her, but it did not come from the hearth, for the log did not catch right away. *This is work for a slavegirl, not a sorceress,* she burned as she blew. *Why does he not call for her instead?*

She took her place, silent as steam, beside Dana while Broichan paced between them and the two visiting priests of the valley.

One tall and stiff, the other hunched and winter-white, they stood like memorial stones, their chiseled faces stern. They watched Broichan's pacing with anxiety. Their news had put rows in the ArchDruid's high brow, misaligning his dotted tattoos. Ainu noticed how his manicured fingers massaged his V-shaped chin, a sign of distress.

Ainu kept her mouth as an arrow, straight and hard. She masked her displeasure at learning of the approach of the strangers-in-white-habits so late. If Broichan had known for so long, why was she not told? First she seethed at Broichan's secrecy, and then at herself for not reading the omens. The hidden reason for the Rite of the Sea Beast became clear.

"He is still on the way, you say?" he repeated with disbelief. "Nothing we do dissuades him?"

"He has great power," said the tall one with a dry voice.

Broichan, dissatisfied, stirred the ashes of the hearth with his staff till the tip smoked. The log caught fire. He cast a criticizing glance at Ainu, and then said to the men, "He has no power in himself. Did you not conjure a storm? Did it not take a life and restore one as nature must do?"

"But the people ascribed the girl's condition to him."

"You allowed them to."

The older man shrugged. "It could not be helped, Wise One. They saw him lay hands on her. They heard the cracking of bones . . ."

"So you, also, ascribe it to him?"

The white-headed magician eyed him warily, chin high, holding his dread. "We ascribe it to the powers of Hy."

"Which you have lost to him." Broichan stroked his chin.

"Why does he now leave Hy to come here? To claim more lands?" He said it more to himself.

"We do not know, Wise One," said the older druid. "He is a Gael. Perhaps he seeks to assure the king he means no harm though he is bordered on his territory, or perhaps he is on a mission from the king of DalRiada, as he comes with only five companions."

"Then they are spies," said Broichan, his face darkened. "I will warn the king to turn them away. There will be no terms of peace for invaders of Alba. If they come to seek new terms for the tribute or release of their hostages and slaves, they will fail."

Broichan clapped his long hands. From the hall a maiden entered, carrying a pail. Nettle-fiber towels draped her milky arms. She knelt before Broichan like a rebuked house dog, and Broichan looked pleased.

Ainu admired the silver fringe on the young girl's dress. Her own white robe felt plain and ugly. The girl's white face bore no tattoos of station, yet by the way Broichan examined her, he preferred her. Her braided hair, like woven brass, was pinned in place by shiny clasps which reflected in Broichan's proud eyes. Her jeweled eyes, sad and lost and too large for her face, waited for Broichan's command.

It is easy to see why he saved this one from the will of the warriors in DalRiada, Ainu thought with contempt and curiosity. As if reading her mind, the slavegirl looked to Ainu. The liquid eyes filled with despising. *Broichan should have left this one to the men's sport,* Ainu mused. *She is too bold.*

"Tend to our guests' feet, Etain," Broichan ordered softly.

The men of Hy dropped onto a wallbench and kicked off their sandals. Etain wet and toweled their veiny feet.

"After a meal, you will return to the Glen," Broichan instructed. "Firmly rebuke any who may listen to them."

"We will," promised the thin man.

"Ainu," continued Broichan coldly, "alert the king to my coming. I will speak to him about these invaders after the meal."

Ainu padded away, relieved to be out of his sight. From the hall she heard Broichan say, "They will no more free DalRiada from the tribute than they will free this slave from me."

Ainu quickened her pace to a soundless run. *The moon goddess is sending the strangers to free me from you,* she smiled. *If they are as powerful as they sound.* She thanked her stars for her extraordinary luck, and her mind reeled with possibilities as she hurried towards Brude's bedchamber. She heard the clank of Etain's water pail on stone, but she did not hear the ArchDruid's order for Dana to follow her.

■

In the courtyard of jagged shadows, Ainu felt her cheeks glowing with satisfaction. She could still intimidate Broichan's foster son. Though Brude held sway over the Highlands and the north islands, he still shook like a cornered hare upon seeing her. She liked how her venomous voice could still make his bowels squirm with equal fear and desire, and that whenever she released his unmarried lusts, he felt more shackled to her spirits. Though he had become more swaggering with each new hostage in his possession, Ainu understood whom the Pictish vassals truly feared. It was Baru, the bear-strong champion, who had conquered them.

And so it was Baru she must conquer as well.

She watched him ride through the wide gates at a full gallop just as they cracked open. Fat capercaillies hung upside down on his saddle, their bloody beaks swinging. He paraded his kill through the standing stones, up and down the courtyard with his men hollering. Baru himself rode stone-faced, with his hunting bow slapping on his bare chest. He passed under the image of Cernunnos, the horned hunting god, who looked on the kill with a single benign eye from atop the high pole next to the well.

Baru's horse kicked up dung and dust, frightened by the hounds baying and leaping for the dead birds. Baru swatted them away and ordered his men to restrain them. The hunters rolled up the long leashes around their forearms, hauling in the dogs like fishers pulling in salmon on the run.

Baru dismounted at the curing house, loudly dismissed his fellow riders with the promise of a feast to come, and pushed the reins into the hands of a ready lad. He swung his game over his shoulder. He raised a knee, etched with a bear's face, and kicked the door with his bare heel. Inside, he hung his catch on ceiling hooks for the blood to drain and for the women to pluck. Matted feathers tumbled to the straw. But Baru heard a crunch too loud for falling feathers.

"Who's there?" he growled, his jeweled dagger suddenly in his fist.

Ainu swished through the door connecting the storeroom, the smell of straw and salted meat heavy on her tunic, and Baru's nose twitched.

"Put away your knife, Baru," she cooed, "unless you plan to carve the bird before it is cooked."

"And you are here to pluck it?"

"I will pluck a different bird. But I need your help."

Baru sheathed his blade. "What do you mean?"

Ainu sauntered close to his chest which was streaked with bird's blood. "We both know you do not take your orders from the king whom you protect," she said. "There is another who orders the king. He alone says he knows the signs for luck in war and hunting."

Baru backed away into the door, clicking it shut. "You speak of Broichan."

Ainu stepped closer. "I speak of one who despises you for not being one of our people, but of Maelchon's in the south. Such a one, he says, is not to be trusted for too long."

"Why do you speak this way?"

"I do not wish to see you gone." She drew circles around his hardening nipples and smoothed her tatooed palms over his slick chest up to his shoulders. She curled her sinewy leg around his knee and slid it up to his thigh like a serpent wrapping a tree trunk. Outside, the dogs yelped, their necks squeezed by ropes, the scent of prey strong. Ainu whispered, "It does not become you to be ordered about like a hound."

Baru's neck veins thickened as though restrained. "What do you gain by this?" he gruffed.

"Broichan is not the only one to read the sky signs. Mark me. The moon goddess will kiss the earth when she is full and begin to rise again, turning red."

"This does not concern me."

"It means a woman is to rise as High Priestess, but only with the shedding of blood." She brushed her lips on his sturdy neck with her wide mouth parted and ignored the sweaty taste. "Do you understand?"

"He cannot be killed. He will come back."

"I can prevent that."

229

"Why should I help you? So you would command Brude instead of Broichan?"

She nuzzled her soft black hair against him. "I cannot command Brude in war as Broichan does. He would not listen to a woman. But he would follow you."

"Why should I believe you?"

"Stand at the sun-stone at midnight on the night of the full moon. Look south. You will see it glide on the altar yourself." She mimicked the motion by gliding her moon-white leg up and down his prickly thigh.

"That is a secret of the priests," Baru said, sounding tentative.

"It is to be our secret and a sign to you. Let no one see you there as no one sees us here."

She lifted her other leg around his hip, attached to him like mistletoe on an oak. Baru gripped her waist, kneading with his thick fingers, and carried her into the inner storehouse. His eager lips moved like caterpillars against hers as they lay in a pile of straw stained with old blood and salt.

■

Broichan found the king in the dining room cackling at a story from one of the warriors. Brude's chest medallion caught the hearthlight and sent a sliver of light into Broichan's disapproving eye.

From beneath a bronze headband, the king's tangled hair swished on his ivory-hued satin tunic. The square designs of the Welsh embroidery reminded the ArchDruid that his foster son was half foreign. *He could harbor a dangerous sentimentality towards forces that pressed upon the Picts' ancient ways,* he thought. *Did not his father Maelchon tolerate a school of the priests of Christos on his lands? If not for his Pictish mother, the boy might have fostered with them.*

But thank the gods, he comforted himself, *the royal line is preserved.* The nephews and half-cousins once removed and all other rivals of the complex matrilineal succession had been subdued. When he heard Brude's nervous giggle again and saw him pick his teeth with the bone of an eel and raise a weasel-skull cup, Broichan closed his weary eyes with disappointment. *All the more reason to shut the gates to these spies,* he thought.

The room hushed as the men recognized Broichan's tall, dark figure. They moved away from Brude as small scavengers on a carcass yield to a more formidable predator.

"Leave us," said Broichan.

The men collected their shields and spears and filed past him at a safe distance. Broichan watched them pass from the corner of his eye. Their callused heels scuffed on the stones, then faded.

Brude stood, dabbing his drawn mouth with his sleeve. He put down the skull cup. It wore a satirical smile. Brude offered a winsome smile himself, but nothing more until Broichan spoke first. He coughed with a sound more like a stifled giggle.

"I must prepare more elixir for you," said Broichan, walking gently to him. He felt each stone warmer as he neared the fireplace.

"It is just the smoke, Father," said Brude. He coughed — or giggled — again.

"But I wish you health and a long reign."

"So shall it be as long as you are with me." Brude's knees rustled on his tunic, and he would have backed away if he could. But he sat at Broichan's signal.

"There are those who would try to separate us."

"Who would try such a thing?" asked Brude, sounding more hopeful than disturbed.

"I have news from the Glen," Broichan replied in a warning voice. "A detachment of men from DalRiada is on the way to Inverness."

Brude's froglike eyes bulged with alarm. "How many?"

"Only six."

"Armed?"

"Only with deceit."

Brude's narrow shoulder slumped in his relief. He wiped his watery eyes. "Why do they come so far? I have summoned no one."

Broichan stroked his chin as though shaping it into a peak. "They are spies."

"How can you be sure of this?"

A frown worked at the corners of Broichan's mouth. He was not used to being questioned. "They come to trick you, thinking you are easily fooled. For they dress as Wise Ones in white robes with razored heads and with staffs of power."

231

Brude's eyes rolled as he remembered. "If they are from DalRiada, then perhaps they are priests of the god Christos."

Broichan's eyes, irritated from the smoke, narrowed. But he was more irritated that his years of training had not cleared the boy's memories of his real father's errors, permitting the poison of the new religion to spread. "It is more likely that they are messengers of the DalRiadan king seeking to alter the tribute. Or bargain for the release of those who are in your hand as pledges. It does not matter. You will close the gates to them."

Brude considered his fingers, cluttered with the rings of conquered chieftains. "Are you afraid of only six men with a message? If they are harmless priests, let us hear them."

"Have you been with me so long and do not remember?" Broichan scolded, not raising his voice but deepening it. "Your mother and your father sent you to me not only for your throne but for your proper training. They knew that we, not the Christ-ones, guard the old truths. We know the forces which give order and life to nature. Can they bring rain? No. Can they summon the sea beasts? No. They pray to a man who was slain."

"They say this Christos was raised from the dead."

How much he yet remembers, Broichan cautioned himself. "It is a feast they call Easter," he said with a dismissing gesture. "It is, even in name, like the feast of Ish-tar, the rebirth of nature in the spring. They take all the old festivals and give them new names. They do nothing original."

"They write."

Broichan laughed. "Yes, they write. They scratch away on precious hides more needed as clothing or saddles. And with what effect? Writing makes the mind lazy. It is for the mentally weak and forgetful. It gives men a show of wisdom but not the substance. Speech is the breath of man's thoughts, inhaled and joined to the being of the hearer. Speech and music mingle with the vibrations of nature. Once written, a word loses its power."

Brude nodded, wordless. He looked unconvinced.

"Besides," Broichan added, "in this ink-spilling they are like the Romans. Like them, these men are also invaders. They even use the Roman language. But they are worse than the legions. Look to the hills and see the high towers built long ago to resist them. In like manner, you will show they have no part with us. You will close the gates. You will not do as your father and invite them in. Does the farmer invite the rats into the grainhouse? Does the weasel bid the wolf into the den?"

Brude fingered the weasel-head cup, evidently pondering the lesson, but his reply took Broichan aback.

"If they do not read the sky as you say, why do they come at the time of the moonswing?"

Broichan narrowed his dark brow. He, also, had pondered the same disturbing mystery. Masking his concern, he moved in deliberate steps toward the door. "As the moon presses upon the earth, so we shall press upon DalRiada. And as the moon turns to blood, such is the price to those who resist us."

He found the entryway suddenly blocked by Baru, sweating like a run-down boar, flecked with straw and stinking of salt. Broichan waved him aside and held his breath as he passed.

■ -

On the appointed night, Ainu lifted her hands to the full moon. Her body was smeared with blue woad and fragrant oils prepared by Broichan. The clay coating, smooth and elastic, stretched like a second skin as she went through the moon-dance motions. Her full sleeves fell back, and her arms glistened in the dim light. The whetted designs in her flesh showed through, dark as the heavy fall of her perfumed hair. As she moved around the circle, miming the path of the moon, her dance steps synchronized with those of the other priests. The night air brushed her slicked skin and raised pleasant goose-prickles. In the middle of the circle, representing earth, Broichan droned a repetitive chant, wooing the sky goddess. With a tall torch in hand instead of his usual yew-staff, he guided her lower.

With each pass at the north side of the ring, looking south, Ainu saw the goddess closer to the distant altar, the recumbent stone flanked by two upright pillars. The black spire of the left aligning pillar showed against the moon's rusty red. Ainu wondered if the great disc, when touching the horizon, would set it aflame. Perhaps at one time it had ripped across Caledonia to carve out the Great Glen itself. *Will the earth quake when they meet this time?*

Ainu's dipping and rising dance steps brought her around to the ring's south side. She looked north into the woods for

Baru. Seeing nothing but the trees, she told herself, "Of course, he is well hidden. He is a hunter."

She took care not to let Broichan notice her searching looks. She moved in the prescribed, well-practiced manner until Broichan stopped his spell. Then the white-robed celebrants gathered behind Broichan, as Ainu and Dana flanked him, like the altar pillars.

The moon rolled on the far-off hills, seeming to pass through the stone marker on the left. Broichan focused on the altar, his face orange and angular in the torchlight. He stood as rigid as the menhirs.

Anticipation rushed through Ainu as she saw the last sliver of moon pass behind the stone. At any moment it would emerge fully over the altar. The time was upon them, but no animal was brought forth. "Where is the offering to make her rise?" she asked, rubbing her fingertips.

"Dana was to bring it," Broichan said stonily.

Dana smiled at Ainu across Broichan's chest, empty-handed.

Ainu bristled. *There must be a sacrifice,* she thought. *Her oversight will not spoil my destiny.* "Why did you not bring one?" she fired.

"I did," said Dana, the smile unbroken.

Ainu glowered. *She lies to avoid Broichan's anger,* she thought. "We came together. I did not see it."

The moon swung between the pillars onto the stone cradle.

"Nor have we seen the guest you invited to the ceremony," said Broichan.

Ainu looked into his unwavering eyes, the moon full in the place of his pupils.

"It is not permitted," he said as he touched the torch to her smock.

The fabric and oils ignited with a whooshing noise. The scream stuck in her throat. The scented hair blazed and crisped; the skin blistered and split.

The sky goddess, unblinking and blood-red, kissed the altar and began her slow ascent.

■

When the sun burned away the night and the tips of the firs glowed with morning, Baru mounted the breastworks of the fort. Beyond the sun-stone and the moon-markers which led in a long avenue to the cliffs, he thought he could make out the charred circle where the moon goddess had claimed her sacrifice. The image was still fused in his eye — in one moment, Ainu had spoken, ever so faintly heard from where he was hidden. The next moment, as the coppery-pink ball brushed the earth, she had flared into a torch, merging with the sky goddess.

Perhaps she foresaw the moon's choice and feared it, he pondered as he tightened his primitive tartan. *Is that why she wanted to be rid of Broichan, to be in a position to select another in her place? Yes, she knew it,* he grumbled, *and she tried to use me to escape it.*

He pressed on his helmet, feeling the deep etching and the rough enamel on the brim. At just a few words from the ArchDruid, she had been sent into the sky, he remembered. He had slipped away then. He did not wait for the end of the ceremony when the standing stones awakened and walked to the water for a drink, killing anyone in their path. He felt for his sword, and he knew it was useless against the stones or Broichan's power.

He rubbed his wristguard made of polished stone and fastened with bronze rivets, made to protect his forearm from the rebound of his bowstring. It chafed, and he did not like to wear it. Why had Brude ordered him into battle gear along with the men and commanded that the gates be bolted upon Broichan's return from the dawn ceremonies?

Did the moonswing portend an attack?

He doublechecked from his platform. The thick bars were locked in place, the bolts properly closed.

He looked over the lake, smooth as glass, unbroken by boat wakes. The steep cliffs careening to the rock-ragged beach were spotted only by nesting gulls. The mist shrouded the more distant woodlands and seemed to cling to the woods nearby. It was murky enough to hide an army, but Baru heard no clink of mail or creak of shields or thump of hooves.

Instead, he heard a song.

At first, it sounded like one voice, pure and deep, on a haunting high note like a druid's incantation. But he knew Broichan and the others were all in from the ceremonies and the morning measurements. He still simmered from the caustic glance Broichan gave him as he hastened the warrior to bolt the gates. The words stuck like a bit in his mouth, and he spat to remember it.

So it could not be Broichan and his bats out there, he glared.

A litany of male voices intertwined the first, solemn and otherworldly. As no man could be seen, it appeared that the mist itself raised the eerie canticle. The crags of Craig Phadrig echoed the music in reply as though in recognition or welcome.

Baru barked to his men. The fair-haired guards leaped to the ramparts. They snatched spears from the racks and put their small square shields to their chins as they peered through the pointed timbers into the haze.

From the woods, dressed in the white mist itself, so it seemed, drifted six men. They emerged from the cloud in pairs, as though stepping into the world from an ethereal realm. Their chant continued in a language strangely beautiful. At the front glided the tallest man Baru had ever seen.

His face was ruddy and radiant with the eastern sunrise, the eyes luminous. The shaven pate shined like a helmet, and the red hair flamed behind his neck. He stepped in time to the song. When he ended it in unison with the others, he stopped before the gate.

The sentries raised their spears. The shafts hung still in their upraised arms, the menacing barbed tips pointed down.

Baru glanced across his shoulder to the courtyard. The strange chant and the scramble of the guards had cleared the yard of people at their chores. A bucket swayed at the well. Beyond it, he could see King Brude at his council chamber window, leaning on the ledge and gnawing at his knuckles.

Baru looked back down to the visitors. They remained in a double column, staffs without points at their sides. He noticed leather straps on their shoulders, but no quivers. To his astonishment, the tall one lifted his fiery head and spoke to him in a confident, royal Pictish: "Open the door! I will see Brude, your king!"

Baru caught his eyes, wolf-gray and lined with silver as though lit from behind. *For the sake of these few men*, he marveled, *does the king bar the gate?* He thought of Broichan's haste to close them. *They look like him in a way*, he observed. *Perhaps*

Broichan knew of his coming and feared him, he reasoned. With an unseen smile of cunning, Baru considered opening the gates. If only Brude himself were not watching.

"It is a prince of an unknown clan," remarked one of his trusted warriors standing near, "or a wizard. Shall we open to him?"

"Let the gates be," said Baru. "We will see if he is a wizard or not."

The stranger called again, but Baru kept his mouth as sealed as the gate.

The stranger then opened his mouth in a sweet song, joined softly by the others. He raised his right hand up, down, right, and left. Baru turned his face away from the mystic sign to avoid bewitchment. What he saw when looking down sent a constricting panic through his chest.

The iron bars trembled, rattling the heavy gates. The gate-keepers grabbed them, but drew back their hands with cries of pain. They blew on them as though burned. The vibrating bars slide aside with an earsplitting squeak. The guards dropped their spears with a clatter and scattered like roaches from a table. Baru meant to yell at them, but the words would not come. The great bars settled, steaming, with the smell of charred wood.

The stranger knocked three times.

The thick doors parted and gaped wide open, as wide as Brude's mouth.

The white-robed stranger and his companions entered slowly. Their footwraps crunched on the gravel, the only sound in the yard. They stepped around the dung piles and goat pellets and puddles where the women had dropped their pails in fright. Unwashed children watched them from doorways. Penned-up swine grunted. The hunting dogs, smelling danger, yelped from their cages. The soldiers drew their swords and crouched.

By the time the tall stranger reached the central well where Cernunnos, the one-eyed god, stared down threats from his pole, Brude was stumbling out his residence door. The leading men of his council trailed him, gathering their cloaks and fastening them. Baru clenched his teeth at the king's rashness, exposing himself so easily. Then he noted that Broichan was not among them. It was a good sign.

Brude's face looked ashen, as powdery gray as his squirrel

collar. He walked with a nervous hop, his arms open. When he approached the towering visitor, he dipped his head in a gracious greeting.

"I bid you, most honored guest, a welcome," the king stammered, "and I beg you to share your name that we may know upon whom the peace of Brude MacMaelchon, king of the Caledonii, may rest."

The towering visitor, more princely in his homespun than Brude in his finery, replied for the entire fortress to hear. "I am Colum of the Clan Conaill, son of Fedlimidh, son of Fergus, son of the Great Niall of the Nine Hostages, a prince and heir to the High Kingship of Tara, and a messenger of the High King of the Otherworld."

16
ETAIN
A.D. 565

THEY ATE A SOUP MADE WITH PICKLED GAME BIRD, SALTED to the bone and chewy, poured into stone bowls. Shapely servers bore silver platters weighted with boiled sheep-stomach sausage stuffed with oats and chopped mutton suet, lungs, and hearts. Leather-loined warriors sliced off chunks with their daggers, carving the kirncheese and clearing a space to sit with swings of the same bronze blades. Lean greyhounds competed for the bits of onion and offal that spilled on the straw from the low tables where Colum's men reclined.

A hooded historian crooned of Brude's conquests. He compared the chieftain and his champion to ancient heroes Colum did not recognize.

Two beardless princes of Orkney and Skye squirmed on their pillows while the historian reviewed their kingdoms' defeats. He likened their capture to that of the birds in the soup. Colum heard a growling and looked for which dog near him had lost a scrap, and then realized it was Baru laughing with his mouth full.

The hunter thumped his dagger handle on his shield, and others followed. The trophies on the walls rattled. Strings of bear claws, boar tusks, captured helmets. Several still had the heads of their owners in them.

The skulls gaped at Brude, hunched in his seat. The edges of his taut lips, shadowed by new mustache hairs, curled up whenever the historian mentioned his name. With the singer's final note, Brude hoisted his mug in salute and splashed muddy mead on his own cloak. The warriors raised, then drained their goblets. They banged them on the packed floor for more. As the female servers tipped their swan-necked flagons, the men pulled them down by the skirts for sport. Colum heard a woman scream. The hall fell silent.

All eyes shifted to the antechamber curtains. The scream came from the curtain rings sliding on the bronze rod. The heavy brocade was pulled aside for a tall, black-browed druid.

With his sharp chin high, his angular shoulders squared, and his arms stiff by his sides, the wizard stood as a raven on a birch branch. His midnight eyes scrutinized the visitors with disfavor. As his suspicious scan passed across the hearth to Brude, the fires flickered with a sudden chill.

"My father, Broichan," announced Brude in a squeaky voice. "These are our visitors, Father, who . . ."

"I know who they are."

Broichan advanced with warriors clearing his path. Behind him stalked a painted priestess. She smirked when she saw Baru. The sinister swirls on her cheeks turned like wheels, and her ice-blue lips took the shape of a canoe. Baru's face squeezed into a fist, and Colum sensed the woman's warning look was one of vengeance accomplished or a rival humbled.

Brude nodded to his foster father. "Did you know that Colum of Clan Conaill is also a king by birth?"

Broichan wrapped his robes like wings and perched on a cushion pushed beneath him by the tatooed woman. "If you are a king," he said coolly to the guest, "where are your colors?"

Colum felt the ArchDruid searching his eyes, probing. "I come as did the Prince of Peace, God's own royal Son. He gave up a great throne, as I have, for a great mission."

Brude leaned forward, eyes wide with puzzlement and interest.

Broichan scolded the boy back with a glance and said icily, "What is your mission?"

Colum motioned to Lugne for his satchel. As he opened it, he saw Baru reach for his spear. The crowd murmured uneasily.

Colum scooped his hand in the bag. He lifted a fistful of black barley seeds.

Brude arched his thin eyebrows as he watched the seeds sift through the stranger's fingers.

Broichan cocked his head and narrowed his eyes with distrust. "Seeds," he said with a tightening throat, "you have come all this way to bring seeds?"

"This is the seed of our finest, hardiest grain," said Colum. "It is bred for our climates. We bring you many years of experience, for planting, for harvesting, for feeding your . . ."

"Is what is set before you not enough?" said Broichan, offended. "Or do you not think we have our own seed? Or do you think us so weak from hunger that we cannot take what we need from others?"

Colum let fall the last seeds and brushed his palms. "It is the seed of peace between our peoples that I have come to plant."

Broichan took a platter laden with a bloated gray sausage. "If you speak of DalRiada, there will be no peace until a Pictish king loyal to Brude lives in DunAdd. Or it will be pushed into the sea."

He tipped the platter. The stuffed stomach flopped to the floor and split, gushing its juices.

The dogs struggled for the spoils, snatching bits of heart and snapping at each other. The warriors called encouragements to them. Broichan's palm drifted up to receive a goblet from a female attendant. He did not look at her, but coldly concentrated on Colum's face.

The rings which held the girl's braids flashed in Colum's eye. The firelight glinted through her hair like red gold after burnishing. Colum broke from Broichan's challenging gaze and followed the girl's graceful movement to the entryway. She kept her eyes downcast, serving no one else, and no man dared to touch her body as she passed.

Comgall cupped his mouth and exclaimed to himself in an uncertain whisper, "Etain?"

The girl heard it and glanced up, pinched her lips and turned her moist eyes away.

Colum seized his interpreter's forearm. "You know this slavegirl?"

"It is Etain," said Comgall with a growing conviction. "Galway's daughter, of DalRiada."

Colum watched the girl hug the bright flask to her silver-fringed dress, as though clinging to an impossible hope. He felt his brow warming.

Broichan touched his drawn lips to the glass just filled and wet them. "If you come to plant seed and reap favors, you are mistaken. If by this offering you hope to wiggle DalRiada free of the tribute, remember this — we will take grain, and gold, and slaves as we please."

He held up the empty platter in time for Etain to take it. He bent forward in a gesture to rise and depart. The druidess behind him knelt to remove his cushion.

Colum pointed to the seat and said, "We are not finished."

Startled, Broichan sank down. With a flick of his wrist, he granted the guest a final indulgence.

Colum noted the fear in Etain's jeweled eyes, and he remembered Maire. He felt the blood rush to his temples and throb in his neck. Broichan sat higher as if drawing strength or pleasure from his anger.

"Life for life," said Colum, his teeth set, eyes piercing. "As this seed will bring life to many of your people, you will give life to one of ours. I ask you to release to us this slavegirl, Etain. She is one of our people."

Broichan clutched the cushion with his long talons. "You have not traveled so far a distance for so small a request," he said, sounding insulted. "You would have her to be the first of all DalRiada released. I will not."

"Release her." Colum's command, not louder but sharper, flew like a well-aimed javelin across the room.

Brude wrung his hands and his rings clicked.

The ArchDruid lowered his head and his voice. "Know this, Colum of Clan Conaill. I will keep this woman as we keep DalRiada. And each will give whatever the master asks."

Colum scissored his legs to launch his body up. In his white robe he stood as high as a waterfall and spoke with a voice as thunderously loud. "Know this, Broichan. If you do not release for me this pilgrim captive before I depart this province, you shall die!"

The hearthfire fanned into leaping tongues. The dogs lowered their tails and found their corners.

"And when will you depart?" asked Broichan, his mouth curved to an amused smile.

"I give you two days. Then, God willing and life lasting, we sail."

"You will not be able," said the magician, raising his goblet to his lip as a warrior raises a sword to accept a duel. "I have power to raise a wind against you and a mist to blind you."

"Then the Spirit of God will fill my sail, and His light will guide me!"

Colum pivoted and stomped from the hall. Behind him he heard the brethren's robes rustle as they hastened to follow him. He heard the crackle of new faggots fed to the flames. Broichan's bark to Etain to refill his glass fueled the fire that burned within him.

■

Wordless, Colum descended to the shallow inlet on the River Ness where his curragh rested among the rocks. He stabbed the dirt with his walking stick, handling it like a javelin. He sliced aside the low bushes and chided himself under his breath. The brothers thought he was offended over Etain the slavegirl. But he was angry with himself.

How could he win Pictland if he could not conquer his own temper? In a single impetuous burst he had jeopardized the whole mission. Could the Fiend exploit his weakness so easily at so critical a moment?

It was not even righteous indignation, he knew, but a boiling up from the well of memory for Maire. Even as he thought it, he saw her image shaped by stones in the lake. He slashed his stick through the water.

The men set to unworking the mooring knots. Diormit urged the abbot into the boat in order to reach their camp by nightfall.

But Colum watched the ripples smooth, and then dipped his hand in the water. Under the sparkles of the surface, the worn pebbles and floating mica looked like shattered shards of glass.

He selected a polished, pure white stone and shook off the water. He displayed it like a valuable coin.

"Mark this stone," he called, "how it lies among so many broken pieces. This is a fragile kingdom. But a new one will be built upon it."

"Or it will be built upon our bones," said Comgall. "Look!"

Colum followed his frightened gaze to Brude's battlements. The gates groaned open and poured forth a stream of horses that clanked with bronze harnesses and pounded the path into billows of dust. The riders' helmets gleamed in the salmon sunlight, and their speartips looked like licks of flame.

"Quickly, brothers," said Diormit, "to the oars."

"Stay," said Colum, fascinated.

"But look how many there be," protested Diormit, "and we without weapons."

Colum rubbed the white stone. If round, it would suit a sling.

Within a hurler's distance he saw Baru spurring the lead horse, a storm-gray stallion with a black mane. The champion kicked and cursed in as furious a charge as Colum had ever seen. The hooves fell with the drumming noise of shields beaten before battle, as at Culdrevne. Colum fastened his fist upon his staff. It could parry only the first few blows if he chose to resist.

Baru heaved his body back and jerked his horse to a halt within a spear's throw. The other riders pulled up beside him, their horses clicking on the stones. Like his mount, Baru shone with sweat. His eyes, no longer cautious, opened wide like his steed's.

"Speak for me!" he ordered Comgall with a jab of his finger, and then pointed to Colum. "The king asks that you return at once with no delay. Broichan is near death."

He spun in the saddle and snapped a command. A warrior brought forward two saddled but riderless horses.

Baru pointed to them. "You will ride now."

"First you will tell me what happened," said Colum.

Baru frowned. "You already know," he said, impatient. "You are the one who cursed him. His drinking glass broke in his hand as he swallowed from it. There are pieces in his throat. The king wishes your magic to save him."

Comgall translated and then added his own aside. "Do we believe him, or is it a trick to separate us?"

"Even so, it is God's opportunity," said Lugne in a rebuking tone.

Baru wheeled about his snorting horse. "Enough talk. Come now."

"Lugne and Cainnech," waved Colum, "go for us. And go with this." He held high the white stone, and Baru regarded it as he would a raised ax.

"If Broichan first releases the slavegirl to these two men," pronounced Colum, "then let him dip this stone in water and let him drink of it, and he will be well. But if he will not release the woman, he will immediately die and the stone will be useless."

"The king asks for you, not these men," gruffed Baru.

"The king asks for my help. I am giving it."

Colum pressed the stone into Cainnech's hand. "Now he will do it," he said.

The monks mounted the horses. The escort closed around them. The Picts thumped away, racing up the hillside with wild whoops and singing whips.

Drostan watched them climb up to the fortress and crossed himself as the doors shut like jaws behind them. "Will the stone heal him, Uncle?" he finally asked.

"Stones heal no one," said Colum. "It is God who heals and love that releases His power. Kneel with me. We must pray for Broichan. And for Etain."

She'll not be pulled away from my arms this time, he swore as he knotted his fingers and set his hard knees to the rocks.

■

The sun, a great brass shield polished for war, settled on the gray hills as upon a warrior's belt. The birds chattered their evensongs. The larches threw long shadows across the praying monks. The waters of Loch Ness darkened like the mood of the waiting men.

"You did say two days, Father," sighed Diormit, "and it is now late. If we come back tomorrow . . ."

"We won't have to," said Colum. "Listen."

The squeal of the opening bolts of Brude's gates whined across the valley.

Comgall sprang up and grimaced as though expecting another sortie to take two more of them to their deaths.

But only two horses wended down the steep embankment. Each bore a rider in a white smock. When the huffing beasts ran onto the beach, Cainnech's bobbing body was easily distinguished on one of them. Lugne drove the other.

"The girl!" moaned Diormit. "Where is the girl?"

Lugne angled aside to steer his mount through the rocks. Behind him bounced another figure in white with silver glitter at the hem and a stream of golden hair snapping behind like a pennant, unbraided and free.

The men clapped their folded hands as Lugne pulled in the reins to a stop. Colum offered a steady hand to Etain while she slipped from the saddle to the ground. She gripped his hand tightly and genuflected. She kissed it before laying her soft cheek upon it.

Colum touched her head in blessing. "And Broichan?" he asked his envoys.

"He must be well," Lugne said, dismounting. "He accused us of using a chip from one of his own Standing Stones in his sacred circle."

"Then called to his priests to meet there at once," said Cainnech.

Colum raised Etain and checked the sunset. "Then we must leave quickly. There is no time to lose."

The men shoved the boat into the shallows. They wrestled with it as with a skittish horse to hold it steady against the lapping water. The curragh creaked in the stiffening breeze that blew damp and cool on Colum's face.

"Hurry," he said, helping Etain over the slippery rocks to a place in the back of the boat. In the woods, an awakening owl's hoot joined the whistle of the wind. Etain gasped at the sudden snort of the horses as they bucked at the sound and bolted away as though driven by demons.

For a moment Colum thought the owl had spooked them. He turned and saw what did.

Broichan stood on the battlements, his dark sleeves outstretched like bat wings. The hooting was the sound of his sonorous chanting. The ArchDruid swung his staff in wide circles, stirring the sky.

The tumbling violet clouds of twilight gloomed with gray.

The colors drained from the opposite shore, which was shaded with a fine mist. The ropes on the mast vibrated like harp strings in the buffeting wind.

Colum thrust the rocking boat out against the incoming wash and climbed in. Diormit hauled the paddles from beneath the benches and began to hand them out.

"Put those away," Colum said, unlashing the halyard ropes. "Move aside for the sail."

Colum yanked the leather sail loose. It opened and shivered in the adverse wind. The boat lurched backwards into the rocks with a splintering crunch.

The jolt threw Etain over the side. She grabbed Colum's leg in time to steady herself and pulled herself back in. Her pale face streaked with tears and terror as the first puffs of a milky mist passed over the boat, enshrouding it.

Colum bent down to comfort her. She shuddered and tightened her hold on his leg as the druid's ghostly chants turned to exulting caws in praise of the setting sun.

"Hold fast to God," Colum quoted as the great orange disc dimmed in the fog. "He is a shield to all who seek refuge in Him."

A wet gust jerked the sail in reply, with a screech like a banshee. The ropes slid through Colum's palms, stinging them. The prow reared up, and the men, shouting, threw their weight to one side to avoid capsizing.

Colum wound the ropes around his wrists as at the chariot races. His raw hands bled and burned as he trimmed the sail and intoned the rest of the proverb:

> Who has cupped the wind in the hollow of His hands?
> Who has bound up the waters in the folds of His garment?
> What is His name? Or His Son's name?
> Surely you know!

The boat, with its bow so high, rode over the next wave. It surged forward, plowing through the next wave with a great spray and scraping the rocks. Tilted to port, the boat tacked at a severe angle away from the shore. Colum felt an undercurrent catch the keel like an unseen hand and pull. The curragh cut through the choppy waves like a new sword. The drone of the druid's song diminished, and then faded completely as the mist peeled away like layers of wet-weather cloaks.

The sun rested, and the first star winked through the dusk like a far-off angel pleased with the outcome of its work.

AFTERWORD

Columcille displaced Broichan as King Brude's foster father and soul-friend. While there is no record of Brude's conversion, Columcille received permission to preach broadly in Pictland where today countless schools and churches bear his name.

Columcille returned to Erin in A.D. 575 for the Synod of Drumceatt. He came with clumps of Scottish sod strapped to his sandals in order to fulfill his vow never to set foot on his beloved land again.

There he overturned an edict calling for the suppression of the bards, founded a system of bardic schools for the preservation of Gaelic culture, and affirmed his appointment of Aidan as king of DalRiada (from whom descended the Stuart line of Britain).

Afterwards, he retrieved his father's body for burial among the kings laid to rest on Hy.

He is known to have engaged in at least two more battles.